# Tico lay with his eyes closed, trying to catch the breath that had been knocked out of him.

Meg Flores's laughter mingled with her teammates', penetrating his mind like a double shot of whiskey. If she spoke the same way she laughed, the woman had one sexy voice.

His senses homed in on the sound of footsteps coming toward him. A cowboy boot stride with attitude. He'd bet a month's pay he knew who the boots belonged to. Wondering if she'd act the part of rescuer, he kept his eyes shut. All hope was dashed when, still chuckling, she whispered to his horse, "Good job for throwing this bozo, fella."

He opened his eyes in time to see the sole of a cowboy boot press down on his chest. The curious stare of one Meg Flores flattened him more than he already was. Damn, she was smoking-hot! The reins dangled from her right hand. Diablo glared at him from over her shoulder.

Traitor horse.

"Can I get you a taxi back to New York, Detective?"

Dear Reader,

As many of you know, I find inspiration for my stories from real-life people and situations. *Desert Heat* grew from my unbounded admiration for my niece and her spouse, two California detectives who face danger practically every day to fight crime against two elements: gangs and drugs.

Amanda and Nic are only two people, but they work from a mind-set that it only takes one person to make a difference. These two professionals train and work tirelessly to be as skilled as possible to keep the streets safe. They have been targets of the criminal element, had bounties on their heads, and still go to work eager to make a change for good.

After I listened to Nic and Amanda's stories, Tico Butler and Meg Flores came to life in an Arizona border town and took action against two of the most notorious crime elements: drugs and human trafficking. While hunting the bad guys, Tico, a former gang leader turned cop, clashes with the one woman sworn to run him off her turf: Adobe Creek detective team leader Meg Flores. Heat rises in more ways than one while these two battle danger from the criminal element and their own emotions to get the job done.

I hope you enjoy *Desert Heat*...it is hot in so many ways!

All the best,

Kathleen Pickering

# KATHLEEN PICKERING

—

## Desert Heat

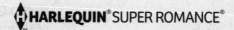

**H**HARLEQUIN® SUPER ROMANCE®

Recycling programs
for this product may
not exist in your area.

ISBN-13: 978-0-373-60873-7

DESERT HEAT

**Printed in U.S.A.**

TM www.Harlequin.com

## ABOUT THE AUTHOR

Kathleen Pickering is an author whose goal is to touch readers' hearts by creating worlds of adventure, love and intrigue. Given her upbringing with a strict Irish-Catholic mother and a gregarious German-Protestant father, coupled with a family tree about which one tends to only whisper, Kathleen is convinced she's living proof that life is stranger than fiction. She brands herself as the author with more than just a story to tell and draws her characters and stories from real-life situations. She loves to travel and finds traveling to research her work an added perk. Just be aware, if Kathleen meets you, you may very well end up in one of her stories.

**Books by Kathleen Pickering**

**HARLEQUIN SUPERROMANCE**

Other titles by this author available in ebook format.

Dedicated to Amanda and Nic...and every law enforcement agent who refuses to let danger destroy the power of love.

# CHAPTER ONE

DETECTIVE TICO BUTLER stood outside a stable in the scorching southern Arizona heat, more out of his element than a scorpion in a snowbank.

His gaze slid from the dust-covered silver Harley Road Glide he'd ridden across the country to the strong, brown, wild-eyed stallion he'd rented to take him the final mile to his destination: the two-bit town of Adobe Creek.

He'd only been on a horse a few times as a kid in New York. It was something his father seemed to think was important, but the horses they'd ridden were from a local riding stable and docile. This horse looked much more muscled than the mounts Tico remembered and way too unmanageable.

The stable hand holding the reins eyed Tico's leather vest and fake sheriff's badge, letting his gaze rest on the cowboy hat as black as Tico's hair. Shaking his head, the old man beckoned Tico closer. "Well, *Sheriff.* This here is Diablo. You good with animals?"

"Deal with 'em every day." Tico didn't want to mention the animals he dealt with were the two-legged kind and usually fleeing a crime scene in Brooklyn. "Are you Charlie Samuels?"

"Nope. Charlie's off today. I'm Seth." He held out the reins. "Diablo was out this morning. Gave him a good run. He should be a pussycat now."

The grin on Seth's face didn't match the horse's agitation; the animal threw his head back as Tico approached. Tico used two fingers to push his hat back on his forehead. "Got anything tamer?"

Seth shook his head. "You said you wanted to look like the Lone Ranger. Diablo is the closest I got to big and white."

"This horse is brown!"

He spit a wad of chewing tobacco into the dirt. "Yep. Closest I've got."

Tico took the reins. He wasn't getting anywhere with this guy, and he was running late for his meeting at the Adobe Creek Police Department. The horse sidestepped as Tico put his foot into the stirrup.

"Hey! Easy, fella."

Diablo continued to move away from him. With one foot in the stirrup, Tico had to hop on the other to keep from falling.

The stable hand chuckled. "Don't worry. If Diablo tosses you out there, he'll know his way back."

The horseman's gibe was all Tico needed. He grabbed the saddle horn and leaped into the seat, coming down hard on the horse's back. Diablo bucked once, then bolted. Tico almost went flying.

"Whoa!"

Tico kept his seat, but the hard landing jammed his back something awful. Seth yelled, "Bring 'im back by five. He gets ornery without his dinner oats."

The horse ran for a good quarter mile in the dirt along the two-lane highway that led into Adobe Creek. Tico bumped his butt for most of the ride until something clicked. He got a better grip with his legs, leaned forward and found a rhythm with the horse's gallop. Reins wrapped around his hands, he continued to cling to the saddle horn— the only thing that saved him from falling on his ass when the horse had bucked. He wasn't about to let go now. No telling if Diablo would buck again.

It was nothing short of a miracle that he was still in the saddle, and a sense of excitement zinged through his system. Riding those narrow paths in the reeds along Brooklyn's shores as a kid had never offered the power and freedom of galloping in the open, barren desert. The sun was hot on his shoulders, and the air filling his lungs was cleaner than anything he'd known. It felt as if his Judumi blood was waking up. Not a good thought. If his father hadn't been such a dirtbag, maybe Tico might have liked the idea of being half Indian.

No need for that nonsense now.

The unexpected flash of emotion about his Judumi heritage left him unsure whether he'd made a good decision taking this job or using this horse to break the ice with his hosts. He'd already gotten feedback on how the investigating team in Adobe Creek had blown a gasket when they'd learned he'd been brought in as a consultant. Opinions flew.

Ex–gang leader.

Strings pulled to place him in police boot camp.

A hard-ass cop who lost a partner in a drug raid.

Tico had been cleared of any wrong, but rumor on the force was that Tico had betrayed his partner to the gang they were breaking. Nobody except his mentor and the two remaining men on his team trusted Tico anymore. He was bone weary from having to prove himself over and over again. Even as a gang leader he hadn't been all bad, just angry. He'd learned the difference a little too late.

So this time, he wanted to take the Adobe Creek team totally off guard. No doubt they expected a tough, opinionated, half-Judumi outcast to ride in and throw his weight around. Instead, Tico had decided to ditch his Harley for a horse and use comedy to make the team think twice before judging him. He didn't have time to earn their trust. Too much was happening too fast on this case. He needed to win them over, complete this assignment and get his tail out of Dodge as quickly as possible. He had a job to do. It didn't help that Adobe Creek was his father's hometown and a place where Tico claimed he'd never step foot.

Ever.

Now it was time to take control of this damned

animal if he was going to make his joke about being the lawman-to-the-rescue and get this frustrated team to work with him. The profile picture of the team leader rose in his mind. Meg Flores. Something about those dark brown eyes, the determination in her jaw, had him thinking she'd be just as stubborn as this damned horse. He sensed a kindred spirit there, and the idea had bothered him for the entire ride across the country. But he wouldn't jump to any conclusions until he met her in person.

He focused his attention back on the horse, gently pulling both reins to slow Diablo, but the damned fiend bucked again. In a blink, Tico flew out of the saddle, giving him a bird's-eye view of a police cruiser heading toward him before he hit the desert floor hard.

So much for being one with the animal. Good thing Tico was in shape. The momentum from the blow to his left side sent him rolling onto his feet. The fall had knocked his hat off. Half his hair had been pulled from his ponytail. With every inch of him aching, he watched the horse run toward the police cruiser. The car stopped. An officer leaped from the passenger side to intercept the horse. The animal slowed to a walk as if to greet the man.

"What the…?" Tico picked up his hat and slapped it on his leg. That damned horse liked everyone but him. *Why should a horse be any different than anyone else he knew?*

Taking a step, he felt as if he'd suddenly become bowlegged. He could already feel where the bruises would rise on his left hip. He made himself take shorter strides to keep from limping. The officer who detained the horse wore sunglasses, so Tico couldn't read his eyes, but from the way his mouth twitched, the burly man was trying to keep from laughing.

"Your horse?"

Tico waved a hand. "Yeah. Thanks. We just met and aren't getting along."

The cop gave a pointed look at the sheriff star pinned to Tico's vest. "Did the outfit come with the horse?"

Tico chuckled. This guy had a sense of humor. His police badge said Quinto. Tico turned his gaze to the mountains in the distance, doing his best John Wayne. "Never been out West. Trying to get a feel for the area."

"You staying in Adobe Creek?"

"For a little while." Tico put his hat back on his head to shelter his eyes from the glaring sun. "Been hired to work with your detective squad."

The officer didn't even flinch. "The expert from New York?"

Tico held out a hand. "Tico Butler. NYPD. I'm better with investigations than horses."

Ignoring his offered hand, the officer gestured to the desert. "What are you trying to do, kill yourself out here?"

No surprise, the guy wouldn't shake his hand. Wiping his palm on his pants, Tico stared at the unruly horse. "Thought I'd have a little fun before work. Didn't think my horse would mind as much as he does." He scratched his chin. "He sure seems to like you."

"Horses have keen senses. If you're afraid to ride, he'll know."

"I'm not afraid. Just been a long time since I've ridden."

"Well, I'm sure you'll earn the horse's respect by the time you get into town."

Tico shook his head. "Can horses be bribed to behave?"

Not quite suppressing a grin, Quinto glanced at the horse. "This is Charlie Samuels's mount. I'd say not a chance in hell." He handed Tico the reins. "It's about twenty minutes to the station. Good luck."

Tico stared Diablo in the eye. "No more games, buster. We've got a job to do."

This time, the horse let him mount, then stood there. Tico made sure his feet were secure in the stirrups. He flicked the reins. "Giddyap!"

The horse didn't move.

Officer Quinto had already climbed back into the patrol car. Tico could see the driver shake his head slowly as Quinto no doubt explained to him what was going on.

Yeah. He looked like a clown to these guys. He

didn't mind, but he needed this damned horse to cooperate.

He kicked the horse's flanks with both heels, and Diablo took off. "Whoooooooaaaaa!"

Tico worked to keep his seat while the horse galloped along the road into town. He'd be one sore son of a gun when this was over, but he had no choice. It was taking Tico years to regain the respect of his New York peers with his hard-nosed, unflinching approach to detective work, but he didn't have time to prove his worth here. He had to win over the Adobe Creek team. While humor had been his intent, he wanted to make his new colleagues laugh, not make a goddamn fool of himself.

The horse had taken to the pavement from the desert. He'd slowed his pace to a brisk walk but was hogging the center of the road. Tico used the reins as he remembered, but nothing he did convinced the horse to move over. From the way the traffic was being held up behind him, then passing him with dirty looks, it seemed that this freaking horse would sabotage his plans. He was losing to Diablo by the minute. Best he could do was pretend he wanted his mount to be unruly.

Tico let out a breath as he viewed the footprint of the small town nestled in the foothills. The mountains in the distance framed what looked like something out of an old Western mining town. From the elevation in the road, he could see Main Street—the busiest part of town. Not one high-rise dotted the vista. Just low adobe structures and wood-front buildings painted brown and white, or yellow or barn-red, with shutters on windows and signs over the doors.

In the foothills, the whitewashed adobe enclave of the Quarry sprawled like a wedge of Hollywood among the tumbleweeds. He'd read all about this celebrity hot spot in his review of the case. The Quarry, a now defunct silver mine, had been back-filled, landscaped and rebuilt into a spa community that managed to attract the rich and famous who wanted anonymity and seclusion. Celebrities owned private homes there, but vacation haciendas were available for anyone with means to pay the outrageous rent.

Tico used his sleeve to swipe the sweat off his brow. Damn climate roasted around here. He wished he'd thought to bring a canteen of water to round out his outfit. He looked like a goof in his *City Slickers* cowboy costume.

Softening his tough-guy reputation for the detectives of Adobe Creek had seemed like a good idea while driving across country. Especially for Meg Flores, who was the squad leader and hadn't asked for Tico's help. He'd been called in because the task force leader in that area wanted to make sure level heads led this sting. Once Meg Flores discovered who specifically had requested his help, she'd like him even less. That wouldn't do when he needed everyone's cooperation to get the job done.

Tico didn't underestimate the loyalty investigative teams held for each other. He'd learned that fact early on through the gangs he'd once known all too well. He'd also learned that the way into enemy territory was easiest when your adversaries thought you were harmless. From the line of cars—including the police cruiser—following him now, he'd say he was achieving the desired effect. The derogatory comments flying from drivers' windows were proof enough.

The procession on the two-lane road grew longer and agitated the horse even more. With every sounding horn Diablo grew more skittish. Thankfully, the Adobe Creek Police Department, the only modern facility in this currently one-horse town, was a stone's throw away. *And look there.* A welcome committee stood in the shade of the carport by the front door, watching him. The woman standing between the two men was Meg Flores. And no surprise, she looked better in real life than in her photo—even from this distance.

Tico concentrated on maneuvering Diablo under the overhang. He pulled the reins to the left, leading them toward the entrance, when the stallion reared unexpectedly, came down hard, then reared again. Arms flailing, hat flying, Butler landed flat on his back in a cloud of dirt. Passersby in cars yelled for him to trade his horse for a car and sped on. Folks on the sidewalk clapped and hooted with glee.

Tico lay with his eyes closed, trying to catch

the breath that had been knocked out of him. Meg Flores's laughter blended with the guffaws of her two teammates. Her voice penetrated his mind like a double shot of whiskey. If she spoke the same way she laughed, the girl had one sexy voice. He would have laughed, too, if breathing wasn't so difficult. Inwardly, he grinned, despite his discomfort. He'd gotten the reaction he wanted, although not exactly how he'd intended. If only it didn't feel as though he'd just broken every bone in his body.

With eyes still closed, he absorbed the jokes flying at his expense. His senses homed in on the sound of footsteps coming toward him. A cowboy-boot stride with attitude. He'd bet a month's pay he knew who the boots belonged to. Wondering if she'd act the part of rescuer, he kept his eyes shut. All expectations dashed when, still chuckling, she whispered to his horse, "Good job for throwing this bozo, fella."

He opened his eyes in time to see the sole of a cowboy boot press down on his chest. The curious stare of one Meg Flores flattened him more than he already was. Damn, she was smoking hot! The reins dangled from her right hand. Diablo glared at him from over her shoulder.

Traitor horse.

"Can I get you a taxi back to New York, Detective?"

Tico laughed out loud. His sides ached. His butt hurt. He didn't care. So, this was Meg Flores.

Tough. Defensive. Acting exactly as he'd expected she would in the face of his arrival. He'd heard she had guts, but no amount of research could have prepared him for the way those dark, proud bedroom eyes leveled him faster than the horse had. For one dazed moment he forgot he was on his back as he inhaled a scorching breath. Unwilling to succumb to his reaction to her, he let an easy grin cross his mouth.

He pointed to the horse, who he swore was looking smug behind her. "You guys really ride those things around here?"

She watched him a moment, her face unreadable. "I've never seen a horse look more embarrassed in my life. This must be your first time out West." She tapped the toy sheriff's badge on his chest with the toe of her boot. "Did the kids at school give you that star as a goodbye gift?"

He pushed her foot away and pulled himself upright. He'd be sporting yet another fine bruise on his hip from this latest fall. He used his hat to dust himself off—especially her boot print on his shirt—only to give up. This dirt was impossible to remove. He totally ignored the insult that had been aimed at his ego.

He took a moment to size up Meg and liked what he saw. Curves in jeans, a tailored white shirt and a navy blazer. Fit. Judging from the roots at her part, her once dark brown hair about as long as his own had been dyed blond. A heart-shaped face, sweet lips and those big brown eyes made her look too gorgeous to be a police detective. She was just a few inches shorter than he, and, from her bearing alone, he could see she'd be able to hold her own in a tussle. Something in the challenge of her stance had him wanting to test her. Her chin might give away her attitude, but those pursed lips nipped at his heart in an unfamiliar way.

Tico ran a hand through his hair. "I thought anyone could just hop in the saddle and ride. It sure looked easy in the movies."

Her laughter held a grudging tone. He didn't mind a bit. Even more, he liked the sound of her voice.

"You're the first out-of-town consultant to make a complete ass of himself at first sight. Well done," she said.

He popped the hat back on his head. Damn cowboy hat. Hated them, but it was part of the getup. He stole a quick glance at the two men clearly enjoying the spectacle he'd created. Winning over the men wouldn't take long. Cracking Meg Flores? Now, she would be a challenge.

Meanwhile, he could benefit from regaining some semblance of dignity. He hadn't expected that he'd have so much trouble with the horse. When he'd come up with the plan, he'd imagined that the horse would behave and not have a personality completely foreign to him. And he wasn't kidding about thinking anyone could simply jump on a horse and go. Damn. He'd ridden before. That beast was more of a bitch to ride than a rigid-frame chopper on city streets. He hesitated about claiming the reins from Meg, who already seemed to have tamed the animal. Yet, from the look on the detective's face, he just might prefer to take his chances with the horse.

He reached for the reins. A smirk crossed Meg's face as she handed them over. The horse turned his head away in total disinterest, pulling at the reins as if testing Tico one more time. Tico held firmly. The horse got the message and stood still. Looking the horse in the eye reinforced his earlier thoughts about riding. He'd never trade his Harley for a horse.

He cleared his throat. "I have an eleven o'clock appointment with Eric Longwood."

One of the men, who looked to be of Mexican descent, thumbed toward the newly renovated precinct. If memory served Tico from the files he read, this was Jose Lopez, the rookie detective on this case.

Lopez gestured over his shoulder. "Inside. Chief's expecting you."

Tico made sure to have eye contact with each of them. "Thanks for the reception."

Meg planted a hand on her hip. "We got a call that a circus act was riding in. Couldn't resist."

Ignoring her dig, he looked around. He wasn't

finished working the joker card. "Where does one park a horse around here?"

Meg shook her head. "Idiot."

He liked the challenge in her derision. When she didn't answer, he said, "I heard your precinct had a mounted unit. Can my demon on four legs hang out with your horses until I'm done?"

She gestured to the corner. "Stable is behind the building." She glanced at her watch. "Better get a move on, cowboy. Eric doesn't like to start late."

Tico walked the horse away, leaving a wave of chuckles behind him for not mounting to ride. For once, Diablo followed dutifully behind him. The beast was probably glad he didn't have to deal with Tico again. He rounded the corner to the stables. In any other city they could have been mistaken for a four-bay garage with doors that swung open instead of up.

The renovated police station reflected the wealth that funneled into Adobe Creek from the celebrity resort nestled in the foothills. While the rest of the city maintained its historic Southwestern architecture, the modern brick precinct looked out of place amid the older adobe and wood buildings and outdated warehouses farther down the narrow street. Adobe Creek needed about fifty years to catch up with the rest of the world.

Tico looked around with a sense of disbelief, unable to accept he'd taken this job. Yet, here he was, his hip already hurting from his two throws, facing off with the squad team that wanted nothing to do with him, and wondering what Meg Flores looked like when she wasn't angry.

His reception had proven to be more or less what he'd expected. What had surprised him was the gut wrench that hit when he'd ridden his Harley past the Judumi reservation outside of Adobe Creek. His dad had told him stories of the Judumi tribe, but any group that had spit out his dad and forgotten about Tico, even though they knew he existed, was no group he ever wanted to join.

Yet, he'd come, even though he didn't relish the meeting with Chief Eric Longwood and the detective team. Under other circumstances he'd bet Meg Flores could have been a friend, along with the rest of her team. But, no. Once again, he had to be the hired gun. He arrived as the threat to their reputations because they couldn't move this investigation forward. None of them wanted him here. Diablo snorted behind him, pulling on the reins as if punctuating his thoughts. Tico picked up the pace. The sooner he unloaded this animal, the better he'd feel.

Did the team know that Tico had originally refused the job? It wasn't until the man behind Longwood's request had called him and explained the personal investment he had in solving this case that Tico did some soul searching and accepted the assignment. The huge pay hadn't hurt either, but refusing would have been morally wrong.

He'd done stings similar to this before. He'd never tackled a group as far-reaching as the Mexican Carlito cartel, but stopping their drug and human trafficking ring in Adobe Creek outweighed his personal desires never to set foot in this part of the country. Diablo's hooves clicked on the pavement as if counting out the seconds that would lead to the hours and then days he would spend in Adobe Creek. He'd get the job done as quickly as possible and get the hell out of town. Maybe take a long vacation. Ride his Harley up the Pacific coast. After fifteen years, he needed a break. He was so damned tired of playing the tough guy with his peers.

An older man with a day's worth of stubble stood in the door of the stables. He took one look at Tico and began to laugh.

"Long ride from Tombstone, son?"

Another joker. Yeah. Maybe he shouldn't have taken this job, even if he did set himself up as a fool. Why was he always right?

# CHAPTER TWO

MEG SAT IN the conference room with her team members, Bill, Jose and Mitchell, awaiting her boss and the Rattlesnake—Tico Butler's nickname in the underground world, according to his profile.

She swallowed a gulp of coffee with disgust. Wasn't it her bad luck that even though he arrived dressed like a clown riding down Main Street, Butler looked like someone she'd find attractive? She'd worried about that since seeing his photo. Almost forty years old, Butler had a tough look, his face chiseled by a life lived hard, but there was something strong, magnetic and downright sexy about the expression in his eyes in the profile photo. His features smacked of his Judumi heritage. Her family ranch sat adjacent to the Judumi reservation. She'd been friends with the tribe her entire life.

She'd learned that Tico Butler's father had belonged to the Judumi tribe. Her most trusted teammate, Bill Mewith, was also from the Judumi and had been her childhood friend. She glanced at him sitting beside her now. He'd mentioned that he was curious about the tribesman they were about to meet who'd never known his heritage. Meg had always admired everything about the Judumi native culture. She might be Mexican-American, but she'd spent her childhood with her Judumi neighbors and felt like one of them.

Bill caught her glance. "So, what if we're wrong about this guy, Butler? I could see my brother pulling a stunt like his this morning."

At Bill's words, Jose sat back in his chair as if expecting bullets to fly.

Palms flat on the table, Meg leaned closer to Bill. "After all we discussed, you're caving?"

"Not caving, girl. We have a serious issue here. Maybe we should rethink our opinion of him."

"Because he made an ass of himself for all to see?" She waved in the direction of the street. "You don't know who he is. *I do.* I did my research. Did any of you? That whole show was to get you on his side. And you're playing right into his hands."

Jose whistled softly. "*Cojones,* man. His must be made of steel."

Bill chuckled. "Especially with the way he was riding. An insult to his heritage, for sure."

Meg cringed. She didn't mind the slang. She minded that they were admiring Butler when they'd all agreed to be unified in their attempt to muscle him off the case.

"Look, I don't argue that he's probably good at what he does, but we don't need him."

Bill leaned toward her at eye level. "He took us

by surprise with his antics. He'd probably be just as effective infiltrating a place we can't get into."

"Must have been quite an entrance. Sorry I missed it," Mitchell said.

Meg swallowed her anger. "Look, he'll be here any minute. I don't want you wimping out on me when you were all outraged that we'd been circumvented. We can do this job without some city slicker."

Mitchell cleared his throat. "We've been working to crack this ring for almost two years. It's been a week since the latest women were taken, Meg. Not one stinking lead. We've probably already lost those three girls."

"No!" Meg could feel her face flush. She didn't like her emotional reaction one bit, but she couldn't bring herself to accept the fact that the missing high school girls were gone for good. At least, not yet. Unsolved, the missing persons files could stay open forever. Meg didn't want those ghosts haunting them. "I'm not willing to give up on these women yet, Mitchell. If they've been snatched by the cartel, too many bad things will happen to them. We have to keep looking."

He shrugged. "Maybe you're right. But we've combed the county. What's your next great idea?"

The sarcasm in his voice had the other men looking up. *Easy girl,* she told herself. Mitchell might be Longwood's hired consultant, but he wasn't hers. In her mind, he'd retired two years ago. He didn't need to be here now. She took a slug of coffee and let the hot liquid burn down her throat. "Seems to me, Mitch, that generating great ideas is why you're still here. You know? Resident expert? Why are you asking me?"

The room fell silent. Mitchell was the longest-standing detective in the precinct. Although he had retired two years ago, he kept coming back as a consultant because he'd experienced more stings and busts than any of them, at least until this latest cartel. The cartel operated along the border but had never intruded on Adobe Creek. Until now.

Mitchell slammed the table with his fist. "Well, little girl, I've run out of ideas this time. Maybe that's why your daddy enlisted Tico Butler."

Her *father* had brought Tico Butler on to the case? No. Eric Longwood had hired him. She wasn't going to split hairs with the man who always tried to push her buttons.

Meg slid back her seat. "Daddy my ass, Mitchell. Maybe if you spent less time with your buddy *Jack Daniel's,* you'd be clear enough to respect that *kids* like us know what we're doing."

Her accusation was like a bucket of ice water thrown on the room. Everyone knew Mitchell tipped the bottle now and then, but no one dared talk about his problem since he didn't venture into the field anymore. After all, he was a legend in his own time. Now that he did mostly desk work, what did the occasional drink matter?

Bill held up both hands. "Dammit, you two. Enough! Nothing productive is coming from this argument."

Meg blew out a breath. Bill was right. She let herself drop back into her chair. "See? The snake hasn't even gotten here, and we're sniping at each other. I'm not backing down."

"We don't have a choice, Meg. Butler is here," Bill said. He leaned toward her. Speaking quietly, he pulled his usual stunt when he thought she was wrong. "I'll bet fifty bucks you're the first one who caves to this guy."

She shook his hand, gripping it more tightly than normal. This was one bet he'd lose. "You're on."

Jose looked apologetic. "Mitchell is right, Meg. We have to listen to what Butler has to say. We've run out of leads."

She pointed a finger at each of them. "If you think Tico Butler is useful, then you get what you need from him before I send him packing." She looked each man in the eye. "Are we all agreed on this?"

Bill nodded. "Might take longer than one meeting, but I get your drift."

Jose held up a hand. "You're the boss."

Mitchell shook his head. "Good luck with that one."

That was all she'd get out of Mitchell. She didn't expect much else.

She listened with half an ear to Jose and Bill

making small talk with Mitchell, which was pretty much the routine for clearing the air after a heated exchange. Football. The latest drug bust. But, now that she'd had an exchange with Butler, all she could think about was how to keep her balance and stand her ground, even if the others disagreed. Butler's stunt with the horse was nothing any of them had expected. More reason to run his unwanted help out of town. A lot was at stake here. She wasn't about to let an outsider screw things up, no matter what his reputation.

She addressed Mitchell. "What do you say we let Eric and Butler do all the talking before giving our input?"

Mitchell shrugged. "That'll do."

She sensed motion in the hallway outside the conference room windows. She sucked in a fortifying breath to settle her heart rate when Tico Butler looked right back at her.

"Okay, guys. Here comes trouble."

PLASTERING A SERIOUS look on his face after joking with the amused officer at the desk, Tico followed the officer's directions to the conference room down the hall. The blinds on the floor-to-ceiling windows were open. He registered the scene with a glance.

Meg Flores, her two teammates and Mitchell Blake were seated around the fake wood table, a pitcher of water, glasses and manila files on the table. An empty whiteboard filled the wall behind the head of the table. A red light blinked on a coffeemaker holding a freshly brewed pot.

From reading their profiles, Tico knew that Bill Mewith was the Judumi Indian seated next to Meg, his hair hanging in a braid down his back. Jose Lopez sat drumming his fingers on the table. Mitchell Blake looked worse than his profile picture. Stress lines around his eyes and mouth, faded red hair and the start of a paunch at his waistline made him look world-weary and badly in need of exercise. Tico had read that they were all good at their jobs. Right now, they all looked pissed as they watched him pass the window.

Exhaling a long breath, Tico was about to push through the door when someone called his name. He recognized Eric Longwood heading toward him. He was taller and rangier than he'd expected from the face-to-face Skype conversations they'd had last week. With blond hair in need of a trim, and a mustache that could rival any biker's, Longwood was as distinguished as his light blue eyes, intent and intelligent.

Eric held out a hand. "Nice to finally meet you in person. Welcome."

Tico let a grin play across his face. "I managed to arrive alive."

Longwood motioned to his clothes. "What's with the getup?"

"Trying to ruin my reputation."

"How'd you do so far?"

Tico tapped his badge. "Stellar."

Longwood shook his head, a look of disbelief crossing his features. "I can just imagine. I've seen the video already. Come in and meet the crew."

Tico followed the chief into the conference room ripe with the smell of coffee and animosity. Inwardly, he sighed. Another round with the angry birds.

Longwood put his own folder at the head of the table. "Everyone, this is Tico Butler."

"We met outside," Meg said. She looked as though she was still stewing. From the subdued expressions on the other men's faces, he figured she'd just given them a good tongue-lashing, as well.

The chief took a seat. "Good, then the introductions don't need to be made. Tico, why don't you have a seat."

Tico pulled out the chair next to Meg. "I haven't been formally introduced to anyone. My horse made that hard to do."

Longwood shook his head. "I know. Your horse made quite a debut on the security cameras. Don't be surprised if you end up on YouTube."

Chuckling, Blake was the first to offer his hand. "Mitchell Blake. Retired. Not sure why I still hang with these kids."

The younger man followed suit. "Jose Lopez."

"Bill Mewith," said the Judumi. His handshake was strong, and his eyes held the guarded look of a man recognizing a stranger as one of his own. "I read your profile. Your father was Judumi."

Tico appreciated the guy's direct approach. "So I've been told. You look like a tribesman."

Mewith nodded. "As do you, brother. You'd fit right in around here."

That hit Tico like a gut punch. Did he want to fit in where he didn't want to be?

"Next you'll be inviting him home for some fry bread and roasted quail," Meg Flores said, looking miffed with her colleague.

Tico leaned back in his chair. "I can see we'll get along just fine, Detective Flores."

"You need riding lessons."

"And you could use some manners."

Chief Longwood took over. "That's enough. Let's get one thing straight right away, Meg. Tico didn't ask for this assignment. He agreed to come after lots of persuasion. So a show of respect is expected. We have a job to do. Let's all get along or go home." He looked pointedly at Meg. "Am I clear?"

Meg nodded once. "Shall I pass out the latest files?"

Tico took a moment to peruse the file she handed him, even though the others probably knew he'd already seen a detailed report. Staying impassive when staring at the smiling faces of the three missing women was still hard for him to do. A case was simply a puzzle to be solved until photos revealed the people involved.

The kidnapped women in Adobe Creek were what had triggered the call for Tico to assist in breaking this case. The mayor of this town worked on a special task force to fight human trafficking, a crime that had become more prolific over the years. The miles of unpatrolled border made abductions child's play for the underworld. Adobe Creek's finest worked hard to keep the cartels away from their residents and, up to this point, had been successful, but someone had crossed the line. Not wanting to waste a minute, the locals had summoned Tico—three times until he'd finally agreed. Tico didn't miss the set of the detectives' jaws as they perused the files in front of them.

Chief Longwood began the discussion. "The Adobe Creek Police Department doesn't like having women go missing within its boundaries. Heck, we don't like women going missing at all, but when it happens on our turf, it's war.

"Tico, as you know, we've been tracking the Carlito ring coming from Mexico for two years now without a whiff of a lead once they cross the border. Can't even figure out where they're crossing. Now that they've hit our town, they're in our backyard. Not acceptable."

"Where do you lose the trail?" Tico asked.

Longwood thumbed over his shoulder. "Adobe Creek is adjacent to the Nogales-Phoenix corridor, which has eight thousand square miles of the most inhospitable land in southern Arizona."

"They also trespass across the reservation, coming on foot and with trucks that destroy fences and vegetation," Bill Mewith added. "The tribe has men we call shadow wolves on the hunt all the time. Sometimes they get a lead, but the trail turns dry by the time they get over another rise."

Mitchell said, "Last week a load of drones headed straight for the sensors, pulling every lawman in a five-mile radius. All bogus. We learned later that the drones were sent to distract our forces while they launched over fifty mule trains from different points. They get a kick out of jerking us around with decoys."

Tico frowned. "They're not using planes, I take it?"

Longwood shook his head. "The feds have some pretty sophisticated tracking equipment, but the cartel scouts have technology that hasn't even hit the States yet. They don't need to use planes. Too noisy. The ground works just fine."

Meg Flores had been surprisingly quiet. Tico was glad when she finally spoke. "We've come up dry in all directions," she said grudgingly.

Tico liked the velvet-smooth sound of her voice, like a blend of bourbon and honey. Her words lit a fire in her eyes. He didn't blame her for being angry. What concerned him was whether or not her outrage would cloud her judgment.

"You investigated the celebrity resort?" He made a show of checking his file although he knew the name. "The Quarry?"

"Last time we checked the resort, everything looked clean," Mitchell Blake said. "And none of the missing women live there."

Meg looked at Tico. "The chief thinks you can infiltrate the area more easily than the rest of us."

Tico tapped his badge. "Can I take my horse, too?"

Meg groaned. "God spare us."

Bill leaned toward Tico. "Word of advice, brother? Don't ever let a tribesman see you riding. They'd put you to shame for not being able to man a horse."

Tico almost winced. Mewith had called him *brother,* twice. He didn't like being recognized as a Judumi, even though he had the traditional almond-shaped eyes and angular face of his father's people. He had enough of his mother's New York Irish in him to stand apart in both attitude and lineage.

The other men laughed.

Tico pointed to the pitcher of water. "Mind if I help myself?"

At the chief's nod, he reached for a glass and felt his muscles pull all the way down to his left hip. Damned horse. He wanted to groan but just kept reaching. The others kept silent as he poured water. He held up the pitcher. "Anyone else?"

Blake stood and headed for the coffeepot. Flores

already had a cup of coffee. No one else answered. Tico drank, glad to wash the road dust out of his throat. "Who reported the missing women?"

"Family. Tina Marks and Cheryl Hall are high school seniors from Bisbee. Came to Adobe Creek to tube on the river with friends. They went out on an errand to the shopping mall and never came back."

Tico appraised the three photos. The high school seniors were blonde and brunette. Both long hair, but different looks. The other woman was a local resident, a mother of two small children. Janice Carlton was older than the other two but not by more than five or six years. Again, with dyed blond hair falling at her jawline, she had a different look. So, no common element here except for the fact that they were women.

"You've questioned boyfriends, neighbors? Janice Carlton's ex-husband and friends?"

Meg shot him a quelling glance. "All of our investigations are in the report. We've been to all suspected areas—twice. Did *you* not read your copy?"

He let a grin play on his face. "Night reading. I usually fell asleep before finishing."

She slapped her forehead. "Chief, I beg you. Do we really have to talk to this guy?"

Eric let his gaze slide from Meg to Tico. "What are you getting at, Tico?"

"I'm suggesting that perhaps we need to go back

to all the original points of investigation one more time."

The room fell quiet. The burnt smell of coffee invaded Tico's nostrils. The hot plate sizzled with coffee Blake had spilled when pouring his cup. Tico took another sip of water, if only to give the others time to digest his suggestion.

"See if there are any contradictions the third time around?" Bill asked.

"Yes. It's hard for people to remember the details they tell when they're lying. And sometimes when the stress lets up a bit, people have time to remember facts." Tico tapped the page. "I see the mother was recently divorced. Lived alone with her children."

"*Lives* alone," Meg said, sending a heated glance in Tico's direction. "She's still alive."

Tico ignored her but changed his verb tense. "Does she have a morning routine? Stop for coffee before work? Work out? Walk a dog?"

Meg answered in clipped tones, "No pets. Has a gym at home. Doesn't drink coffee. We've covered all that."

Taking a fortifying breath, Tico gestured to Bill and Meg. He was about to ruin their day asking a question they wouldn't want to hear. "I understand your impatience. It must feel like hell sitting here when there are three women missing and no leads. The pressure can make a detective edgy— especially when another woman goes missing after two years of investigating the ring. Can you handle this case?"

Bill's face grew stone cold. Meg's jaw dropped. She turned to Longwood.

"Chief, are you going to let him insinuate that *we* are incapable of conducting this investigation?"

Longwood brushed his fingers along his mustache. "I know we've been over this, Meg, but I'd like to hear you answer him." He nodded toward Bill. "You, too. For the record."

Meg scoffed. "For the *record?* I'm sure Mr. Rattlesnake here knows all the details from his discussions with you before he got here."

Bill sat straighter in his chair. "Is this really necessary, Chief?" When Eric didn't answer, Bill turned to Tico. The cut in his voice made it perfectly clear that he'd been insulted. "My neighbor and two other tribal elders were murdered by passing drug dealers while they were harvesting ceremonial plants in the desert last year. Meg and I tracked and caught the bastards without shooting a bullet or losing a man. Do you seriously think I need to answer your question?"

Meg pointed to Tico. "And you want us to be nice to this guy?" She leaned back in her chair. "Look, Detective Butler. We are working against all odds here. We know it might be too late to rescue these women. But I believe their captors still have them holed up locally, waiting for a window of opportunity to funnel them to safer ground." She stared at Tico as if he were a dung heap. "As you know, the women are probably being drugged to keep them docile. Once the abductors get them away from here, they will be raped, beaten and tormented to break their spirits."

Tico didn't flinch. "I understand your concern better than you think, Detective Flores. However, you didn't answer my question."

He saw her decision to hate him flick like a switch in her eyes. The tension in her face drew those full, kissable lips into a fine line. He watched her, unblinking. This was what Longwood had hired him to do. He'd dealt with anger, death threats and his share of fights. Yet, seeing her animosity rise was like swallowing battery acid. A new reaction. The feeling jolted his senses. That irritated him something fierce.

The other men might recognize that he was only doing his job, but this woman and Mewith were taking his question personally. He had to admit— he'd do the same if some out-of-town show-off tried to take over his investigation when he had so much at stake. But Tico already knew Mewith's story. He also knew that Meg's family had lost women to human trafficking. He needed to make sure these two could be impartial, not caught up in a vendetta. Feeling everyone's eyes on him, he

watched Meg Flores while tension thrummed the
air, waiting patiently for her to answer.

MEG SEETHED INSIDE but she kept her expression as
neutral as possible. No wonder they called Butler the Rattlesnake. He'd sat perfectly still during
the case discussion. Only the flash in his eyes had
warned her he'd been about to strike. This son of a
bitch pushed her buttons on first contact. She didn't
need a ruggedly sexy jerk from New York point-
ing out the possibility of her own shortcomings in
front of her boss and her team.

Sure, this case was critical. Sure, Butler had
street know-how that her team could use. But damn
it all. She didn't want to have to answer to him. *She*
was the team leader—and now she was feeling as
emotionally unfit as he suggested she might be.
Yes, she was pissed.

This investigation needed to move forward—
and now. Everyone around this table needed to quit
flexing their muscles. Someone had to give, but
Meg couldn't relent. Not yet. Not until she knew
that she could trust this one-time gang leader from
New York. Rumor had it that he didn't even have
the required high school education to get into the
police academy. Guts alone and the recommenda-
tion of his mentor had gotten him accepted, and
not without a fight.

Could she trust a man like that? The only way
to find out was to not back down.

Meg closed her file. Laying a hand on the folder as if it were a Bible, she looked pointedly at Butler and said in a low, controlled voice, "I am more than capable of executing my duties in bringing these women home quickly and efficiently. Do you have a problem with that, Detective?"

Tico closed his file, returning the stare. "Not at all, Detective. That's all I wanted to know."

Butler swallowed. The movement had Meg staring at his neck. Corded. Defined. His collar, open at the neck, hinted at muscles beneath the denim shirt with her boot print still shadowing the front. His black hair, pulled into a ponytail as with most Judumi men, glistened beneath the overhead light. That intrigued her. If the man was as set against his heritage as he seemed, why did he imitate his people, who believed long hair enhanced their senses? His dark eyes seemed dangerous, probing, and watched her with an unsettling curiosity.

Lines etched around his eyes and mouth betrayed his expressiveness. A scar crossed his jaw. He had a nice mouth. Good teeth. Gawd! She was checking him out as if he was horseflesh. Worse, he realized she was staring and simply stared back. The room had gone quiet while these two appraised each other.

Eric Longwood cleared his throat.

Tico kept his attention trained on Meg. His voice lowered. "Okay, then, Detective. What's your plan?"

Just like that? He was giving up after putting her and Bill on the spot? She shook her head. This guy was not going to manipulate them into cooperating by intimidation.

"Is this a test, Detective Butler, or are you already out of ideas?"

Tico smiled. "I'm full of ideas, Detective. I'm simply wondering if you are ready to listen to them."

# *CHAPTER THREE*

MEG PRACTICALLY TURNED her white pickup on two wheels into the quarter-mile drive for Rio Plata Ranch. A cloud of dust rose behind her. The open, arid land on either side of the road passed without notice. Meg couldn't get her mind off the meeting at the precinct, where Tico Butler had invaded her world. Her concentration had been shot for the rest of the day while she'd stewed over what to do.

The answer had struck like lightning. Now she headed for her parents' house. The only way she'd be able to get Butler off the case was to ask for her father's help. Don Francisco Flores was mayor of Adobe Creek. Next to the Judumi reservation, Don Francisco was the largest landholder in the county. He also owned the Rio Plata silver mine in Mexico on which he'd built his fortune. Don Francisco knew every public official within a one-hundred-mile radius and had funded the Adobe Creek unit against drug and human trafficking years ago. If anyone could send Butler packing, Don Francisco could—and would if Meg asked him to.

Meg reduced her speed to lessen the dust as she

passed the cabins for the ranch hands. Two horses
were still in the split-rail corral next to the courtyard and cantered to the fence at the sight of her
truck. Her parents must have been riding before
dinner. Nice. They really knew how to enjoy their
life now that they'd both retired from the mining
industry. Well, her father would never truly retire.
But Meg's brother was doing a fine job of running
the business in Mexico, which freed Don Francisco
to concentrate on his twin passions—politics and
Adobe Creek.

Pulling her truck up to the courtyard leading to
the front door of the low-slung, rambling adobe
ranch, Meg caught sight of a silver Harley-Davidson
parked in the shade of a mesquite tree. Her breath
caught in her throat. The bike had a New York tag.

She froze. "No way in hell."

She pushed open the arched heavy wooden door,
ready for battle. The familiar, sage-scented cool-
ness of the living room welcomed her, but no one
was around.

No *one* person in particular.

She headed for the kitchen at the back of the
house. "Mom? Dad?"

"Señorita Flores, is that you?"

The housekeeper's teenage daughter came burst-
ing through the kitchen door. Her eyes were bright
with excitement.

"*Hola,* Ana. Where are my parents?"

"Oh, *Señorita*. We have a guest. Such an interesting man."

Of course. A rugged, sexy stranger rides in on a Harley looking as if every inch of him offers excitement, and any teenage girl would go gaga.

"Easy now, Ana. Where are they?"

"The veranda. Mama is preparing *ropa vieja*."

No way was that creep eating dinner in her house. Meg took the few steps to the back doors and looked out. Sure enough, Tico Butler sat beneath the shade of the roofed pergola at the far end of the stone-walled veranda, holding a glass of beer, leaning back in the upholstered chair, looking very much at home in her parents' company, attentively listening to something her mother was saying.

Damn his bones. Meg charged out the door. All three looked up at the sound of her footsteps. Barbara Flores smiled at her daughter's approach. Once she sensed Meg's intention, her brow creased with distress. Though her mother could read her every mood, anyone watching would know Meg was angry. Her father and Tico seemed to share the same expectant, if not guarded, look.

She smelled foul play at her expense. There was more going on here than she suspected. She pointed to Butler. "Dad, what is he doing here?"

Still wearing her riding clothes, Barbara Flores sat straighter, if possible. With her silver-streaked black hair pulled back in an elegant chignon, her blue eyes a striking contrast to her hair, her mother was a woman of sophistication who always stood her ground, especially in the world of academia, where she'd made a name for herself. She would not tolerate Meg's impoliteness, unless she understood her daughter's reasoning.

"Meg?"

Meg didn't want to cause a scene, but really? Did she have to come home looking for help, only to find the root of her problem charming her parents before she even had the chance to talk with them?

"I don't mean to be rude, but I can't think of anything else to say." She gestured to Butler. "We met today and do *not* get along. I can't understand why he is here."

Don Francisco stood. At sixty-four, of medium height and build, he was every bit the dark, handsome Mexican aristocrat in his jeans, boots and crisp white cowboy shirt. He'd worked his way up from the streets to earn his fortune and carried his success with pride. He took Meg's hands, kissed her cheek. "It distresses me to see you upset."

Her father's patronizing tone was way too familiar. "You haven't answered me."

He ignored her prod. "Detective Butler told us about the meeting this morning. We understand your concern."

"But that doesn't explain why he's here."

"Because I invited him to dinner."

Meg looked from her father to her mother, who didn't look happy with Meg. At all. "You what?"

Tico stood, placed his beer on the low table. "I don't want to cause any trouble. I'll be happy to take a rain check on dinner."

Don Francisco held up a hand. "Unnecessary, Tico. Meg will regain her manners, and we shall continue our conversation."

"Dad!"

Don Francisco signaled to Ana, who hovered in the doorway. "The beer is ice-cold. I think you can use one."

Ana acknowledged Don Francisco's request for Meg's beer and shot Tico a smile before leaving.

Barbara tapped the orange cushion on the wicker chair next to hers. "Sit down, Meg. We were having an interesting conversation about horses."

Tico's easy grin did nothing to sway her. Meg understood exactly why Butler had arrived on horseback, and it was for no one else's benefit but his. "Maybe another time, Mom. I won't stay. I'll catch you in the morning." She turned to go.

"Meg, stay. You most certainly do not want to miss our conversation," Don Francisco said.

Her father's displeasure wasn't lost on her. He was a man of few words, but when he spoke, he made his point. "Why not?"

"Because it concerns you."

Tico was still standing, watching her. He stood maybe three or four inches taller than her, but his strong physique made him seem bigger. He'd lost the goofy vest, and she couldn't help but notice how his denim shirt fit the planes of his tanned chest.

The curiosity in his eyes was unsettling. He lifted a hand as if in a gesture of peace. "I'm not the enemy, Meg. I swear."

Oh, hell, no. He wasn't going to win her over with false sincerity in front of her parents. "Yet you questioned my integrity in the presence of my boss and my team?"

Barbara frowned. "Meg, is this necessary?"

Her mother's soft voice made her uncomfortably aware of the venom in her own words. She released a breath. "Look, everyone. I apologize. I'm a bit keyed up. Women are missing, and we're getting nowhere because everyone is trying to prove who is tougher. Meanwhile, those women could be suffering. I don't like seeing important business neglected while everyone jockeys for control. I just want to get back to work."

Her father gestured to the seat his wife had offered Meg. "Sit. Let's talk."

Reluctantly, she took the seat as Ana returned with a frosty mug of beer on a tray. Meg took a long draft of the cool amber liquid and let her gaze fall past the veranda to the acres of open land framed by the mountains. The lowering sun cast a golden glow on the arid ground and low trees, the cattle in the north acres settling in for the evening. Two ducks paddled across the still lake bordering her own two acres on the back lot. The sun reflected on the windows of her cabin nestled among paloverde trees at the lake's edge. She'd love to take Whisper on a run before sunset, but not tonight.

When she turned her focus back to the veranda, Tico was watching her. Again.

"What?"

"I'd heard this land was beautiful, but I never imagined how much."

Adobe Creek didn't need another resident, especially one whose rugged sex appeal was derailing her intentions. "Don't get too comfortable."

"Meg! I've never heard you be so unkind." Barbara fanned herself.

Don Francisco sat once more. "No more of this nonsense, Meg. You will have to find some common ground with Detective Butler. He came to Adobe Creek at my insistence. It doesn't help anything to have my own daughter disrespect his ability to get the job done."

Meg's jaw dropped. So, once again Mitchell Blake was right. "*You* brought him here?" She blew out a hot breath. "I can't believe my ears! What makes you think my team can't do our job?"

"*Mi hija,* in my life, I've already lost two sisters to human trafficking. I will not stand idle at the possibility that you could be in harm's way, expressly because someone may want to target me to stop this investigation."

"I'm perfectly capable of taking care of myself!"

Don Francisco nodded. "I believe you are, but you are my only daughter. I will not take the chance." He gestured to Tico. "I believe with Tico's help you will not only be safer, but more efficient."

"I don't need a chaperone. That's why I became a police officer in the first place. God knows you hammered self-defense into my head since I could walk."

"In this situation, your training does not matter."

She knew what was coming but had to stop it. "Dad, nothing will have me taken off a case faster than insinuating to Eric that I can't handle this task on my own. If there's any doubt whatsoever, I'm removed. You know this." She pointed to Butler. "He knows this. Do you want me to lose my job?"

Don Francisco grew silent. Her mother said nothing.

Her parents' silence said it all. Holy crow. The two of them had been reluctant to support her decision to become a detective because of the dangers involved, but they *had* supported her. From their grim expressions now, they were about to betray her. They'd never been comfortable with the fact that she put herself in harm's way, but they were never ones to dissuade her from her vocation. Now, because of the abductions, Don Francisco was panicking based on his own personal losses.

She scoffed. "You can't be serious."

Barbara laid a hand on Meg's knee. "We don't

want you to lose your job, honey. It's just this case. It's too dangerous."

Meg could have been hit with a wrecking ball. She sat back in her chair, using every ounce of willpower to keep her cool. One glance at Tico and she saw he'd already had this conversation with her parents. A single line furrowed the brow on his poker face. Was that concern about her reaction? Did he like the idea of taking over *her* case? Was that why he was here? Was that why Eric hadn't defended her against Tico's question at this morning's meeting? Was the plan to remove her already in place? How could Butler sit there so cool and unflappable? What would he do if he was in her situation?

Inwardly shaking herself, she leaned forward to keep her mother's attention. "Mother, this is my job. I am completely qualified, with or without this so-called expert." She hoped Butler saw the anger and distrust burning in her eyes.

His voice gentle, Tico said, "I can help, Meg."

She sat back in her chair. He actually sounded as if he cared. What a load of horse manure. Refusing to look at him again, she glanced from her mother to her father. "I can't believe you two have turned on me like this. What is wrong with you?"

Don Francisco expelled a breath. "I have every confidence in your ability as a law enforcer, Meg. But the Carlito cartel? They are arrogant. Ruthless. They will think nothing of infiltrating your unit and hurting everyone they can possibly reach. I already told you. Because I am mayor and I lead the Mexican task force, you are a prime target for revenge. This group has deep pockets and moles everywhere. I'd rather you step aside this one time and let Detective Butler do his job."

"*His* job is in New York. My team can do this."

"My dear, the only way I will permit you to stay on the case is if you let Detective Butler lead the squad. You follow his instructions, or Eric will pull you off. Your mother and I prefer you work this case from a desk, anyway."

And she'd thought this morning's meeting was bad. She'd just been sideswiped by the two people she trusted most in the world while the object of her derision watched. She wiped her mouth with the back of her hand. "And to think I came here to ask your help to remove Detective Butler from the case."

Don Francisco shook his head. "No, Meg. He's our guest. I've invited him to stay in one of the vacant cabins."

That did it.

She stood, placed the half-finished beer glass on the table, her insides quaking with anger. "I've heard enough. Enjoy your *ropa vieja*. Good night."

TICO SAT IN the rocking chair on the porch of his cabin, feet on the rail, roasting the end of a Catelli cigar for lighting. The orange tip glowed in the dark as he drew on the cigar. Slowly exhaling the smoke, he relaxed his muscles, letting the stillness of the evening settle into his senses.

He'd showered off the day's dust and bad attitude, and changed into his favorite worn jeans, black T-shirt and boots. With his hair tied back, he felt physically refreshed, but his thoughts were weary.

Once again, he was the odd man out. As much as he could have happily spent the evening alone, especially after pissing off the sexiest woman he'd seen in a very long time, he'd stayed for dinner with Don Francisco and Barbara.

They'd seemed genuinely interested in learning more about him, asking in-depth questions about his parents and his upbringing, which Tico patiently answered, though he didn't appreciate the invasion of his privacy. He suspected Don Francisco already knew the answers, but figured the man wanted to see Tico's take on his childhood. Tico could understand the man's motives, which was why he'd answered. He wouldn't have been as understanding with anyone else. As his employer and the father of the sultry team leader he'd been hired to supplant, Don Francisco deserved respect and ease of mind.

He'd worn his long-sleeve shirt through dinner because he hadn't wanted Barbara Flores to see the rattlesnake tattoo circling his forearm. The ink was a permanent reminder of a time he was no longer proud of. But the tat? The snake's meaning had changed with him.

Now, in the dark, he didn't care. He needed to unwind from the day but was too wired. His newly relaxed muscles tightened up once more as he thought about Meg's fine ass as she strode from the veranda tonight. He really liked everything about her. Felt a pull toward the woman in a way he'd never known. If the situation were different, they'd make one helluva team.

He took a moment to exhale a stream of cigar smoke. His entire left side ached from the falls this morning. He'd been so outraged at the horse after the morning meeting, he'd called Charlie Samuels and told him he'd pay extra if Charlie would send someone to pick up the horse and give Tico a ride back to his Harley. The son of a bitch had laughed on the other end of the phone, but sent Seth with a horse trailer.

A chuckle escaped his throat. The look of amusement on Meg's face before the horse threw him had been priceless. She may have treated him rough, but he'd seen the intense way she had checked him out while all huffy and pissed. The others might have been fooled, but he could tell she was arming herself against her own thoughts in his favor.

He'd take a chance on that instinct in the near future.

Even though her father had hired him, the last thing Tico wanted was to ambush Meg as team leader of the investigation. Don Francisco had brought him in as a top detective, but not until tonight had he made it clear that his desire to keep his daughter safe from the cartel was enough for him to sanction Tico taking over Meg's job—permanently. He'd couched his concern by saying that he wanted Tico to do anything necessary to keep his daughter unharmed. Tico had heard Don Francisco's veiled message loud and clear, and didn't like it. At all. In an equally correct manner, he'd replied that Meg had an excellent reputation, and he looked forward to working with her.

Tico had no desire to take Meg's job. He wanted to get the bad guys. Period. Don Francisco's double standard put Tico in a difficult position with both Meg and her father. Would he be able to solve this case and keep his integrity intact with either party?

In the past, Tico had never had trouble bulldozing anyone out of the way if they impeded an investigation, but Meg hadn't done anything wrong. In fact, she and her team had done everything right. Smugglers had the upper hand with stealth and technology, and were terrorizing local residents to remain invisible—and untouchable. The cartel's advantage made law enforcement almost impossible. Every detective knew that no matter how big the sting, they could only scratch the surface of the black market. The answer to killing the underworld was to have public demand dry up. People had to stop feeding their addictions—and their dark sides—in order for the good guys to win.

That would mean changing the world. Given the world he came from, Tico was determined to do just that, one case at a time. The one person he thought who didn't need changing at all was Meg Flores. He'd seen how she had put her heart and soul into this investigation. He'd react exactly as she had, if the tables were turned. No doubt, Meg's helplessness at her powerful father's demands was infuriating.

He stood and leaned against the railing. Overhead, stars filled the night. Until driving across the country, he'd had no idea what the night sky truly looked like. Now the inky darkness attracted him with a haunting familiarity, though he'd never seen anything quite like the stark blackness littered with so many points of light. His imagination soared as he looked into the depths of the sky.

Maybe it was the dry, hot air. Maybe the occasional lowing of cattle on the range, or coyotes howling in the foothills. Whatever the reason, this place stirred a need in him he'd never known. He wanted to belong to an environment as wide and clear as this place. Nights like this simply did not exist in one-bedroom apartments in the lower Bronx with car horns blaring, trains clanking and kids who yelled to each other from the sidewalks. He exhaled a long breath. He could get used to life in the desert.

His gut knotted at the realization. Inwardly, he shook himself. This place was haunting his good senses. He'd learned early on not to attach himself to anyone or anything. He'd chosen to be an undercover detective because his parents had been crack addicts. Unsupervised, with a lot of pent-up anger, he'd run with gangs until he was finally arrested in his early twenties and scared straight. Even then, working for the law, he found no sanctuary.

Tico was tough. Running with gangs had made him that way. But he was honorable and got the job done. Then, when he lost his partner in a gunfight with a gang, prejudice toward him spiked, and Tico's defenses rose right along with his peers' reactions. He'd learned as a kid and again as a cop that no place was home.

Yet, basking in the peaceful night on the most beautiful grounds he'd ever seen, Tico found himself wishing for the first time in a long time that he had roots—a home like this one. Maybe not so grand, but a place to belong. He hadn't entertained thoughts like these since he was small. Now desires like these did him no good at all.

Yeah. Coming here was a bad idea.

He needed to get his job done and get out as fast as possible. He'd planned on cracking Meg's defenses and winning her over, but he'd liked her and her team on sight. They looked like honest, straightforward folk with whom he'd like to be on good terms. Bill Mewith and he had the Judumi in common, but was his lost heritage something he wanted to explore further?

It didn't matter. Tico had been perceived and received as the enemy. An uphill battle, one more time. It was ironic the way he'd been more accepted in gangs than in the world of law enforcement. The old adage of being judged by the friends one kept followed him everywhere he went.

Don Francisco had set the stage one more time for Tico to be the outsider. But what the hell. He'd do it. The pay was certainly worth it. He'd ignore the pull of the land, of his Judumi heritage, of Meg Flores's soulful eyes. There was nothing here for him except a job to do.

He'd get it done.

His instincts were already giving him ideas for directions he should pursue. Only this time, for the first time in his career, he wouldn't bulldoze the team leader. Again, unfamiliar territory. But he'd read the reports. Met Detective Flores and her team. No matter what Don Francisco wanted, he'd make sure Meg worked with him on this investigation. Somehow, he'd appease Don Francisco. Meg deserved the recognition. Tico could protect her. He had no goddamn idea why he was even remotely entertaining that thought, but he was.

Maybe it was the swirl of stars overhead. Maybe it was this excellent cigar. Whatever. At the moment he felt inclined to meet this challenge. Who knew how he'd feel tomorrow.

The pounding rhythm of hoofbeats rose from behind the ranch house. One horse. One rider. He'd watched Meg's truck pull up to a cabin on the lake in the distance after she'd left her parents' veranda this evening. Sounded as if the rider was coming from that direction.

A rush heated his blood. Damnation, he hoped so.

Standing perfectly still, he watched as Meg rode around the house, heading for his porch. She looked sexy and wild in the shadowed light, her hair flying behind her, the air pushing a white Mexican shirt against her body as she moved—and what a body she had. He moved the cigar to the other side of his mouth. A sweet sight in the saddle, Meg handled the horse as if they were one. The power of the gallop meant she was still fuming. That brought a grin to his face.

She reined in the horse in front of the railing, just a hair's breadth from where Tico stood. In the small cloud of dust, the musky heat from the horse's hide vibrated the air between them but did nothing to match the heat from Meg's flinty stare. He didn't move a muscle. She looked sweet as hell.

He took a draw on the cigar. "Nice night for a ride."

Her voice thrummed with barely suppressed hostility. "As if you'd know."

"Did you race all the way here to discuss my riding abilities?"

"You have none."

He chuckled. "A little rusty. I'll give you that."

"We have to talk, Detective."

She was still pissed. He would be, too. Time to get to the bottom of their first encounter. Tico gestured to the rocking chair next to the one he'd been sitting in. He'd like to know if his inclination to help Meg had been misplaced.

He flicked the ash of his cigar into the dirt. "You climb down off that thing, and I'll be happy to listen."

# CHAPTER FOUR

THE SMUG LOOK on Tico's face had Meg questioning her reason for coming here. Needing to keep her anger, she refused to ignore his jest. Meg laid a propriety hand on the horse's neck. "She's not a *thing*. Her name is Whisper."

"Sounded more like thunder to me."

Okay. So maybe she'd ridden Whisper hard on the five-minute run over here. She didn't want to have this conversation but had no other choice. "Very funny."

He addressed the horse. "Okay, then, Whisper, why don't you deposit your mistress so we can have an eye-level conversation."

"She won't answer. She knows better than to converse with a man who considered himself above the law for most of his life."

He frowned. "Did you really just try to insult me?"

Of course she did. Tico looked like the same type of hard-edged criminal she'd busted dozens of times over the years. The worse ones to handle were the dudes with attitude because they had sex appeal. Those Romeos thought their shit didn't stink. She was sure that Tico fell into that camp. But there was something compelling about him. Attitude had its allure.

The fact that Tico was one of the good guys now made him a curiosity. One she had no time or inclination to explore, though, dammit all, her curiosity egged her on. She felt stupid when her heart thumped as she watched him stand there all arrogant and hot in his tight black shirt and jeans.

She spotted the rattlesnake tattoo immediately and used all her cop training not to stare. Given the many run-ins she'd had with rattlers in the desert, Butler's lifelike tat, which curled around his forearm with the head and forked tongue resting just above his wrist, unsettled her right down to her toes. She honored nature in all its forms, especially with what she'd learned living closely with the Judumi, but she wasn't a fan of snakes. Even more, she wasn't one for tattoos. But that lean, golden brown rattler circling Tico's forearm downright suited him.

She gestured to his tat. "Didn't know you had a pet."

He took a drag on his cigar and exhaled the smoke while watching her, but said nothing. The ash on the cigar between his fingers burned orange in the dark.

If he thought he was intimidating her, he was dead wrong. Meg swung from the saddle and looped the horse's reins around the porch rail. Why did this guy bring out the worst in her?

Tico pointed to the horse's reins. "Do you really believe a single loop will keep her from bolting?"

"She's my horse. She won't go anywhere."

"Like mine obeyed me so well this morning?"

Meg thought it prudent not to comment on his horse abilities this time. "He wasn't really yours. I've had Whisper since she was a filly. If you had a dog you raised from a pup, wouldn't he stay by your side without a leash?"

Tico shrugged. "Wouldn't know. Never had a dog."

A boy and no dog? She couldn't imagine. "Guess city living doesn't make it easy for a dog."

"My grandmother had a Chihuahua, but that's not a dog."

She laughed. "My roommate has one. He's rather charming."

"Charming is not how I'd describe a dog." He waved her up the one step to the porch. "Have a seat. Do you mind if I smoke?"

She crossed her arms over her chest. "That's a stupid question. You already are."

He stuck the cigar back in his mouth. "Just being polite, ma'am."

Meg took the one step to meet him square on. Crossing into his territory seemed appropriate under the circumstances.

"Polite would be for you to back away from the investigation."

He shook his head. "Sorry. No can do."

She planted her hands on her hips. "Are you here to take my job?"

He bit down on the cigar. "Do you want the party-line response, or my true intentions?"

"I want to know why the hell you're in my way."

He leaned back on the railing and tugged the cigar from his mouth. "I am here because I plan on stopping some sewer rats from stealing and destroying innocent women. Drugs and human trafficking are disgusting, and I can help with the investigation."

"That sounds like the party line."

His gaze slid to a point over her right shoulder. A momentary frown creased his brow. "Despite what you may think of me or my motives, I came to get a job done."

"What I think of you doesn't matter at all. What did my father offer you?"

"I'm not going to discuss your father."

"Then tell me about yours."

A short, amused laugh escaped him. "Not a chance." He cocked a brow. "What are you fishing for?"

She stared a long moment, growing uncomfortable as those restless Judumi eyes focused on her mouth, then her neck, before dropping slowly along the flower-embroidered neckline of her Mexican blouse. The scrutiny of men was nothing new to Meg, but Butler's attention irritated her. No, she was wrong. His attention intrigued her.

Was that why she stood her ground in the dead of night, knowing she'd get his attention? Was her intention to do battle with the enemy—or to entice him so she would get her way? Her chin rose higher when his gaze slid down to her hips and trailed the length of her faded denims, stopping at the hole above her knee. She released a breath when his gaze finally fell to her well-worn but cherished tooled boots, then snapped back to hers.

He puffed on his cigar, just one small, easy draw. From behind the veil of smoke she caught his grin as he said, "Nice boots."

She tapped her foot. "I'm not here for your amusement."

"Then why are you here?"

"To tell you to go home. I have a damned good team, and we know what we're doing. Despite what others may think, we can break this case."

Tico used thumb and forefinger to take a piece a tobacco from the tip of his tongue. Did she see regret in his eyes?

"You obviously don't get it. I was *hired* to come here. This is my job. I'm not going anywhere."

"Then stay out of my way."

"Look, Detective. Why don't we make an effort to unroll this investigation by working together? I see no threat here. The problem is yours."

Meg actually snorted. "Clearly you are not familiar with small towns, *Detective*." She exaggerated his title to make her point. "I know my father. I know Eric Longwood. Eric would never have let you question my credibility in front of my team if the three of you didn't have a plan that's been kept from me."

Tico began to speak, but she stopped him with a raised hand. "I worked my ass off to get where I am today. I've chewed up and spit out men with far more brass than yours. Your brash attitude and stupid stunts don't fool me." She repeated her words. "Stay. Out. Of. My. Way."

She'd gone so far as to poke his chest with a pointed finger to emphasize her words and met with sheer solid muscle. Without warning, he grabbed her hand, the snake on his arm flexing with his action. His grip was firm, his long fingers and wide palm warm—and surprisingly soft. A shiver ran along her spine. Damn. Damn. Damn.

"You've got this scenario all wrong, my dear."

*My dear?* "Let go of my hand."

He grinned again, and she wanted to slap his face. God, how he riled her! She wrenched her hand away just as he let go, and she lost her balance.

Again, with unexpected speed, he gripped her waist to keep her from falling. He took a moment to push a lock of her hair from her shoulder and dusted off her sleeve as if she'd fallen. When he spoke to her again, his tone was low and danger-ous. "The mayor brought me in for this job. If you think you have enough influence with him, why don't you have me sent home? Until then, I'm work-ing with or without you."

He pointed from her to himself. "The way I see it, *we* have a tough job ahead of us. So, it's in your best interest to be nice to me."

"Is that a threat?"

"Oh, no. You'd recognize a threat, Meg."

She hated the sound of her name on his lips. "I should have known better than to try to reason with you. And I'm *Detective* Flores."

She climbed onto Whisper, her heart racing. The horse sensed her tension and tossed her head. Meg shifted her weight in the saddle, and with a flick of the reins, Whisper turned back toward home. Rein-ing her in, Meg stole one last look at the outsider watching her from the porch of her father's cabin.

Tico held up a hand. "Do cowboy cops eat do-nuts? I'll bring some to the meeting tomorrow."

"Rot in hell, Butler."

Meg kicked the horse's flanks. Whisper bolted, but not before she heard him grumble, "I'm already there, lady."

TICO DROPPED THE cigar into the ashtray, disgusted. He'd let Meg goad him into another argument, the last thing he wanted with her. Damn it all. They had a very serious and very dangerous case to crack, and now they were in a pissing match. If she couldn't get her emotions under control, she would have to step aside. He'd read the reports. She and her team had done everything right. All he wanted to do was advise them. Why did she have such a hornet in her hat over his arrival? He'd come a long way to help.

He'd done a lot of self-talk the entire ride from New York to convince himself he could blend with this group. Having team members bucking him was the norm. He was comfortable with that. Yet, for some reason, he didn't like crossing swords with this woman. He'd done his research. He understood how Detective Flores had poured her heart and soul into a law enforcement career despite only grudging approval from her demanding father. And now, Don Francisco was withdrawing his support because he was afraid.

When all was said and done, Tico was a loner, but he wanted to work with Meg. Curiosity more than anything had him wanting to spend more time in her company, and damn it all, if she blew this case, her career could tank. That would devastate her. Which was why she was attacking him now. He understood that. But he wasn't the enemy. How to make her believe that?

Earlier, while watching her with hands on hips, hair tossed back, chin high, he'd noticed that she'd traded her work clothes for faded blue second-skin jeans and a Mexican shirt that could bring an angel to tears. He imagined her on the back of his Harley, arms wrapped around him. When he'd saved her from losing her balance, he'd had an urge to slide one arm around that tight little waist of hers and pull her against him so she could read his lips when he answered her challenge. Instead, he'd stood there and they fought.

What did he care? This place was doing strange things to his very set, very comfortable convictions. He had to get out of here as soon as possible.

In the silence, a coyote howl rose from the foothills. Farther away another howl echoed in response. It was as if the pack was calling to gather. Overhead, the stars still held their ground. He pulled his cell phone from his pocket to check the time. Nine-thirty. Damn. It was going to be a long night.

MEG SLAMMED HER heavy front door. She was still so damned frustrated from getting nowhere with Tico Butler. The smell of popcorn invaded her senses. Her roommate, Penny Riggs, appeared from the kitchen, bowl in hand. Bruno, her Chihuahua, scurried around her feet, focused on the bowl of popcorn. Behind her the television was on, volume muted.

Penny frowned. "I waited for you to start the movie, but from the look on your face, you're in no mood for watching a romance."

A mocking laugh rose in Meg's throat as she

reached down to pet the dog. "A murder mystery would be better."

"Your detective didn't cooperate, I take it?"

"Nothing but aggravation." Meg turned in a circle out of sheer frustration, fists clenched. "I could just scream!"

Where Meg had curves to her athletic, lithe figure and long hair, Penny's petite frame was lean and trim like a ballerina's. Tonight she'd gelled her short platinum hair into spikes. Gleaming silver hoops dangled from her ears, complementing her turquoise camisole and brown gypsy skirt. Penny had been blessed with green eyes that usually held mirth. She offered her hand and led her friend into the den. Glass doors opened to the night, warming the room decorated with Indian pottery, overstuffed furniture and woven rugs.

"Why do you have the doors open, Pen?"

Penny grinned. "Because there's something you should see. Step outside."

Penny led Meg to a cactus garden bordering the covered patio. The light from the den glowed softly on the cholla, barrel and fishhook cacti beneath the bottlebrush tree that was meant to shade the area during the hottest part of the day. In the center of the narrow garden, a hip-high, barren-looking, tangled and twiggy cactus of no real beauty held center stage.

Pen pointed to the small bulbs dotting the ends

of the plant's sticklike branches. "Look what happened today!"

Meg caught her breath, immediately forgetting her anger. "The Queen of the Night is going to bloom!"

The women grinned at each other. Penny said, "It's been almost two years. The bulbs look ready. If we sit out here, we may witness it firsthand."

Meg let out a breath. "That would be the first nice thing to happen all day."

"It's a beautiful night. I'll pour us some wine, and we'll wait and see if she opens."

Penny put the bowl of popcorn on the table. Bruno followed her into the kitchen. Meg moved two of the patio chairs to the edge of the garden.

This particular cactus was a rarity in the desert. Meg had planted the Queen of the Night herself when she'd moved into the cabin six years ago. Back then the plant had been simply a round tuber root with a stick. It had grown and spread into this sparse, leggy plant. Unless you knew what it was, you'd think it was dead. When those buds opened, the beautiful blossoms were large and white with yellow centers. Their vanilla fragrance suffused the air like heaven. The flowers hadn't appeared last year. Now more buds emerged on the plant than she'd ever seen.

Penny returned with two glasses of white wine and a camera hanging from her shoulder. She handed Meg her wine, then scooped up Bruno and dropped into the chair beside her. She rested the camera next to the chair. "This sure beats watching the movie."

As she spoke the first bulb popped open. "Oh!" Meg leaned forward. The rest of the unfurling would be slower, but once one opened, the others would follow. It was as if the plant had some sort of communication system where all the buds waited for each other. She stood, not wanting to miss a moment of this precious event. "Look, they're all opening."

Pen grabbed her camera and began clicking photos of Meg smelling the blossoms. She shook her head. "I can't believe they waited for you. Don't they usually open after sunset?"

"They must have known I needed their magic." She inhaled a deep, sweet breath, feeling as if her lungs were taking oxygen for the first time today. "How I missed this amazing fragrance."

Pen leaned forward to breathe the flower's essence. "Nothing like it in the world."

Meg sat back in her chair, ready to let the conflict of the day fall away. She let her gaze roam into the distance where a few dim lights shone from her parents' house on the other side of the lake. They'd disappointed her today beyond belief. They'd always known her line of work was dangerous, but had always had faith in her abilities to do her job. She'd simply have to stand her ground with them until they understood she wasn't to be swayed.

Butler's cabin wasn't visible from where she sat, but she knew he was out there. She tried to push the thought of him from her mind. She wanted to relax, but he kept crowding her thoughts. Dammit. Returning her focus to the blossoms, she sipped her wine.

"How was work today, Penny?"

Pen ran a hand through her hair. "Busy." She sat back down, but not before clicking another photo of Meg.

Meg shielded her face to stop Pen from taking any more. "You still like the job?"

"Oh, yeah. As a matter of fact, today was my six-month anniversary. Enrique finally gave me keys to the spa this morning."

"Sounds like you passed the training period."

"With flying colors, according to Enrique."

Pen had always wanted to move from the small salon in town to the spa in the foothills that attended to the elite residents of the Quarry. With her friendly personality and keen fashion sense, Pen had a style and sassiness that made her a perfect match for the spa community.

She managed to hide the fact that she was a celebrity groupie. Nothing excited her more than primping the hair and nails of a movie or rock star, politician or business tycoon. Yet, to all outward appearances, she behaved with sophistication and the perfect touch of reserve around those who preferred anonymity at the Quarry.

Meg tapped Pen's wineglass with her own. "Congratulations, girl. You've reached the top."

Penny chuckled. "I can't tell you how hard it was resisting the urge to ask Katrina Ripley for an autograph while prepping her for a pedi-wrap."

Meg laughed out loud. Katrina Ripley was well known in the fashion world as the latest leggy, angel-faced model. She'd been discovered living on the streets in Berlin by a French photographer when documenting the city. That photographer had done an exclusive on Katrina with photos before and after he cleaned her up, which shot her to international fame.

Any clothes, accessories or jewelry she modeled sold out so quickly that one lingerie mega-store had nabbed her, offering an obscene annual salary to be their exclusive representative. She'd met and married Josh Ripley in a fast and furious love affair that had been plastered all over the tabloids for months. "Wow. Even I'm impressed."

"I know! Katrina Ripley is amazing."

Meg shook her head. "No. I'm impressed that you made it through two hours with the woman and didn't ask her to sign your arm."

"Or ask her for a pass for tonight's concert. Enrique would have fired me on the spot. Bothering the celebrities is the best way to lose your job." Penny tapped her lip with a finger. "But it might have been worth it for front-row seats to see Joshua Ripley perform."

"I'd prefer an Eagles concert any day."

Penny grinned. "Well, sure, but he's here, and they're not."

Meg reached for some popcorn. "So, do you like working with Enrique?"

"He can be a ballbuster, but he's protecting the privacy of the residents. Once you get his motives, he's pretty easy."

"I guess he's like Eric Longwood. In charge of everything, so has to run a tight ship."

"Exactly. I like Enrique. He's not bad on the eyes, either." Pen's attention fell on the cactus blooms. "I can't believe that by morning, these beautiful flowers will be withered and gone."

Meg got up from her chair to touch one silky flower petal. This moment wouldn't come again for another year—or longer. Cupping the bloom with a hand, she bent to inhale the intoxicating fragrance, her hair falling about her shoulders.

Pen clicked another photo of her. "That's a good one."

Meg took the camera. "Go ahead, Pen. Strike a pose. Let's prove to your spa friends that you really saw a Queen of the Night in bloom."

Pen's eyes lit up. "Great idea." While she angled herself by the cactus blooms, careful not to get too close to the spines, she said, "I saw Mitchell Blake talking with Enrique by the pool this afternoon. Are you guys coming back to the spa to investigate?"

"Butler is insisting we retrace our steps, but

I don't think Mitchell was there because of the case. More likely a disgruntled resident with a complaint." Meg snapped a profile shot of Pen sniffing the bloom. "Okay, Pen. Look at the camera. Big smile."

Pen took the camera Meg returned to her and checked out the photo in the viewer. "I know Enrique works with the police department to keep security tight at the Quarry, but Mitchell looked annoyed."

"Mitchell and I argued this morning, but that had nothing to do with the spa."

Pen chuckled. "Well, we all know what he thinks of rock stars. The Ripleys have been having some pretty wild parties at their house. I think some of their neighbors were complaining."

Meg could just imagine Mitchell's irritation at needing to placate some snooty resident because their neighbor's music was too loud. "Enrique usually goes straight to Mitchell. The spa likes to get the big guns in the department to deal with their own breed of riffraff."

Meg inhaled a deep breath at the thought of Tico Butler. Funny how he popped into her mind with the mention of riffraff. Two more blossoms opened, filling the air with their essence. She closed her eyes, letting the scent of the flower embed itself in her mind. She wanted to discuss Butler with her best friend and not get agitated all over again because he, like the flower, would soon be gone.

Pen must have sensed her agitation. "So, talk. Let me hear what's bothering you."

Meg shook her head. "Butler was pretty clear in letting me know my father wants me off the case."

"What about Butler? Does he want you off?"

Meg shrugged. "Oddly enough, I get the feeling he wants to work with me and the team, though I haven't missed his veiled threats."

"Threats?"

"That he's not going anywhere since Dad hired him. And that either I work with him or he'll follow Dad's wishes and take me off the case."

Pen shook her head. "It's awful that Don Francisco lost confidence."

Meg released a long breath. "I wouldn't have minded Dad bringing in an expert, except for the way he did it. He and Mom are scheming and actually want me to stop doing undercover work."

"Like they could make you stop?"

Meg sighed. "They'd simply force me to move to another city. They want me to find a guy and settle down. I'm not meant to stay home, marry and have a passel of babies."

"Ever?"

Meg laughed at the concern in her friend's face. "You know I'm not the marrying type."

Pen shook her head in amazement. "You've said that for years, but I can't believe it. Nothing would make me happier."

"Then *you* get married and have babies."

"That's what I mean. Nothing would make *me* happier."

Meg grinned. "I know. You've told me that for years, too."

"Now all I need is to find someone worth marrying."

Meg turned her attention back to the blossoms. "Happy hunting, my friend."

"Is your detective Butler a handsome man?"

"He's not *my* detective Butler."

Pen waved a dismissing hand. "You know what I mean."

Was Butler handsome? Meg mused as she realized the first flower had opened completely. "He's not stud-handsome like in the *GQ* magazine sort of way. But sexy? Yeah. He has an imposing presence."

Grinning, Penny raised a brow. "How imposing?"

"Hmm. Oh, I don't know. Like no woman has been able to tame him yet. He's half Judumi and looks Native American. About fortyish. He's had a tough life. His face is strong and angular, but the stress lines around his mouth go all soft when he smiles, and his eyes get a mischievous look."

"Eye color?"

"Brown. Almost black. Expressive." She thought about it. "I'd go so far as to say soulful."

"Hair?"

"Long and black. Ponytail."

She had Penny's attention. "And his body?"

Despite her anger earlier tonight, Meg hadn't missed how snugly Butler's jeans fit his muscled thighs while seated on her parents' veranda, or how his denim shirt, opened just enough at the neck, stretched across his chest, or how his lean, strong hands looked as if they knew the power of touch.

And tonight. With the rattlesnake tattoo circling across his tanned forearm. The way he'd watched her with those dark eyes while toying with his cigar. Then when he'd saved her from losing her balance, she found herself breathing deep to get enough of the fresh-soap scent of his skin beneath the cigar smoke.

Meg blew out a long breath. Not good to indulge such thoughts, and Pen's grin irritated her. "I've been so busy arguing with him that I really haven't noticed his body."

"After the blow-by-blow description you just gave me on his looks, you expect me to believe that?" Pen narrowed her eyes. "Come on now. It's me you're talking to here, kiddo."

"Okay. So he has a hot body and a wicked rattlesnake tattoo on his right forearm. But believe me. Tico Butler holds no appeal to me."

Penny used her glass to shield her grin. "Sure. I can tell you mean every word." She chuckled. "Wish I could be a fly on the wall for your team meeting tomorrow morning."

*It's in your best interest to be nice to me.*

Butler's words invaded Meg's mind. He'd said them playfully, but she'd been able to tell he was serious. "My last words to him were an invitation to rot in hell."

Pen practically choked on her wine. "You're kidding!"

"No. Clearly my anger is doing nothing but causing trouble between us. I've got to keep a level head when around that man."

"Good idea." Pen pulled Bruno into her lap to keep him from licking her ankles. "Maybe you can call a truce or something."

"He said something about donuts. Maybe I'll bring that New York bozo a box of his own tomorrow." She let a dangerous grin spread across her face. Oh, she could play so nice that Butler would never see the precinct door hitting him in the butt on his way out of town. "Think donuts for a New York cop would work as a peace offering?"

# CHAPTER FIVE

Meg moved a bit more slowly than usual on the treadmill at the gym this morning. She and Penny had finished that bottle of wine last night. She didn't drink often, but the combination of the blooms, the scented air and the wine had worked wonders on calming her after the insanity of the day.

Now she was paying for the indulgence. She usually ran on the treadmill. This morning, jogging made for an easier pace, but she set the timer for an extra twenty minutes to make up for lack of speed.

In two hours she'd be face-to-face with Butler at the team meeting. God only knew what direction the investigation would take. She'd spent part of yesterday rehashing the notes on the people interviewed who'd last seen the young mother and two teens. There had to be a lead somewhere, though she still couldn't find it. She wondered what Butler would suggest they do when there were no clues, and nothing but miles of barren desert filled with caves, nooks and crannies in the hills surrounding the town.

On the other side of the gym, Penny traveled from one weight machine to the other on the cross-training circuit, her usual routine. Meg would do the same after she finished her cardio segment. The girls went to the gym together but worked out separately. Penny had a longer commute than Meg, so they'd decided they could forgo gossip for efficiency. They had plenty of time to talk at home.

It felt good to be in motion. Meg closed her eyes, concentrating on her movements. The perspiration rising on her skin felt good. Cleansing. She'd pulled her hair into a knot on her head; a sweatband circled her forehead. The new running shoes she'd purchased felt like clouds on her feet. She reached for her water bottle to take another swig and stopped with her hand in midair.

Penny had just gotten off one of the machines and was chatting up none other than Tico Butler, looking particularly buff in a blue T-shirt and baggy gray gym shorts. His hair, caught in the usual ponytail, gleamed under the overhead lights. He'd fastened his attention on Penny with that intensity Meg was coming to recognize as Butler's style. As a former object of his scrutiny, she knew it could be either disquieting or comforting, depending on his intent. Penny must have been feeling his welcoming side. By the look on her face she was flirting, big-time.

Shit!

Pen's focus moved from Tico's face to the tattoo on his right forearm. The momentary widening of Pen's eyes and her quick glance at Meg betrayed that she'd realized who he was. Butler followed Pen's gaze, saw Meg and gave her a curt two-finger salute.

Ignoring him, she continued to drink water, her insides heating up. From Pen's gestures, it was easy to tell that Pen was explaining her relationship to Meg. Tico nodded, smiled at her roommate and moved on to one of the other machines.

Wiping her mouth, Meg acknowledged that the man took his physical well-being seriously—his honed physique was a dead giveaway. Any good investigator active in the field would. Darn it all if now her gaze didn't wander in Butler's direction over and over. The man was clearly familiar with the equipment; his bulging biceps responded to the repetitive motion as he exercised. Nice. Angry at her gut reaction, she punched the buttons on the treadmill, increasing the speed.

A major run ought to distract her.

Ten minutes later, sweating buckets, Meg slowed the treadmill for the cooldown. She glanced across the room. Butler, seated at an ab cruncher, blatantly watched her with admiration on his face. Penny had finished her circuit and, bless her heart, headed toward Meg, blissfully distracting her from the urge to flash Butler a rude hand gesture. So much for last night's decision to be nice.

Penny jerked a thumb in Butler's direction. "Look who I just met."

Meg slanted her an impatient glance. "You mean, hit on?"

Unapologetic, Penny fanned herself. "A new face. A new possibility. Sorry, Meggie, but he is hot!"

When Meg glared at her, Penny laughed. "Twenty more minutes before we go?"

Meg peered over Penny's shoulder. Butler concentrated on his crunches. She refused to start her routine on the circuit with him nearby. "I can leave now."

"Oh, don't be a spoilsport. I told him we're roommates."

"Not best friends?"

A devilish grin tugged on Pen's lips. "He might not like me if he knows how close we are."

Meg swatted Pen's arm. "Traitor!"

"No way! Desperate."

Meg laughed. Pen was stunning with her dancer's body, glowing skin and bright green eyes set against hair mussed just enough to look like sex and fun rolled into one. "Prospecting is more like it. Guys usually don't know what hit them when they meet you."

"So bring 'em on!"

Meg stopped the treadmill, taking a moment to blot her face with a hand towel. "Butler isn't going to be in Adobe Creek long. Don't waste your time."

Pen stole a glance in his direction. "I think you should heed Detective Butler's suggestion and work very, very closely with him, Meg." She tapped her friend's hand with a perfectly manicured finger. "A bit of advice from someone who cares."

BOX IN HAND of a dozen homemade donuts from the coolest little bakery he'd ever seen, Tico barged into the conference room to find everyone present except Eric Longwood. The guys grinned at the sight of the pure white box with the red bow.

Not Meg.

She looked as sexy as ever in a black V-neck shirt beneath her gray suit. That alone was enough to make him think one more time that he'd love to see her perched on the back of his Harley.

But her glare ruined any fantasy of the kind. He saw why when his attention fell on an identical box of donuts already opened and half empty on the table in front of her.

Tico laughed. "Hey, I said I'd bring the donuts."

Meg shrugged. "I took you for a plain-donut type of guy. I didn't want to be disappointed, so I brought the jelly-filled and the éclairs."

Damn. She'd pegged him. "Nothing in here but glazes, plains and cinnamons. Good character read, Detective."

Mitchell reached for a glazed donut when Tico opened the box. "I'll take one. A real donut doesn't need a dressing."

Meg held out a hand. "Then I'll take back the two jellies you just inhaled."

Mitchell grinned. "Check with me after lunch, sweetheart."

Jose grimaced. "Oh, that's disgusting, Mitchell."

Bill lifted a hand. "What is this, a donut face-off?"

Meg's phone rang. She checked the caller ID, then clicked the phone off without answering.

"Another bad date trying for a second time?" Mitchell kept just enough playfulness in his voice to keep from sounding patronizing. Tico shook his head, surprised at the animosity this man was showing toward Meg. And here he'd thought this was a tight-knit team.

Meg shot Mitchell an impatient look. "No. My roommate has developed a sudden interest in this investigation. She can leave a message."

"Speaking of roommates." Tico took the seat next to Meg's and crooked a finger to beckon her closer. He liked the reluctance in her body language before she finally leaned toward him, a lock of hair falling on her forehead. Was she wearing perfume, or did her skin smell like heaven? He indulged in a slow, deep inhale before speaking. He felt strongly about what he had to say and hoped Meg wouldn't take it wrong.

"Your roommate was flirting with me this morning."

Meg lifted a brow. "And?"

"You might want to warn her that starting conversations with strangers around here could be more dangerous than she thinks."

"Penny can take care of herself."

"I'm sure the woman who disappeared a few days ago felt she could take care of herself, too. Just do me a favor and warn her to lay off the friendliness. She didn't know me from the devil. She's asking for trouble."

Meg didn't get a chance to reply. Eric Longwood entered the conference room, looking disgusted. He dropped his file on the desk. "Bad news. Another woman was reported missing this morning. A twenty-three-year-old. Melissa Collins from the ranch lands outside town."

Tico sat back in his chair, quick to gauge the reactions of the team. What he saw surprised him. For now, he'd keep his counsel. While Meg, Bill and Jose looked surprised and as disgusted as their chief, Mitchell Blake sat back in his chair with an expectant look on his face, as if he already knew. When Mitchell saw Tico watching him, he leaned forward and gave Chief Longwood his full attention.

Eric continued, "Mitchell, Bill, Jose, I want you to check out the Collins woman's car found in the mall parking lot. Talk to people. Look for leads. Tico, Meg, come with me to speak with the family. Let's go."

Out front, Tico opened the door to the backseat of the unmarked sedan Longwood brought from the precinct garage. Again, Meg gave him that lifted brow. "Not going to fight for shotgun?"

He grinned. "And have a dangerous blonde sitting behind me? Not today."

Eric put the car into gear. "So, are we working any closer toward camaraderie among teammates?"

When neither answered, Eric heaved a heavy sigh. "I had a complaint from Mitchell yesterday, Meg. Says you sniped at him."

Meg shook her head. "Sorry about that, Chief. I'm just trying to hold my own here. I'm getting flak on all sides. My career may not be as long as Mitchell's, but I've earned my place, and he keeps trying to slap me down."

"Your bio is pretty impressive," Tico added in a show of support.

"Flattery will get you nowhere, Detective," Meg said over her shoulder. "Besides, Chief, I have a bone to pick with you."

Tico leaned back in his seat, waiting to see how Eric handled Meg. He knew exactly where she was steering this conversation.

Longwood reached for a pair of sunglasses from the dashboard and slid them on, shielding his eyes from the desert glare. "Before you jump to conclusions, Meg, you need to understand that Don Francisco may tell me what he wants done and as mayor can fire me if I don't follow orders, but he respects me enough that I believe he'll trust my decisions. I simply need your cooperation."

She thumbed to Tico in the backseat. "You mean cooperate with him?"

"There's a good start."

"Meg and I had a conversation last night that I'm sure helped bridge that gap between us," Tico said.

At the look of disbelief on her face, he added, "And you have to admit, Eric, you and I would be pretty upset if our credibility was being challenged. Detective Flores and I are finding a common ground."

"We don't have time for you two to find common ground. You need to own it. Now. Do you understand me, Meg?"

"I'm being coerced here."

When Meg folded her arms across her chest, Tico found himself stretching his neck to see what effect that had on her cleavage. He rolled his eyes at his own actions and sat back.

"Look, Eric. No team leader likes to be circumvented. I get that. What's worse is that Don Francisco is making decisions based on his own fears when his daughter is the most qualified detective for the job. I say, we offer the mayor lip service and get the job done with Meg's team as fast as we can before he can object."

Silence fell like dead weight in the car. From the look on Meg's face he'd stunned her. Good. With another woman missing as of this morning, it was time to pull the team together.

Meg cleared her throat. "Sounds like you're undercutting the mayor, but I thank you for the vote of support, Detective."

"You're welcome." He held out a hand. "Now, let's get to work."

Meg looked at his hand a long moment before shaking it. Her hand felt small, soft and warm in his, triggering some foreign desire to keep her safe. Where the hell did that come from?

He cleared his throat. "So, what are your thoughts?"

Meg glanced from Eric to Tico. "If another woman went missing this morning, I'd say the others are still around. Seems like some arrogant son of a bitch is rounding out a stable of women to ship out all at once."

Tico nodded. "Agreed."

"Here in Adobe Creek?" Eric asked.

Meg nodded. "If not here, then in that damned barren corridor. My gut tells me if they're using the corridor, there's a hole somewhere close to our boundary. Well hidden and soundproof or locals would have reported unusual activity."

Eric pulled the car into the driveway of a low adobe ranch off the highway, not far from where Tico had rented that damned horse. A split-rail corral circled in front of a small barn with doors still open to the arena. As their car pulled up the drive, a man emerged from the barn. Baseball cap, T-shirt, faded jeans. About forty-five, his face lined from years in the Arizona sun. At the same time, the front door opened. A dark-haired woman, a wad of tissues caught in her hand, waved to them.

The man approached the car as they exited. He held out a hand to Eric. "I'm Jake Collins. I'm the one who reported my daughter missing this morning."

Eric was quick with introducing Tico and Meg. "Usually we require twenty-four hours to accept a missing persons report, but given the current situation, rules don't apply. Tico and Meg are part of a special task force. We want to act immediately."

"Do you think Melissa's been taken by the same people who kidnapped the other missing women?" Jake Collins asked.

"We hope not, but we're not taking any chances."

Jake watched his wife approaching. "That would kill her mother," he said, his voice low. He slung an arm around the woman's shoulder when she arrived next to him. "This is my wife, Ellen."

The woman blotted her eyes. "I'm sorry. I can't stop crying. Melissa always comes home. I'm worried sick."

"When did you last see her?" Meg asked.

Ellen wiped her nose. "Last night. She and her friend Vicky left here around four o'clock to drive to a rock concert in the desert outside the Quarry. She said she'd be home late."

"And Vicky?"

"She got home around three this morning. She and Melissa went to a party at the Quarry afterward." Ellen frowned. "Vicky said one minute Melissa was there, the next she was gone. She had her own car and it was gone, too. So Vicky thought she'd left."

"Would she have driven to the mall?" Tico asked.

Concern creased Jake's brow. "Makes no sense that her car was found there."

Meg touched Ellen's arm. "Can you remember where the party was in the Quarry?"

"I couldn't remember earlier when we filled out the report. I was too upset. But I remember now. Melissa called from her cell phone late last night. Jake and I were already asleep. She was all excited because they were going to the rock star's house. Josh Ripley." Confusion filled her eyes. "Why would Melissa have been invited there? She doesn't know him."

Tico almost fell over when Meg looked at him and not Eric to indicate the lead.

"Mrs. Collins, did your daughter have problems with anyone? Boyfriend trouble? Anything?" he asked.

"No. No one. Melissa had a boyfriend, but they broke up when he moved to Tucson."

"Does she have a job?"

"She works in town for a travel agency. Been there for two years. She likes it."

"Has she met anyone on the internet that you may know about?"

Ellen waved a hand. "No. Melissa has a few social media accounts, but she's very private and keeps a tight circle of friends. She would tell me if she'd met someone online." She started choking up again. "It's not like her not to come home. Even if she became involved with…a boy, she would have called by now to tell us she's all right."

Meg handed the woman her card. Tico followed suit, handing his to the father. "Please, call if you hear anything or remember any more details."

"We already filled out a report."

Meg shook the man's hand. "We understand. My team has a special interest in ensuring Melissa's safety. Please, call if you have any questions."

Back in the car, Tico tapped Meg's shoulder. "Doesn't your friend Penny work at the Quarry?"

Meg held up her phone. "Dialing her now." She turned to look at him. "Wow. She told you a lot in a few minutes."

"Like I said, she was way too friendly."

Meg checked her watch. Penny would have been at work for two hours now. When she didn't answer the call, Meg disconnected the line. Penny was probably with a client.

"No answer."

Eric turned the car back toward Adobe Creek.

Meg turned to Tico. "I'm thinking we should head up to the Quarry and look around."

It was on the tip of his tongue to invite her to hop on his Harley, when she said, "I'll drive."

So much for that. "No problem. It'll give me a chance to enjoy the scenery." Including the woman who rivaled Diablo in temperament but was as beautiful to watch as the mountains in the distance. Tico blinked a few times and stared out the window. Where in the hell were these thoughts coming from? Now he was a damned poet?

When Eric finally pulled into the station, he said, "I'll send word to the other three. Let's meet in the conference room at sixteen hundred to debrief."

Meg laughed. "Sixteen hundred, Chief? Whatever happened to four o'clock?"

He grinned. "Holdover from my navy days. Later, you two."

As he drove away, Meg pointed to her truck. "I'd rather not take a squad car. Don't want to attract any attention."

"Wouldn't we need a sports car to fit in up there?"

She snapped her fingers. "You're right. And I know exactly where to get one. Let's go."

MEG PUT THE black Maserati into gear and eased out of the precinct garage like a pro, shifting gears as she accelerated north on Main Street.

"Bet you wish you were driving now," she said, teasing.

"Watching you is more fun. You drive this like you own one."

She laughed. "I do. This is mine."

"So much for thinking this was confiscated in a drug bust."

"Nope. Eric lets me keep the car here. It's safer than at the ranch."

He leaned over to check out the dashboard. "I see you've put some miles on it."

"This is great for night runs up to Tucson, or better yet, road trips to Sedona."

He'd heard Sedona was a cool place where the town had been built to blend into the scenery. "Maybe someday I can get you to try the road trip on the back of my Harley."

She shook her head. "Really? Because I'm a woman I get the back?"

"Do you have a motorcycle license?"

"No, but I'd probably do better driving a bike than you did on the back of that horse."

He laughed. "I'm much better with a Harley. So, how about going for a ride?"

"No, thanks."

Wow. "Just like that? Do I turn you off that badly?"

She grinned. "No."

"You don't like motorcycles?"

"Like them just fine."

"Okay. Then what?"

She slanted him a quick glance. "Women don't turn you down much?"

He didn't even blink. "When I'm interested, no. They don't."

She turned her attention back to the road. "Cocky bastard."

"Hey! We agreed to get along."

She laughed. "You're right. I apologize. How about I rephrase that to there's no accounting for taste."

He slapped a hand over his heart. "Cruel woman."

"So they say."

Meg sped along the empty road leading to the foothills. Tico's attention drifted to the desert fanning out to the distant mountains, dry and abandoned. Almost how he felt right now. The vastness of the desert, Meg's perfume, this challenging case, all were having a disquieting effect on him. He didn't belong anywhere, and never had it been more apparent than since he'd arrived in Adobe Creek.

"So, if you're so hell-bent on being a simple cop, why the Maserati?"

Meg laughed. "I have a soft spot for fast cars. I couldn't give this up."

"You can afford this?"

Meg pulled up to the gate of the Quarry, slid a card into the ID box and revved the engine a bit while waiting for the gate to slowly open.

"I hate to admit this, but I'm a trust-fund baby. I try not to make a big deal of it. But, hey, it comes in handy sometimes. Like now. No one will give us a second look."

"These tinted windows help."

She laughed. "Never want anyone to see who I'm traveling with."

He grinned. "Slum a lot, do you?"

Keeping her expression deadpan, she said, "Not until today."

She'd delivered the barb so effectively that Tico wasn't sure if she meant it or not. He must have looked stunned because Meg burst out laughing.

"That razz was worth your reaction." She patted his arm. "I'm only kidding, cowboy. Just wanted you to stop goading me."

Composure regained, he held up a hand. "Okay, then. Done. I'll give you this one."

Tico relaxed into the seat, more at ease with Meg than he'd expected, as she turned her attention back to steering the Maserati along the narrow, winding road toward the resort center. A golf course, invisible from the valley they'd just left, spread between the road and the foothills that seemed close enough to touch. Low haciendas sprawled along the course and up the graded steps in the hills. White stucco walls and terra-cotta barrel roofs gleamed in the sun, seemingly unpretentious, though the amount of water channeled into this enclave to keep it lush would be extravagant. While a desert landscape enhanced the locale, the blend of color and symmetry in the vegetation made it clear the scenery had been professionally groomed. The talent required to carve luxury into a barren mountain was not lost on Tico. The air practically shimmered with wealth. The few exotic cars dotting the parking lot at the spa when they drove up emphasized the point.

Meg gestured to a vintage powder-blue BMW. "Penny's car."

"Wow. That's a beauty for how old it is. In New York that would have rusted out years ago."

"The desert air preserves cars out here."

"So I see." Tico gestured toward the spa. "Let's talk to Penny first. She'd know about the concert last night."

They walked through the courtyard, where a small pool shaded by a bougainvillea-covered pergola held huge golden, orange and white Japanese koi. The air smelled of incense that must have been burning earlier, unless some of the small flowers on the miniature trees were emitting the fragrance. Soft music accented with chimes and nature sounds filtered through hidden speakers, wrapping the atmosphere in a blanket of calm.

Tico followed Meg through the arched doorway into the spa. He did a double take when he glimpsed the pool area through an open-air hallway. Plush lounges and palm trees surrounded the huge pool. A few well-toned, tanned bodies in bikinis lay facedown on the chaise longues, shocks of blond hair tied in knots on top of their heads, bikini tops undone. The women decorated the scene as if the landscape designers had placed them deliberately. He'd never seen scenery look so lush. He'd never felt more out of place.

"Nice," he said under his breath.

"Not my cup of tea," Meg replied just as quietly.

"Oh, no?"

"I'd take a beach on Maui over this any day."

"Right there with you, sister," he said. Especially if he could take her there, say, right after this investigation was closed? He shook his head, wanting to dislodge such a thought. What the heck had happened to his equilibrium since meeting this woman?

She led him through the glass doors of the spa. A man in a white shirt and shorts that set off his dark tan stood at the counter crafted from granite and wood. His dark brown hair was slicked back into a ponytail. Surprise lit his blue eyes when he spotted Meg.

"Adobe Creek's finest graces our spa," he said to Meg in a rich tenor voice. He held out a hand. "Hello, Meg."

He clasped her hand with both of his, letting curiosity show in his eyes when he looked at Tico. "What brings you here today?"

"Hello, Enrique. It's always a pleasure to see you." Meg gestured to Tico. "Please, meet Tico Butler, NYPD."

Brow raised, Enrique shook Tico's hand. "Enrique Comodin. Welcome."

Strong grip. Soft hand. Not a speck of dirt under

those buffed fingernails. Tico thought, *Wouldn't
trust this guy if I had a sister.* "Nice place you have
here," he said.

"We're proud of our spa," he answered. "So,
what can I do for you today, Meg?"

"I wanted to have a word with Penny, if it
wouldn't be too much bother."

Enrique frowned. "I'm not sure she's here." He
tapped two numbers on the phone. Listened. After
a moment, he shook his head. "She's not in the
back. Let me check the schedule. I just arrived myself, so don't know what the morning held."

He turned to a small computer screen tucked discreetly beneath the counter and clicked the mouse.
"Looks like she's doing a house call. A mani-pedi."
He checked his Rolex. "She'll probably be another
hour."

"Then I'll catch up with her later."

"Excellent. Oh, and, Meg, she's a terrific addi-
tion to our staff. Every bit of high praise you gave
her in your referral was well deserved."

Meg smiled, and Comodin seemed to light up.
Tico realized she had yet to smile at him. And if
she did, would he react in the same sappy way as
this guy?

"I'm glad it's working out. I know she loves the
job. I hope you didn't mind that she used me as a
reference."

He shook his head. "No problem. We've known
each other long enough that I could rely on your

character reference. I know how careful you are with your praise."

Meg laughed. "You make me sound like a hard-ass."

He grinned. "No. That would be your father."

As THEY HEADED back to the car, Tico said, "Did you check out his watch?"

"His Rolex? Sure. What about it?"

Tico shrugged. "Oh, I don't know. Gold. Diamonds in the face. I've seen that watch in more drug busts than I can count. Never sits well with me."

Meg laughed. "Enrique is *not* a drug dealer. He's been working at the spa since he carted towels by the pool in high school. He's catered to more celebrities in his lifetime than we've seen on television."

"What does that have to do with the watch?"

"Enrique told me he bought it from Sotheby's in New York after a client pulled strings for him. Supposedly, it belonged to Frank Sinatra."

"How long ago was that?"

Meg looked surprised. "I don't know. Four, five years ago."

"Your family knows Enrique well?"

Meg nodded. "His father used to work for my dad before he died in a plane crash in Mexico. We were still in high school."

"That's rough."

"Yeah. He was a good man. His death trashed

Enrique pretty badly. His mother and sister, too. But they've carried on pretty well since."

"They still live around here?"

"His mother, yes. His sister moved to San Diego for college and never came back."

"How do you know Penny?"

Meg frowned. "What's with the inquisition?"

"Just getting a feel for the neighborhood."

"We met at college in Tucson."

"So, you're a college girl?"

She shook her head. "Lasted a year. Wasn't for me. I preferred officer training instead."

"Did that bug your parents?"

A hard look crossed her face before she gave him a knowing glance. "You're good, Detective. The University of Arizona is Mom's alma mater. What do you think?"

He whistled softly. "I'm sure it didn't go over well at all."

"They got used to the idea in time." Meg clicked a button on her key. The Maserati taillights flashed, and the doors unlocked with a satisfying click. "Hop in. Let's grab a sandwich before the meeting."

Tico rubbed his belly. "Oh, I don't know. I'm still full from the donuts."

At the look of incredulity on her face, Tico smiled. "Only kidding. I could eat a horse."

Meg slid into the driver's seat. "Can you use another analogy, please?"

"Oh, yeah. Sorry." He took a moment to inhale Meg's powdery perfume in the confines of the small space. He could feel her body heat from the seat just inches from his own. Her profile reminded him of classic Mexican beauty with the sweep of dark lashes framing her dusky eyes, the straight line of her nose above those sensual full lips. If he leaned a little more to the left he could bury his nose in her thick blond hair, which he swore should be dark brown.

He snapped his seat belt into place. "I have a great idea. Why don't you take me to your favorite lunch spot? You can treat."

She started the engine, a look of annoyance creasing her brow. "*Cojones,* Butler. You're sporting a major pair."

He grinned. "What, are my pants too tight?"

Shaking her head, she turned the sports car back toward the valley. Tico pulled his focus away from her profile and the urge to tangle his hand in her hair. If he had his way, he'd have her grow her hair back to its natural color. Especially with those dark bedroom eyes. He'd seen a photo of her in her parents' house taken before she'd dyed her hair. She looked sultry and romantic with that fall of almost-black hair framing her face. Sure, she looked hot and provocative as a blonde now, which worked well for her line of undercover, but he preferred her softer side.

He turned his attention to the passing scenery, shifting uncomfortably in his seat. "Yeah, but you didn't say no to treating."

## CHAPTER SIX

MEG PULLED THE Maserati into the dusty parking lot of a low adobe building just out of town. A green, sun-faded wooden sign saying Cantina hung over the door. An outdated gas pump stood on the edge of the parking lot, clearly not used in years.

She grinned, knowing full well that Butler was watching her. "If you can eat one of Pepe's *chiles relleños* without drinking a glass of water, I'll buy you lunch."

He eyed the restaurant. "This looks pretty authentic."

Meg smiled and was taken aback when Tico settled against his seat watching her with a slow, lazy smile on his mouth. Something inside her gut shifted at the satisfied look in his eyes, and she didn't like it.

"What?"

His grin widened. "You have a beautiful smile."

Suddenly the confines of the car were way too close. She'd been inhaling the warm incense of his skin since they'd started driving. The Arizona sun had a way of rendering the true essence of any living being—animal, vegetation or human. And Butler's particular blend of cigar smoke and whatever he used to wash that gleaming black hair had put her senses on alert for most of the day. This particular man was becoming more enticing by the moment.

Against every argument she could muster, she was beginning to like this New Yorker who'd invaded her territory. If Eric and this case didn't demand she comply, she'd have ejected Butler from her space immediately. Her self-preservation demanded it.

She opened the car door. "Get out of my car. Keep talking like that and you'll not only be buying lunch but walking back to the precinct."

He looked at her from over the roof of the low car. "Sorry, I was surprised. It was the first time you'd smiled at me."

"Don't be a jerk, Butler."

He caught up to her. "If I eat two of Pepe's chili-whatever-you-call-'ems, will you buy dinner, too?"

She laughed. This guy had such cheek. "Let's see you get through one first, then we'll see who buys dinner."

She headed for the cantina before Butler did something stupid like try to open the door for her. Had she just agreed to have dinner with him? Was she out of her mind? She'd find a way to regroup before they finished their meal.

The aroma of roasted meat, cumin and Mexican

oregano had Meg's stomach grumbling the minute she walked through the door. Butler walked next to her. Though he wasn't an overly tall man, she'd never felt more aware of another person's presence.

A small, rotund Mexican woman, dressed in traditional white lace top and tiered skirt, saw Meg and threw her arms wide open. "Margarita! *Bienvenido!*"

"*Hola,* Rita!"

Rita gave Tico a stern glance before speaking in broken English. "Your table usual?"

Meg smiled. *"Si, Señora. Tenemos hambre."*

Tico gave her a questioning look.

"I'm telling her we're hungry."

He nodded once. "So I gathered."

The woman handed them menus. Meg waved them away. *"Dos platos del Pepe's chiles rellenos, por favor."*

"*Picante?*"

Meg met Tico's stare. Should she make them *picante*...spicy? Hell, yes. *"Si, Señora. Gracias Y dos tés helados."* She turned to Tico. "Iced tea work for you?"

"Sure, but I probably won't need it. You can have mine, too."

Meg couldn't help but suspect Tico was up to something. "Ever have *chiles rellenos?*"

Tico unwrapped the paper napkin from around an old fork and knife. "Nope."

Meg did the same, placing the napkin in her lap

to take her focus away from the infuriatingly intriguing man across from her. "Do you like Mexican food?"

"Yup. Taco Bell is all over New York."

She almost choked on her laughter. "Oh, then you're going to love this meal."

Tico's slow grin had her toes curling in her cowboy boots. Time to get the focus away from her. She'd agreed to work with Tico in the name of solving this case. No way around that. So, she might as well dig in and find out just how much she should or should not like him.

"Okay, since we're going to work together, will you answer some questions for me?"

"I'm all about business. Fire away."

She spread her palms on the table. "I want to know about you."

He frowned. "You got my profile, just like I got yours."

She waved a hand. "Yes, but I want your take on what I read."

Tico grew still, his face guarded. "Why? You want to make up your own mind on whether I'm a dangerous criminal masquerading as a cop?"

"Wow. Touchy."

He closed his eyes a moment, inhaling a long breath. "Your father already interrogated me last night."

Don Francisco had probably used his usual diplomacy while filleting the man. "My questions are probably...more honestly motivated."

"Really? How?"

Now it was her turn to release a breath. "We've been thrown into each other's laps. You know I find you a threat to my job. I need to know as much as I can to tell if I can believe what you say."

The intensity in his eyes floored her, and she had to sit back in her chair.

He tapped the table with a finger to punctuate his next words. "Let me insist on one point, Detective Flores. Your job is the last thing I want. Believe me, I do *not* want to be in Adobe Creek. I'm here because I'm good at what I do, and, yes, I can help. Period."

When she opened her mouth to speak, he held up a hand. "I can see you've been blindsided here. I don't like it. Actually, I was asked to step away from a pretty important investigation in New York to appease your father. I agreed to come here because human trafficking isn't something I can ignore. I didn't expect to get caught in the crosshairs of a family argument. Let me go on record with you right now that I don't appreciate the situation this puts me in with you or your father."

His face, body language and choice of words seemed sincere. Meg had to decide if he was deceiving her or saying what he genuinely felt. For the sake of the case, she chose the latter.

"Okay. I appreciate your answer." She let gratitude show in her eyes. "Very much, indeed."

The look on his face changed. Softened. "Are you playing me here? You sound way too earnest."

She chuckled. "No. I mean it."

He shrugged. "Then, okay. Ask away. I'm an open book."

Wow. Just like that, he let his guard down. Maybe he really didn't like being in Adobe Creek. Maybe he really didn't like *her*. But it seemed that a bit of kindness and honesty was all it took to soften him up.

He leaned forward. "Before you ask your first question, let me ask one."

There he went, turning the tables. Throwing her defenses up once more. Yet, she'd lived her life openly, so what could he possibly ask that would bother her?

"Okay."

He tilted his head. "What makes you tick?"

"What do you mean?"

"You're smart. Beautiful. Why are you a cop and not a schoolteacher or a nurse, or something?"

"You mean a woman's job?"

He frowned. "Not at all. Men are great at those jobs, too. I mean, why a dangerous job?"

"Well, it's certainly not for the thrill of the chase."

"Bad as pursuit is, I enjoy the adrenaline rush now and again."

She shook her head. "My heart pounds every time we do a sting. But stopping crime motivates me more than anything. Crime sucks. It hurts people, including the criminals."

"So, why?"

She shrugged. "I'm sure you know my father lost two sisters to human trafficking."

"You became a cop to vindicate them?"

"Not that, as much as wanting to protect others. Also, my dad pounded the importance of being street-smart into my head, so police work seemed like the thing to do. It's a good feeling, knowing I can protect myself."

The waitress brought their plates, the food steaming. Tico pointed at his plate. "So, what is this?"

Meg stifled a grin. "Green chilies stuffed with cheese, dipped in batter and fried. Pepe's famous sauce on top."

He dug up a forkful and popped it into his mouth.

Meg waved one hand. "Careful, it's hot!"

He breathed out of his mouth a few times. "No joke!" He chewed quickly, then swallowed. "I should wait until it cools down more."

Meg's jaw dropped open. The chilies themselves weren't that hot, but Pepe's sauce was killer. A person had to love spicy food to handle one of these entrées.

She cut into her meal, blew on the piece before eating. The spice exploded in her mouth, but damn it all, she wouldn't show it if Butler didn't. Her eyes started tearing, and she wanted to reach for her iced tea. Instead, she took a piece of bread from the basket between them.

Tico held up a fork. "Hey, no fair. We both know bread kills the burn while water makes it worse."

Her hand stopped in midair. "Oh, yeah? They taught you that at Taco Bell?"

"Hell, no. I have a Costa Rican neighbor who likes to cook for me. I learned to appreciate habanero peppers."

The waitress returned and asked in Spanish if the meal was sufficient. Tico answered with perfect fluency. *"Si, Señora. Todo está bien. Gracias."*

Meg put down her fork. "You speak Spanish?"

"Wasn't that in my profile?" He gestured to her plate as he cut another piece for himself. "Now, let's eat. This is great."

Well, the son of a... "Hey! You played me!"

Tico plastered an innocent look on his face. "Me? When you ordered the meal spicy thinking you'd get a free lunch?" He wagged a finger at her. "You should rethink who was pulling the fast one here."

Damn. He'd caught her out. "Touché, Detective. You win."

He grinned. "So you'll buy dinner, too?"

She shook her head. "No dinner, but I will buy lunch, as promised."

"Then I'll buy dinner."

She leaned closer. "No dinner."

"Why not?"

He was devouring his meal just like a local. Amazing. "Have you ever had Judumi cooking?"

That seemed to stop him cold. He wiped his mouth with his napkin. "No."

He answered with a note of finality designed to shut down more questions, but that wouldn't stop her. "But your father was Judumi."

She knew a guarded look when she saw one. Butler's poker face didn't fool her when he said, "So?"

"Didn't your mother cook his favorite food?"

"From what I remember, my mother cooked hot dogs, and those she usually tossed at me cold."

That slowed her down. "Oh. I'm sorry. I didn't realize—"

He cut her off. "That I was a neglected kid? Now, *that* fact wasn't in my profile."

"Do you know anything about your Judumi heritage?"

Tico shook his head. "I didn't think you could find a question that would bother me, but this one does."

"Why?"

He pushed his plate away. "The truth?"

"Of course."

He hesitated. "Because I want you to like me, and my story isn't very likable."

"You care if I like you?"

"What do you think? How would you feel about always being the wild card sent into a contentious situation? After a while, a guy gets a complex, you know?"

She laughed. "I can't imagine."

"I'm sure that's true. I'll bet you've never known rejection."

She pursed her lips. Actually, she hadn't. She hadn't encountered too many roadblocks in her career. As for her personal life, well, she'd chosen to stop dating because it got in the way of her work. No real rejections there, either. She grimaced. "Darn, that sounds awful."

He laughed. "Yeah. It does. I have no idea what such a cushy life is like."

Meg twirled a lock of hair around a finger and stopped herself. Ugh! How flirty! Butler was making her feel desirable, and she liked it. Double ugh! She planted both hands on her legs under the table and pinched herself to keep from losing perspective. Time to get this guy talking about himself again.

"You passed the Judumi reservation before you came into town."

Again, the blank look in his eyes. "I know."

"Have you been there?"

"No."

"I'll take you, if you'd like. I've known the tribe my entire life. Don't know if you noticed, but the nation borders on Rio Plata Ranch."

"I saw that, too." He released a breath. "Look, my father abandoned the Judumi tribe early. Traded that for a life dealing drugs across the Mexican border."

She knew this from his file, but somehow reading it hadn't had the impact that came with hearing the unveiled disgust in Tico's words. "Were you with him then?"

"Not then. He met my mother in Mazatlan. A New Yorker visiting during spring break. He sold her cocaine. She was pretty spunky, and I guess he liked that. He talked her into smuggling drugs for him. They fell in love and got married."

Tico delivered this information with such finality that Meg's heart squeezed. What a shitty story. How the heck did Butler have a chance of becoming a decent kid with parents who broke the law for a living?

She shook her head. "Bad way to begin a relationship."

"You're telling me." Tico grew quiet. "But there were a few times when my dad would talk about being a Judumi." His focus drifted past her. "He talked about medicine men. Smoke lodges. Rites of passage. Riding the foothills bareback on ponies with pretty girls." A frown creased his face when he looked back at her. "Making fry bread on campfires. But he was usually flying high on crack, so I didn't believe him. He made it sound so cool. For me it was like promising a kid to take him to Disney World someday and never delivering."

She took a moment to exhale. Disappointment rolled on every word he spoke. Meg wanted to know more but didn't want to seem insensitive. "He never brought you here?"

Tico laid his hands on the table. "This is my first time being remotely close to the Judumi. From what I understand, the tribe expelled my father because he'd been arrested too many times. Once my folks moved to New York, where I was born, they never left. I don't think I need to see the tribe, nor do they need to see me."

How to sound neutral? She knew the basics about his father, but no details. She knew his family who remained on the reservation, but they'd been closemouthed about Tico's parents and Tico himself. She'd been unable to get Bill to tell her anything he knew about Tico's background because he said what he knew was irrelevant to the current case. She should have known better than to ask. The tribe protected each other from gossip. Tico obviously wanted her to understand but didn't want her to pry.

Meg couldn't help herself. She wasn't gossiping. She simply wanted to understand. "So, you were okay with growing up knowing you had Native American roots?"

"Hate to disappoint you, but my roots are in New York."

"What made you become a cop?"

A small chuckle rose in his throat. "You mean, did I join the force to avoid jail?"

The thought had crossed her mind. "No. I want to know what changed you."

He'd been sitting rock still. Now he leaned forward. The intensity in his eyes was startling. "The single event in my life that influenced me to become a cop is nowhere to be found in my profile."

"I'd like to know what that event was."

He watched her a moment. "This is the part where I think you'll begin not liking me."

She held her ground. She liked him more by the minute, but she'd save that information for when they were on a more solid footing. "Try me."

Tico Butler was proving to be a pro at using silence to make his point. With each empty second Meg knew he was deciding whether to share a personal fact with her. She opened her mouth to encourage him when he began to speak.

"My parents used our home in Brooklyn as a crack house. Usually the drug dealing began before I woke in the morning. Druggies would drift in, get high and hang out for hours on end.

"One day we were raided. An officer found me hiding behind a couch, still in my pajamas from two days before. I'll never forget the look on his face when he pulled me into his arms and told me not to worry. That I was safe. And you know what? For the first time in my life, I believed him. That guy was so strong and confident, while my parents were being herded out in handcuffs and didn't even remember I was there. I felt like that officer rescued me when no one else even knew I existed. I knew right then and there that I wanted to be like him when I grew up."

He may have delivered that information factually, but holy smokes. The hurt still showed. "How old were you?"

He shrugged. "I don't know. Four? Five?"

Absolutely awful. "Did you parents clean up their act?"

"Oh, God, no. Smoking the shit landed my father in jail on and off for the next few years until it finally killed him when I was seven. My mom died of an overdose two years later."

Meg frowned. "But you joined gangs before becoming a cop."

Tico shrugged. "I got sidetracked for a few years." He held up a finger. "But the cop who rescued me as a kid was the same one who recruited me all those years later. Small world, eh?"

Abandoned and forgotten way too young. Meg had had no idea. Figuring the last thing he wanted was her pity, she asked the obvious question. "Who took care of you?"

"My maternal grandmother. She died when I started high school. So I ran away rather than let them put me in a foster home."

A pained look crossed his face. "After my dad

died, I heard my mother fighting with my grand-mother because people from the Judumi tribe showed up for the funeral. My mother refused to let them see me. After my mother died, my grand-mother stopped paying attention to me. It was hard in New York—fighting to stay alive on the streets. At ten, I was sick of constantly defending myself. I kept remembering the stories my dad told about the Judumi. I thought maybe I could escape. I went to the library, looked up the Judumi nation and sent a letter to the chief telling them I wanted to come back, but nobody came for me."

"Did they know about your situation?"

He shrugged. "I have no idea. I just knew they were out there because they'd shown up for my dad's funeral." He hesitated. "I fantasized about running away to Adobe Creek. My dad made the town sound so magical when he wasn't angry over being exiled. But one year melted into another. I got tougher. Angrier. After having to dig myself out of a few holes, Adobe Creek became a hell I promised myself I'd never visit, especially if it spit out a father who left me in a hell of my own."

"But you're okay now."

He frowned. "Am I? Instead of being hunted as a criminal, I hunt criminals. I have no family. No real ties anywhere. The few friends I have are solid, I'll give you that, but in our line of work, you can't get too attached to anyone."

She nodded. "I understand. Too dangerous."

"You've got that right."

They watched each other in silence. She whispered, "Do you think the job is worth the sacrifice?"

His mouth formed a hard line. "Oh, yeah. Every single day."

It all made sense now. "You accepted my father's offer because you don't want these abducted women to feel abandoned the way you felt as a kid."

"Bingo." He grabbed his iced tea and chugged.

He broke the emotional moment. Meg pointed at him. "Ha! You drank first. You buy lunch."

He smiled. "I was planning on it." He gestured to her unfinished meal. "Now, are you going to eat that?"

THE RIDE BACK to the precinct flew by. Not because Meg was driving with a lead foot, but because Tico didn't want to lose the comfortable bond that he'd started to forge with her. As much as he hated telling his life story to people, and rarely did unless interrogated for a job, coming to Adobe Creek had begun unearthing needs he hadn't realized he had. And suddenly, with Meg Flores, one of those needs was to be understood.

Before lunch, he'd almost died when she smiled at him in the car. He'd been so relieved when he hadn't made a complete ass of himself. Actually, he thought he'd handled the moment rather well. He liked that he'd flustered her in return. The fact that he got a belly laugh from her when he asked to finish her plate seemed to finally break the ice between them.

He was glad. They had too much work to do on this case to remain at odds with each other. Besides, he wouldn't have permitted it to continue much longer. Crossing this one hurdle with Detective Flores kept her on the job.

As Tico followed her into the conference room, the familiar aroma of newly brewed coffee betrayed the fact that someone in the room needed a caffeine boost. He didn't even have to look to know Mitchell Blake held the only cup. Meg took a seat next to Bill. Tico grabbed a chair on the other side of the table beside Jose. Eric Longwood arrived just as they settled into their seats.

Tico listened as Eric launched into a recap of their interview with the missing girl's parents. "Bottom line is that she was with witnesses at the party in the Quarry before she disappeared."

"So she met someone there," Bill suggested.

Mitchell Blake shook his head. "Circumstantial evidence. She could have been hijacked on the way home. Would someone from a posh party drop her car off at a mall? I say she left without her friends to meet someone."

Jose nodded. "Makes sense."

Eric asked Bill, "Anything with her car?"

He shook his head. "The car was wiped clean of fingerprints. A few hair samples, but they all matched the missing woman. No signs of foul play. No blood. No clothing. Only desert sand on the floor of both front seats and the passenger seats in the back."

"That suggests Melissa took a full car to the desert concert," Meg said.

Bill agreed. "We got the names of the others from her friend Vicky. They all said the same thing. The group went to the after-party together. Melissa became upset about something and walked out when no one was looking."

"The girl's car was wiped clean of fingerprints. Someone knew what they were doing," Tico said.

Mitchell shrugged. "Might not even be the same group who snagged the first three women."

Tico frowned. "Why not? Are abductions common in Adobe Creek?"

Eric answered, "No. We've managed to keep things pretty quiet around here." He glanced at Meg. "Our mayor is more vigilant than most, given that we're a border town."

"So it's safe to assume all four kidnappings are related," Tico said.

"To assume anything makes an *ass* of *u* and *me*," Jose muttered under his breath. He looked up when the room grew silent, and met the group's stare. He shrugged. "Learned that in training. I assumed way too much, and my instructor was a hard-ass."

Tico shook his head. "Sometimes assumptions are all you have to go on until you're proven wrong." He looked around the table. "Any witnesses around the car?"

Mitchell sipped his coffee. "No one saw it being dumped. We have no further witnesses unless we talk to the folks at the party."

"Do we have a list of partygoers?"

"I can get that," Mitchell said.

"Good. Have we confirmed who hosted the party?" Tico asked.

"The rock star from the concert. Josh Ripley." Bill ran a hand through his dark hair. "He and his band collect groupies for themselves and the posse of friends who travel with them. Ripley likes to party and have a crowd around him."

"We need to get that list," Meg said.

"Better yet, we need to get inside," Tico added.

"No landscape job for you, Butler," Jose said, chuckling.

Tico playfully smacked Jose's arm. "Yeah, maybe I can moonlight as a rock star."

Eric's eyes lit up. "Can you pull that off?"

"Sure. I play a mean radio," Tico said, deadpan.

"Great." Eric shook his head. "Okay, Bill. You and Jose visit the rock star and check with Melissa's friend Vicky again. Let's compile every name from the party—even the catering help. We'll divvy up the names and start asking questions. I want to know who was the last person to see Melissa Collins."

# CHAPTER SEVEN

MEG SAT IN the gloaming on her back porch, the last of the daylight reflecting purple and pink on the still lake. The chaise longue faced the water and the ranch land beyond reaching to the foothills. The breeze from the day was still hot, carrying the dusty scent of the desert. She'd changed from her work clothes into a red tank top and frayed white denim shorts that hung low on her hips. She'd slipped on a pair of Keds, no socks. Bruno had wormed his way into her lap, and she absently stroked the tan fur between his ears while she watched two buzzards circle high in the sky. An issue of *Vanity Fair* magazine lay untouched in her lap. She'd wanted to unwind from the day, but couldn't let her thoughts go.

After lunch with Tico, the rest of the day was a bust. Bill and the other guys returned from their investigation with a decent list of names to go through but no clear clues.

What the heck had happened after the party? No matter how much Meg tried to unwind, she couldn't let the investigation go. Women were missing. Someone would have to trip up soon. How could it be that they'd get so close, only to find no trace of the traffickers once the team got into motion?

Meg headed into the kitchen. Not big on air-conditioning unless she really needed it, she pulled the cords on the ceiling fans to increase their speed. She switched on the internet radio on her computer, the sound of classic guitar filling the silence. A nice cold beer would help her chill out on this hot night. As she poured herself a glass, the throaty sound of a Harley came down the drive. She stopped pouring and put the beer on the counter. Tico Butler was the only person she knew with a Harley. Her hands flew to her messy ponytail. Her clothes—oh, God, they were ancient!

*Whoa!* What the heck did she care what she looked like? She was off duty and in her own home. She hadn't invited company, nor would she explain herself to anyone who arrived at the door. Especially Tico Butler.

The engine cut out, and before she could turn around, there was a knock at the door. Butler peered through the door side window, spotted her and gave her a two-finger salute, as John Wayne used to do in the movies.

This New Yorker must have lived on Westerns.

With Bruno yapping beside her feet, she opened the door. "What are you doing here?"

Butler looked down at Bruno, squinted. "Is that a dog?"

She quelled her impulse to laugh, if only to keep Bruno's dignity intact. "Yeah. A man-eater. You'd better watch it."

"Well, with that noise, he makes a good watch-dog." He pulled a bucket of fried chicken from behind his back. "I would have brought pizza, but it wouldn't fit on the bike."

"Hey, I thought I told you no dinner."

He scoffed. "Detective, this is not my idea of dinner. It's a snack."

"Well, I wasn't expecting company. I'm trying to relax."

He shook his head. "I don't feel like we covered enough ground today in the debriefing. I want to talk a few things over with you." He cast a glance down the length of her, lingering on her legs. Grinning, he said, "Besides, you look nice and relaxed to me."

She rolled her eyes. "Riiight." She opened the door wider and scooped Bruno up with one arm. "Okay. Come in. I just happen to have a cold beer to go with that chicken. But you can't stay long."

Tico whistled as he walked through the living room to the kitchen. "Nice place. Bigger than it looks from the outside."

She gestured with her free hand. "It's the open floor plan."

"Love the woodwork."

Dark wood beams against the whitewashed living room ceiling accentuated the Southwest theme of the house. The wide-planked kitchen floor reflected the wood cabinets, while the huge chopping-block counter had two stools pulled up to it. Tico turned to look back into the living room. "I could fit my entire apartment in your kitchen."

Meg put down the dog. He sniffed at Tico's boots before trotting to his little bed by the porch doors. Meg opened a bottle of beer and poured it for Tico.

"How does a body live in an apartment the size of my kitchen? My kitchen is not that big."

Tico opened the bucket of chicken on the chopping block. "Do you want to just eat out of the container?"

Meg shrugged. "Sure." She grabbed a bowl and two cloth napkins. "Come on. We can sit outside. There's a nice breeze off the lake."

"If you call that a breeze."

She turned to look at him. "Desert getting to you, cowboy?"

"Hot is hot. No way around it." He pulled on the neck of his T-shirt. "Don't you believe in air-conditioning?"

"Sure."

"What? It's broken?"

She laughed. "It's not hot enough."

"I guess you don't sleep with any blankets."

She raised a brow. "How I sleep is none of your business." She wanted to kick herself the moment she said the words. The air temperature seemed to rise a few degrees with the look in Butler's eyes.

They settled into the chairs she and Penny had occupied last night. Meg glanced at the Queen of the Night. The blooms had already withered. Most of the spiky petals lay in the dirt, still white, like wispy afterthoughts of last night's fragrant blossoms.

Tico placed the bucket on the small table between them. Meg handed him a napkin. The scar along his jaw caught her attention once more. Someday she'd ask him how he got it. Ugh! What was she thinking? Butler wouldn't be around long enough for her to ask.

He held up the cloth napkin. "You're okay with me getting grease on this thing?"

"You're kidding."

"No. Paper napkins work just fine."

"I'm big on conserving trees. Don't worry about the grease."

Tico laid the napkin in his lap. "You don't own much when living in a small space. Makes life easier." He offered Meg the open container.

Meg took a wing. "Sounds Spartan. Like living in the military."

"It's not much different." He took a bite from a chicken leg, looking around. "I never imagined that this type of lifestyle or so much open land existed."

Meg took a moment to appreciate her world all

over again. "Dad worked hard to build this ranch. I have never taken what he's done for granted."

"You're lucky."

She inhaled a long breath. "Yes, I am."

"Is this your father's house?"

A tug of pride pulled at her heart. Meg had always wanted a place of her own, and she hadn't waited for marriage to create the house of her dreams. She felt good about that.

"No. I bought this parcel from my parents. Designed the house and paid for the construction. I've lived here about five years."

"Nice."

She tilted her head at the distant look that rose in his eyes. "What about you?"

He shrugged. "I rent. Most of my income goes into a nice fat retirement plan."

"No real estate?"

"With the enemies I've made from work? No. I move every year or so. Don't need any ex–gang members making house calls."

Meg chewed on that answer in silence. After a while she asked, "Do you think you'll ever settle down?"

"I don't know. My Harley keeps calling me out. Maybe after I've explored enough back roads."

Even with all the things Meg had done, she'd never ridden a motorcycle. For a brief second, she entertained trying her first ride on the back of Tico's

Harley. Would she wrap her arms around that bod of his? She met his stare.

"You know, land is still cheap out here. You could set up your own homestead for less money than you think."

He sat back in his chair. "That coming from a woman who wants to run me out of town?"

She laughed. "I didn't mean here in Adobe Creek. There's plenty of space near Tucson or Bisbee. New Mexico is spectacular."

A look of disappointment filled his eyes. "Oh."

Meg's face felt hot with embarrassment. If the situation were different she'd be scrambling to help him find his own parcel. But, no. He was danger in denims. No way around that fact. He couldn't stay anywhere near her town.

"So, what's bugging you about the debriefing?"

Tico let his attention wander over the lake as he chewed on another piece of chicken. "Adobe Creek has gone so long without losing citizens. And now, four in a row."

"I know. Adobe Creek has lived a charmed life, but that's because my father was instrumental in protecting the town long before becoming mayor."

"Really?"

She swallowed the bite she'd been chewing. "Sure. He made donations to the police department so they could afford to hire enough staff to patrol the town, the border and county boundaries. Those donations also allowed the department to acquire state-of-the-art surveillance equipment. It's not quite on the level of the mega technology the cartels employ, but it at least keeps us only a step behind."

"That's a pretty hefty donation."

Meg grinned. "No joke. Dad also makes sure city justices are absolutely merciless on crime when it happens."

Tico looked impressed. "The entire package makes Adobe Creek a nuisance to the criminal element, so they circumvent the area for easier spots with no hassle."

"Until recently."

"Which means something has changed." Tico frowned in concentration.

"Thoughts?"

Tico met her gaze, and it bugged her that her stomach flip-flopped at the intensity in his eyes. He truly was determined to get to the bottom of this case. That determination made him look awfully damned sexy.

"Two points. Either someone is extremely confident that they won't get caught, or there's a new team in town for a hit-and-run—and they know the local system."

The latter option was disquieting. "And the fact that they hit again today means they're still here."

He tossed another leg bone into the bowl. "Exactly. Your investigators checked the outlying ranches?"

"Helicopter runs and door-to-door, but there are so many holes to hide in out there."

"Checked along the river?"

"Oh, yeah. The Rio Grande is a favorite camping ground for smugglers, but we only found abandoned sites. No new activity."

"My concern?"

Meg deposited her finished wing in the bowl. She'd lost her appetite, thinking about the futility of their search. She was grateful to hear Butler's perspective to compare with her own. "What's that?"

"If it's a hit-and-run gang, they'll go after a few more before leaving. Four women aren't enough."

"Unless they're snatching women from another area, as well."

"Have you heard of any?" he asked.

Meg compressed her lips. The only trouble was in Adobe Creek at the moment. "No."

"Adobe Creek isn't that big. Would patrol cars notice new vehicles?" He reached for another piece of chicken.

"You can eat while discussing women getting kidnapped?"

He finished chewing, swallowed. "The situation makes me sick, but if I let every case affect me that way, I couldn't do my job." He wiped his hands on the napkin. "So, yeah. I eat."

She grinned. "A real stress eater, eh?"

He checked his belly. "What? Do I look fat?"

She laughed. Oh, *fat* wouldn't be the word she'd use. She grabbed another piece of chicken. Not good to think that way about her adversary at all.

But sitting on her porch, sharing a meal and discussing the case with him an arm's length away, smelling like the hot desert air he'd ridden through, wasn't something one did with an enemy now, was it?

She shook herself. Despite her greatest efforts to hold out, this clever New Yorker was slowly but surely whittling away her resolve. She dropped her untouched piece of chicken back into the bucket as reality hit. She'd caved. And in only two days. For the good of this damned case, she'd given Butler the benefit of the doubt. She'd have to pay Bill his fifty bucks.

"I could go for a piece of chocolate," she said.

"What? Don't like the chicken?"

Unwilling to share her bet arrangements, she waved away his concern. "The chicken is fine. I'm just thinking about the case."

"Like what?"

"I don't like the idea of some criminal knowing how to manipulate the local system."

"Tell me about your team. I read the profiles, but what's your take on your men?"

The way he said "your men" clearly acknowledged her as team leader. It also sounded as if he had suspicions about her team. She didn't like that. Then again, he was calm and strong-willed. She liked that. His quiet steadiness would be an asset to the team. Who would have guessed that an ex–gang leader would have such a level head?

"What do you want to know?"

He shrugged. "Start with the rookie."

"Jose is still a little wet behind the ears, as they say, but he's good. Fast thinker. Quick response. Born and raised in Adobe Creek. Newly married with a baby on the way any day now. He feels driven to protect his new family and has a strong sense of justice."

"You trust him?"

She couldn't keep the shock from her face. "Of course. Why?"

He held up a hand. "Just let me play devil's advocate here."

Her back stiffened. She didn't like hearing anyone bash her team. "I'm listening."

"Jose would be a prime target for the cartel. With a kid on the way, stashing some large bills could be pretty attractive."

She shook her head. "I understand, but it's impossible." She gave him a quelling look. "Impossible for the entire team. Don't go there. With any of them."

"Okay. If you say so, I'll believe you."

"No. You brought this up, so let's talk about it. I don't want a single doubt in your mind."

"Well, then, I have another concern." He grabbed a chicken wing. "Imagine my surprise when I saw you and Mitchell sparring with each other. Why don't you like him?"

"I don't dislike Mitchell. He's one of the best

detectives out there. But Mitchell and I have been at each other since I became team leader. He retired and I took his job. My opinion is that he can't quite turn off the job." She shrugged. "He snipes at me to keep me on my toes. If I ease up on him, the guys will lose confidence in me."

A frown creased his brow. "That's what you called that little display yesterday?"

"I'm sorry you saw that. I think he was putting on a show for your benefit." She hesitated. "Honestly? We all argued over how we would handle your arrival. It wasn't pretty. We were divided on whether bringing you in was a good idea."

"I understand."

She tilted her head. "Do you?"

"Sure. All I have to do is turn the tables and imagine how I'd feel."

"So why the sheriff getup and riding into town?"

A grin tugged at his mouth. "Come on, Detective. You already figured that one out."

She chuckled. "Yeah, I did. You moron."

He laughed. "I've been called worse."

The front door banged open. "Hey! I'm home!"

Penny's singsong voice, high-pitched and expectant, called out to the patio. Meg recognized that tone. Pen was excited. Either she had great gossip from the spa or the sight of Butler's bike out front had gotten her juices flowing. Bruno must have sensed her excitement, because he raced to her and started yapping again.

Meg rolled her eyes at Tico's questioning look. "We're on the patio, Pen."

Penny blew in like a little dynamo, Bruno in her arms, her eyes bright. A smile as big as the great outdoors was plastered on her face. "So, we have company."

To Meg's amusement, Tico didn't say hello, but instead held up the bucket of chicken. "Hungry?"

Penny's face scrunched. "No, thanks. Vegetarian."

She ran a hand through her short hair, looking every bit the pixie in her turquoise peasant skirt topped with a pink camisole and tiers of delicate, pastel-colored beads around her neck. "I'll get rid of my gear and join you two in a minute."

When she disappeared down the hallway, taking Bruno with her, Tico asked, "Been roommates long?"

"No. Penny moved in last year after breaking up with a boyfriend. We've known each other since college days. She's great fun. I charge her rent because she wouldn't stay if I didn't."

"Has she always lived in Adobe Creek?"

"No, just ten years."

He sipped his beer. "That's long enough."

"What do you mean?"

Penny returned with an open bottle of wine from the kitchen. Tico blew out a breath, then whispered, "That's long enough to know not to flirt with strangers."

Penny obviously heard him. "Are you talking about me?"

She pulled a chair from the table to sit closer to their chairs on the edge of the garden. "Sorry if I came on too strong this morning." She held up a hand. "Didn't realize who you were. It won't happen again."

"Don't get me wrong," Tico said, "I enjoyed your flirting, but I suggest you don't do it at all. Women are disappearing around here. You're setting yourself up as a target, talking to strangers."

Penny frowned. "Oh, come now. If I live like I'm afraid, I might as well not live here at all."

"That might be a good idea."

"Wow. That's not very nice."

He shrugged. "Just trying to keep you safe. Do yourself a favor and don't talk to strange men."

She huffed. "All right, already. Now, if you're done slapping my hand, I have a juicy story to tell you two."

Meg settled into her chair, pleased at how easily Penny had moved past that uncomfortable moment. Tico was right, and she knew damned well Penny would never listen to her advice. She was grateful that he cared enough to speak up.

"Go on, Pen. We're all ears," she said. Penny's stories were usually entertaining since some of her celebrity clients took themselves way too seriously.

"When I missed you two this morning, I was at the Ripleys' hacienda. Katrina Ripley wanted a massage to remedy her bad night, as she called it, and her two girlfriends wanted manicures. Adele and I went over."

Tico perked up at the mention of Katrina Ripley's name. Meg grinned. Wouldn't it just beat the band if they got a lead from Penny, of all people? "So, what happened?"

"Great gossip." She shook her head. "I'm stunned to find someone as beautiful as Katrina is so insecure. Can you imagine? Jealousy is a problem for her."

"I'd think that groupies pawing her husband all the time must get tedious," Meg said.

Penny nodded emphatically. "Enough to cause a ruckus at the house after the concert. The party got out of hand."

Meg and Tico exchanged glances. "How out of hand?"

Bruno trotted back in, and Penny pulled him into her lap. "Katrina didn't like some of the wildlife her husband brought home. One of the little vixens in the party had her face slapped. Started a brawl."

"Katrina hit someone?" Meg asked.

Penny sat back in her chair. "Oh, yeah. Caused the whole lot of them to be thrown from the party."

"Do you know who Katrina struck?"

"Nope. She just kept calling the girl 'that black-haired bitch.'" Penny made quote marks with her fingers.

Tico raised an eyebrow. "That's hostile."

Penny chuckled. "Yeah, but it sounds so charming when she says it with her German accent."

"You're kidding, right?" Tico said.

She lifted a shoulder. "Um, I guess so."

Meg laughed. "You don't understand, Tico. Penny thinks celebrities walk on water."

"No, I don't. They have their moments." She frowned. "I'm actually becoming disenchanted with Katrina. She didn't tip us for the house call."

"Hitting below the belt, for sure," Tico said.

Meg liked the amused look he sent her way. Penny must not have missed it because she glanced from him to Meg, then stood and placed Bruno to the floor. "It's been a long day. I could use a good soak in the tub before dinner."

Penny was making herself scarce. Meg wanted to roll her eyes at her friend but acted as if Penny always took a bath at seven in the evening. "Thanks for sharing the celebrity dirt, Penny. After gossip like that, I'd need a bath, too."

Penny gave Tico a pointed look. "Will the good detective be staying for dessert?"

"No," Meg said.

Not missing a beat, Tico gestured to the chicken. "That was plenty. Thanks anyway. Nice to see you again."

With her glass of wine in one hand, she gave them a brief wave with the other. "Pity."

When the patio door closed behind Penny, Meg grimaced. "Sorry. She can be pretty bold."

"Like I said…"

Meg held up a hand. "I'll talk to her. You don't have to say it again."

"I think we have a situation needing investigating at the rock star's house."

"Yes."

"I'm going to recommend to Eric that we go undercover into the Quarry. Get invited to some of those parties."

Meg swallowed hard. She'd been undercover before, but never with anyone who raised her body temperature the way Tico did. She cleared her throat. "Okay. But I make a lousy rock star."

He grinned. "How about a hot, gorgeous trust-fund baby?"

She laughed. "I could pull off the trust-fund part."

"Oh, I don't know. I think you could pull off the whole package."

Meg practically snorted. "Are you flirting with me, Detective?"

Tico drained his glass and stood. "Well, I thought about it. But given the look on your face, I'd say it's time for me to leave."

## CHAPTER EIGHT

TICO WAVED TO the officer at the desk as he headed to the meeting room. He'd slept uneasily, distracted by a gut instinct that something wasn't right with the investigation.

The other distraction was the team leader herself. Last night, seeing Meg dressed in those white shorts, which accentuated her tanned legs, and that small red top, which hugged her very luscious curves, had made him want to run a hand along her flat belly and pull her in for a long, hard kiss.

Those tumbling thoughts had made sleep impossible. In his line of work, an emotional attachment to anyone could become a target for his enemies. So, he'd been careful. Stayed married to his job. He had planned to keep it that way, until last night. Watching the emotions and laughter in Meg's eyes as they spoke last night had started to change his mind about the possibility of falling for someone. And that chafed the hell out of him.

He was the last one to arrive for the meeting because he'd taken the time this morning to visit Melissa Collins's parents again. He'd interrupted their breakfast, but they hadn't seemed to mind. He didn't usually drink coffee, but he'd had two cups with Ellen Collins while she'd described her daughter's daily routine, friends and interests. Somewhere in this mix was an abductor. Tico meant to take him—or her—down.

Bill looked disappointed. "No donuts today?"

Tico grinned. "Wouldn't want to spoil you guys two days in a row. Maybe next time."

"Maybe there won't be a next time because you'll have this case solved by then," Mitchell Blake said, leaning back in his chair.

Oh, so now Blake was needling him the way he did Meg. Tico turned his attention to Meg and thumbed toward Blake. "How do you handle this guy?"

She shook her head, choosing not to answer. He appreciated her restraint. "Morning, Detective," she said.

Tico grabbed the vacant chair next to Jose. Patted him on the shoulder. "How's the wife feeling today?"

The rookie seemed surprised that he'd asked. "She's doing fine, Tico. Getting big, but she's okay. Thanks for asking."

Eric Longwood looked amused. "Okay, if we're finished with the pleasantries, let's get to work." He turned to Bill. "What progress did you make with the list from that party?"

He shook his head. "About twenty names, but it's

not complete. Jose and I talked with a few of them, but they all tell the same story. Great party. Josh Ripley flirted outrageously with Melissa. Katrina slapped the girl for sitting on her husband's lap. Melissa left the room when one of her guy friends starting yelling at the rock star to rein in his wife. The group was thrown from the party. Except Melissa was already gone and no one saw her leave."

"Any suggestions?" Eric asked.

"Her girlfriends thought she'd gone to the bathroom but decided she must have left because she was upset. They ended up calling a taxi after security showed them outside the Quarry gates." Bill shrugged. "No one has seen Melissa since."

"And then her car was found in the mall parking lot," Tico added. "With the steering wheel wiped clean of prints."

"Meaning?" Mitchell said.

"What do you think it means?" Tico was surprised this professional needed the situation spelled out. "She was abducted, and whoever did it knows what they're doing." Tico stared at Mitchell. "You're a pro. Don't you see that?"

He nodded once. "I do."

Eric said, "So now we need to know if she left the party alone and was kidnapped on her way home, or if she was taken from the party."

"Is Ripley a year-round resident?" Tico asked.

Bill shook his head. "He owns the house, but comes and goes. He's here now because he just came off a world tour. Usually stays for a month or two, then takes off again. When he's in the mood he holds a concert in the desert outside the Quarry, like he did the other night."

"The man is a bona fide rock star who loves to perform," Meg added. "Can't seem to stop. His publicist spreads the word to all the colleges and radio stations when a concert is planned."

"How long do you think he'll stay?" Tico asked.

"Another month, maybe?"

Tico addressed Eric. "I'm thinking we should get ourselves into the Quarry. Always wanted to know how the other side lives."

Eric's eyes lit up. "Keep talking. Sounds like you have a plan."

"Since Enrique Comodin knows us, we should enlist his help," Tico suggested. "Meg and I should crash the community. Maybe get ourselves invited to some of the parties. Renting one of the haciendas might be a good idea."

Mitchell Blake laughed, and it wasn't friendly. "That sounds like a cozy arrangement."

Meg shot him an angry look. "Unless you have a better idea, Mitchell, muzzle the stupid comments."

Meg's response surprised Tico. She'd agreed to a sting last night, but he expected her to balk a little at his hacienda suggestion. The fact that she hadn't showed her dedication to get the job done—and how she was refusing to be left out. He liked that.

Almost as much as he liked the thought of spending a few nights with her in a ritzy spa community.

Mitchell ignored Meg and spoke to Tico. "Won't be a problem with you, Butler, because no one has seen you." Mitchell gestured to Meg. "She'll need a disguise."

Bill grinned at Meg. "And how will you manage that?"

Tico answered before Meg could say anything. "My idea was to use Detective Flores as bait for a flirtatious rock star."

Meg shot him a heated glare. "Enough, Tico."

Eric said, "You'll have to find out what Josh Ripley does for recreation during his private time."

"I can get that info for you," Mitchell offered.

Bill said, "Jose and I can work surveillance."

"We don't have time to ease our way in. We have to break into their circle, immediately," Tico said. "Any ideas?"

"If you're using me as bait, maybe I should go in alone," Meg said. "Nothing kills a guy's attention more than a boyfriend."

Tico grinned. She wasn't getting away with that idea for a second. "Didn't say I'd be your boyfriend."

He was rewarded with a blush that stained Meg's cheeks. "Going in alone is a better idea. You can work as you originally suggested, as part of the grounds crew."

"Won't work," Tico said. "If Katrina Ripley is

as jealous as she sounds, there's no way in hell she will let you get near her husband." He thumbed his chest. "But with me there? No chance of a misunderstanding."

Eric raised a finger. "How soon can you be ready?"

Tico looked at Meg. "Can you come up with a disguise by tonight?"

"Depends. Who am I?"

"Let's make you that spoiled trust-fund baby we discussed. Bored. Coming to the Quarry for some relaxation and maybe some wildlife."

Bill grinned at Meg. "You said you could use a vacation."

"Not what I was thinking, Bill." She indicated to Tico. "And you? What's your cover?"

"We can either play married, or I can be your gangster boyfriend who Daddy hates. That way I can be nosing around the spa while you hang out at the pool and chum it up with our rock star dude."

Mitchell closed his file. "I can set this up with Comodin since I seem to be his direct line for whining."

Tico nodded. "Great. Just get us in and we'll take it from there."

"What can you do to look different quickly?" Eric asked.

Meg thought a minute. "I can dye my hair, for starters."

"Some big sunglasses, a change of clothes and

makeup could finish the disguise." Tico wagged a finger. "And don't forget the bikini, or the snotty attitude."

She shook her head. "You can cut the crap anytime now, Detective Butler." She turned to Eric. "Let me know what our budget is. I'll take us clothes shopping. I know a great place in Tucson."

"Tucson? I passed there riding down here. That's more than three hours away. We don't have that kind of time," Tico said.

Meg grinned. "Trust me. I can get us there in under an hour, cowboy. And the sooner, the better. I don't think your sheriff's badge and black hat are dressy enough for the Quarry."

Eric stood. "I like it. Mitchell, see if Comodin can get them into a house as near to the suspects as possible. Bill, get the surveillance going. Jose, keep working that list from the party and feed the info to the team as you go." He nodded toward Meg. "Do your best chameleon for us. Tico, go in as a bad boy. Ripley might find your old gangland persona an interesting curiosity." He rapped his knuckles on the table. "Let's get these creeps and close this case."

MEG HEARD TICO whistle softly as she led him to her father's private jet waiting for them on the airport tarmac. Although she was proud of her father's accomplishments and the luxuries he shared with his entire family, she felt compelled to downplay her wealth in front of Tico. When she realized the inclination was from pity, she quickly adjusted her thinking. If Tico could be confident about himself despite his upbringing, she needed no excuse for being the daughter of a wealthy man.

This was the last time she'd entertain the notion that she had to protect him from her pedigree. Just because he'd had a rough life didn't mean he'd be envious of those who hadn't. Heaven knew Tico had been pretty open with his criticism, but also generous with his compliments. She led him up the stairway.

"Ever been on a private jet?"

"Nope. I try not to fly at all."

She looked back at him just as he pulled his attention from the seat of her jeans. Raising a brow, she said, "Afraid of heights?"

"Not in the least. It's the crashing part that bothers me."

She laughed. "Well, you're safe with me. A native shaman once told me I'd never die in an airplane."

"Why did he say that?"

"Because I'd had some nightmare about flying and crashing a plane and went to him for explanation."

Tico followed her into the jet. A flight attendant met them at the door of the salon. "Good morning, Ms. Flores. Welcome aboard."

"Thank you, Tara." She indicated Tico. "This

is Detective Butler. We'll be your only passengers today."

Tara smiled. "Captain Murphy is in the cockpit. We should be cleared for takeoff in five minutes. Please make yourselves comfortable. Would you like anything before we depart?"

"No, thanks." Meg looked at Tico. "You?"

He held up a hand. "Nothing for now. Thank you."

Tara smiled, her gaze lingering on Tico a bit longer than necessary. "I'll prepare for departure, then."

Tico smiled at Meg when Tara stepped out of earshot. "She likes me."

"Really?" Meg indicated one of the white leather seats next to a window. "Why don't you take a load off that overblown ego of yours? Or would you prefer the table?"

A wood dining table for four occupied the other side of the salon. He was grinning. "Does it matter?"

Meg kept her face deadpan. "You don't even have to wear a seat belt. Pick a seat."

A wall partially obscured an area toward the rear of the jet. "What's back there?"

"A bedroom. Shower. Bathroom."

"Tell me there's a tub and I'm jumping."

She laughed. "No tub. Looks like you get to live through another flight."

Tico settled into one of the seats near the window as Tara secured the jet door. Meg took the seat across from him. Through the window, they could see the ground crew rolling the steps away from the aircraft. Tico immediately started fiddling with the seat, adjusting the settings, pulling out the leg rest, dropping the seat back.

Meg laughed. "You're like a kid in a toy factory."

He sat up, surprised. "What?"

Every reservation she had about this man dissolved at the look in his eyes. Tico's blatant playfulness came from an innocence that only someone with a clear conscience could have. "Were you one of those kids who tinkered with things until they broke?"

"You mean, was I curious?"

She fought back a smile, trying to act exasperated with his juvenile yet oh-so-endearing behavior. "You could say that."

"I'll answer if you tell me why you were so worried about that plane-crash dream."

That stopped her. She waved a hand. "Not important. Teenage angst. Suffice it to say, I'm your good-luck charm for flying."

"Okay. I like that. And I broke everything I touched."

She laughed. "Well, then, keep your hands off the seat controls."

The jet taxied onto the runway. Tico watched out the window for a while. The engines whined as the craft gained speed. Within seconds, they were off the ground.

"So, you figured there's no other choice for our disguises except a shopping spree in Tucson?"

"You packed clothes for a celebrity spa?"

He looked surprised. "Damn straight. All I need is a T-shirt and jeans."

Meg released a breath. "We have a nice budget for clothes. Let's play the part. My favorite hair stylist is in Tucson. She has a one o'clock slot open. I'm going back to dark."

"You're really going to change your hair?"

She shrugged. "Sure. Anything to get the job done."

He tilted his head. "I'm not convinced."

"Why do you say that?"

He watched her a moment. "I've survived this long by understanding body language and voice inflections."

A shiver ran her spine. Survived. Had the man ever had a chance to simply live? "My voice wasn't convincing?"

"Nope. You're not happy about losing the blond."

"It doesn't matter. Eric wants a chameleon, and he'll get one." She held up a finger. "I could shave my head into a Mohawk if you think it'll help."

He laughed. "We're trying not to attract attention, here."

As if Butler could ever be ignored. The man's energy filled a room. She could feel his presence sitting across from him. Tico drew attention even when silent.

The jet banked northward. Meg found herself sighing. "I'm glad to be away from Adobe Creek until it's time to hit the Quarry."

"Why?"

"If Dad gets word of our plans, he'll stop them."

"Eric won't let him. This is the closest lead you've had."

"Maybe. But if I'm not around, he can't detain me."

Tico laughed. "He can tell the plane to stay in Tucson."

"Then it's a good thing he doesn't know we borrowed it."

"You just absconded with an aircraft?"

She chuckled. "You make it sound illegal."

"Well, it's your family plane, so I guess it's not."

Tara appeared with a tray of sandwiches and pastries. "Coffee?"

"Sure," Meg said.

Tico bit into a sandwich. "So, let's plan our strategy."

"Even better yet, our story."

"How does a rich, exciting heiress like you hook up with a nasty gang leader like me?"

"Match.com?"

Tico laughed. "No. Give me a story."

Meg decided she'd be honest. "You know, Tico, I've busted my share of gang members. I have to say, if I came across you, I'd have second thoughts about how bad you really were."

Tico looked surprised. "No joke?"

"Were you dangerous?"

"I've done harm. I'm not proud of that. I was headed for jail when I was approached by the feds."

She had to know. "Why?"

He didn't hesitate. "I killed a man."

Meg grew still. She'd shot and killed a perp in the line of duty, but had never killed out of anger. "You had justifiable reason, I hope?"

Tico closed his eyes. When he looked at her again, his dark eyes held no emotion. "The prick shot my girlfriend in front of me."

"Oh, my God, Tico. How horrible."

He shook his head. "Walked right up while we were eating burgers in my car. Shot her in the head. It happened so fast, but it only took me seconds to react. I was out of the car and on the bastard before he could turn and run. He was dead in seconds. That's when I got the nickname Rattlesnake."

"You shot him?"

"With his own gun."

A shiver ran up her spine. "You were young?"

"Seventeen."

"Oh, Tico. Gangs are so brutal. I really can't grasp you in that world. Why did you get into it?"

He turned to look out the window. "Why does any kid join a gang? I know I did it for safety. Only problem is you end up with a lot of angry kids who pretty much act out how they've been treated. My gang was the only family I had, and as their leader, I made sure things went the way I wanted them to. No one was going to lay a hand on me or anyone I cared for again, unless they wanted it back in spades."

Silence fell. The high-pitched whine of the jet engines filled the cabin. He'd been rubbing his tattoo while he spoke, but Meg doubted he was even aware of the fact. She tried to imagine what she would have done in the same situation. Growing up in such an unsafe world from infancy could break a person. Yeah, she would have killed, if someone she loved had been shot before her eyes. Given the stories she'd been told about her abducted aunts, as a kid she'd wanted revenge for them strong enough to taste it. She'd become a cop so she'd never have to feel helpless in the face of danger. The fact that Tico had surfaced from the dark side spoke volumes about his character.

"And the tattoo?"

He glanced at it once. "I got this after we buried Jackie."

"Because you can't see a rattlesnake strike?"

He frowned. "Actually, no. Everyone thought so, but I'd done research at the library. A snake symbolizes change, protection and power."

"Pretty clever for a kid."

"Kid? I never had the chance to be a kid."

He held her gaze. "Did you know that snakes are

also considered a symbol for healing and cleansing? For shifting and adjusting to moods and situations? I pride myself on being able to read a room of people in a heartbeat. Now that I'm in law enforcement, I focus on its more positive symbolism." He shook his head. "I may have killed, but I still have nightmares over it. And Jackie. God, she was a mess. So young. And because of me."

"Jackie was your girlfriend?"

His look held regret. "First love. Taught me real fast that a dangerous life and lovers don't mix."

"One of the drawbacks of undercover work, as we already discussed."

When Tico didn't answer, Meg said, "I had no idea snakes held such complex meanings."

As if he needed to lighten the discussion, Tico stuffed another sandwich into his mouth. "Yeah. I'm a deep son of a bitch," he said.

Meg sipped her coffee. Tico might be glib about the depth of his emotions, but he wasn't fooling her. This guy was carrying wounds that hadn't healed.

Her voice dropped low. "We have a lot to be grateful for in life, Tico. No matter what happened in the past."

He sat back in his seat, hands resting in his lap, studying her. "I'm grateful for simple things. Like hearing you say my name. Kindly."

Bammo. He'd hit the mark. Not even joking. He meant it. His vulnerability tapped her compassion. If he was playing on her emotions to win her over, his job was done. She let a smile dance on her lips. "I can do that. Just don't piss me off."

Laugh lines creased his mouth. "I can't promise anything."

Tara appeared from the cockpit. "We'll be landing in approximately ten minutes."

Meg turned to Tico. "Uh-oh. We didn't plan our strategy."

"We'll have plenty of time while we shop."

"Don't laugh at me when my hair goes dark."

He shook his head slowly. "You have no idea. I can't wait to see you as your natural self."

Bammo. Again. Her heart skipped a beat. His matter-of-fact curiosity about her was the sexiest thing she'd heard in a long time. Damn. Either she'd been out of the dating arena for too long, or this guy was as dangerous as his tattoo looked.

Six hours later, Meg watched with admiration as Tico handled their rented Ferrari as if he'd driven one for years.

The sun had set hours ago. While Eric would have preferred them to arrive at the Quarry in daylight to attract attention, she and Tico had gotten all their stuff together and were too hyped up to wait. Arriving after dark suited their adopted personalities better, so Eric let them go. They'd make appearances around the spa in the morning.

Before leaving, Meg had explained their plan to Penny. Mitchell had secured Enrique Comodin's permission for Penny to leak their arrival as wealthy clients wherever she could. Once Penny and Enrique had been sworn to secrecy by a judge, Meg and Tico were off and running.

Penny's excitement over the fact that Meg and Butler would be holed up together in the hottest spa in the Southwest still amused Meg. She'd insisted that her friend get a grip on her amorous suggestions, but even so, Meg couldn't help thinking about Penny's colorful descriptions as Tico's smoky essence invaded her senses.

He'd let his hair down and wore jeans they'd bought in Tucson that could make a schoolgirl sin. A tight white V-neck tee stretched across his chest beneath a jacket. He'd pushed the sleeves up to the elbows, his snake tattoo catching her attention as he shifted gears after a stoplight. After Tico's explanation, the snake seemed less fearsome. She saw the power in his choice.

Tico's dark, Judumi eyes burned as if he could already see how their plan would unfold. The small scar along his jaw was barely visible in the dashboard light, but his mouth was relaxed, making him look sexy as all get-out. A shiver ran down Meg's spine. Time to rein in her libido and act like the professional she was.

As tempted as she was, there was absolutely no room for fooling around with this guy. All her instincts screamed that he might be fun for a tumble, but in the long run, he was emotionally dangerous.

This guy was a heartbreaker whether he admitted it or not. He'd already said long-term relationships weren't an option for him. And Meg's intuition told her that anything short-term would end up with one of them getting hurt. The energy between them was way too volatile to take that chance.

Tico had been quiet since they'd started driving. She openly watched him just as he'd watched her when she'd arrived at the station in her new persona. And judging from the look on his face, he had been truly impressed by what she'd done.

Meg's stylist had dyed her hair back to the rich dark color it had once been. Tico had actually slapped his chest over his heart when she met him at one of the boutiques near where they'd gone for her hair appointment. While Tico's reaction made her feel better, Meg was having a hard time adjusting to the change. When she'd dyed her hair blond five years ago, she'd consciously traded her old, by-the-book, compliant self for the ballsy, aggressive detective she'd become. Her new attitude got the job done.

Going back to her old look, adopting the pampered, wealthy yet rudderless personality of her disguise was disquieting. With her father's millions, she could have easily evolved into a woman just like the one she now portrayed. That's what made the disguise so natural. The women in her father's family knew wealth. Many of her cousins spent their money on frivolity. Hopping on her father's private jet this morning to shop for designer clothes pissed her off just as much as the character she was portraying.

Tico had noticed her reticence when he'd asked her about changing her hair color. When she'd been a brunette she'd almost let herself get lost in the lap of luxury. Don Francisco's jet was at the ready anytime she wanted to shop or take a vacation somewhere.

Although Don Francisco had laid the world at her fingertips, Meg had decided to defy the idea of luxury for luxury's sake. She'd watched her mother succeed in a man's world in the scientific community, establishing herself as a metallurgy specialist. She'd seen how her mother's goals had been achieved with hard work and had decided to follow in her footsteps. That was why Meg was so upset when Barbara Flores had also wanted her off this case.

She became aware that Tico was watching her as he drove. "What?"

He grinned. As if reading her mind, he said, "I knew you'd make a hot brunette."

She pointed out the windshield. "Shouldn't you be watching the road?"

"You're far more interesting. It's a straight, empty road right up to the foothills. I could drive this blind. Meanwhile, you are far more fascinating in your outfit. Those legs should have a license, and—" he pointedly let his focus fall to her cleavage "—I can only imagine where you've concealed your weapon."

She'd indulged in a coppery mesh halter top over a tan suede miniskirt and new slouchy cowboy boots of butter-soft leather. The halter top draped beneath her cleavage, effectively concealing the holstered gun she'd attached to her bra. No doubt Tico had figured that fact out. She held up a hand. "Stop it, Tico. I don't like the flirting."

"Wait. Didn't we decide on the way back in the jet that I'm into you for sex and money, and you don't care because I'm so good in bed?"

She punched his arm. "We never said that!"

He laughed. "I know. I wanted to see you get flustered."

She laughed, while her heart banged around in her chest like a stampeding bull. She liked the idea of Tico's suggestion but didn't want to accept it. Her new persona was pulling her in directions she shouldn't go. Oh, God. Was she going to play a role, or would the role take over?

He patted her hand. "Let's go over the real discussion one more time."

She mentally shook herself. Back to business, and *only* business. "Okay." She tapped a finger. "We met in Los Angeles." She tapped another finger. "My limo was hit at an intersection, and you came to my rescue because the accident was engineered by a gang to rob me."

A grin tugged at the corner of his mouth. "Yeah, I may have been bad, but I have a hero's heart."

"Whatever. You can say that over drinks at the first party we crash."

"It'll sound lame."

"Not to the women." She went out on a limb here. "Looking like you do, they'll be crawling all over you, anyway."

Tico did a double take. "Did you just compliment me?"

She shrugged. "Maybe. How does it feel?"

He narrowed his eyes. "You playing me?"

She wasn't. It felt great to say what she'd been thinking, but it was better for them both if he thought otherwise. "Yeah. I'm playing you."

"Be careful, Detective. Payback can be a bitch."

"You can dish it out but can't take it?"

Still grinning, he turned his attention back to the highway. "That would be correct. Don't forget it."

"I'm beginning to like this sting already."

They drove in companionable silence for a while. Soon the lights from the Quarry appeared in the distance.

"Okay, we're almost there. Let's finish recapping our story."

Meg nodded. "We've been together for a year. My father is a Silicon Valley genius living in Japan with his young wife and three kids. My mother lives in France. I live on my trust fund, traveling around."

"Home bases for you?"

"Paris. Los Angeles. New York City."

Tico nodded. "Got it. And I'll just tell my life the way it went, only taking it into the gang scene instead of law enforcement."

"Right. And if people ask for details in your present life?"

He shrugged. "I'll just say they don't want to know or I'd have to kill them."

She laughed. "Oh, they'll love that."

He arrived at the gate. Tico pulled out the entrance card and slid it into the receiver. Warm desert scents rose on the air through the open window. Oleanders framed the gate. The flowers' sweet perfume belied their poisonous nature. Meg breathed deeply, nonetheless. When the gates rolled open, Tico put the Ferrari into gear. "Which way?"

Meg pointed toward the spa. The whitewashed Southwest adobe structure sprawled low and softly lit in the night. "Enrique is waiting for us. He always accommodates new arrivals."

Tico grinned. "Oh, we're new arrivals, all right. The Quarry will never be the same after we're done with it."

# CHAPTER NINE

TICO SPOTTED ENRIQUE COMODIN, pacing around the pool talking on a cell phone. With his hair pulled back and his tanned skin glowing, the dude looked pretty sharp, as if he knew how to appreciate the spa facilities he managed.

It was after hours, of course, so he could have been on his way out for the evening, but everything from his thin, pricey-looking belt to the matching loafers screamed designer labels. Either Enrique spent every penny of his income on clothes or he had a nice cash flow keeping him comfortable. No matter how much confidence Meg had in this guy, it couldn't hurt to check on his background.

Comodin saw them. Straightened. Waved. Tico's instinct told him the man was discussing him and Meg on that phone. He had no proof, but for Tico that instinct was enough. If he'd still been a gang leader, he would have used his own powers of persuasion to find out what the call was about. As an officer of the law, he'd have to wait. Catch the guy out when he least expected it. Tico hadn't expected his radar to go off so quickly, but something in Comodin's eyes told Tico he was shady and untrustworthy. Right now, he'd give the guy the benefit of the doubt. For all he knew, Comodin could be explaining to a girlfriend why he was late.

A small hum rose in Meg's throat while she watched Comodin, as well. Tico would check with her later to see what her gut reaction was. Comodin circled the pool to greet them. Again, Tico suspected he was taking the long way around to give himself time to pull his shit together.

Tico made a mental note to talk to Bill about this dude next chance he got.

Enrique went to kiss Meg on the cheek but refrained. "Oops. Almost forgot myself there. Your dark hair reminds me of how you looked when we were kids."

Meg smiled. "Well, no one else knows me. Consider us in character as of now."

Comodin shook Tico's hand as if greeting him for the first time. "Welcome to the Quarry, Mr. Sanchez." He smiled at Meg. "Miss Diaz."

Meg slid into her character's personality. "Please, call me Amelia. You can't believe how badly I need to drop off the planet for a while."

Enrique smiled. "I'm sure that's true on so many levels." He gestured toward the spa. "If you'll follow me inside, we can get you registered and into your hacienda as quickly as possible. I trust Harry took your luggage?"

"Yes. Thank you."

He led them to the registration desk by a rock fountain. "Now, I understand you'd like to get to know the Ripleys?"

"Been a fan for years," Tico said. "Can you get us a house close to theirs?"

"The hacienda across the street from theirs is vacant. Their parties tend to get loud, so other guests choose to put distance between them." He looked up from the computer. "Will that do?"

"Should be fine," Meg said.

"I'll take the golf cart. If you two follow me, I'll take you to the residence." He picked up an intercom and instructed Harry where to deliver the luggage.

"That works," Tico said.

"Oh, and from what I've heard, the Ripleys are having another one of their all-night dinner parties tonight." He checked his watch. "This might be a good time to go over."

"Good. No wasting time," Tico said. "Oh, and nice watch."

Enrique smiled. "Thanks."

"So, what can you tell us about our neighbors?"

"The Ripleys have been coming here for several years now. I'm their go-to man when the neighbors complain."

"Will we be intruding?" Meg asked.

Enrique shook his head. "I already told Katrina about you two. Made you sound really rich and interesting. Believe it or not, she's easily impressed by millionaires. And she likes the idea that a rich woman like you found yourself a gangster boyfriend."

Tico laughed. "So, in we go." He clapped Enrique on the shoulder. "Appreciate your help, old boy."

Tico drove the Ferrari behind Enrique, letting the headlights flood the golf cart.

"Why don't you switch on the parking lights? You're probably blinding him," Meg said.

"He can see just fine. I want him to know I'm here whether he likes it or not. I don't like him, Meg."

Meg frowned. "Why? He's a little eccentric, but he's fine, Tico. I've known him my whole life."

Tico glanced at her. Damn, she was beautiful. Hard to concentrate when she was seated mere inches away.

"Maybe you've been too close for too long. I don't trust the guy. What did you make of his phone conversation when we walked up?"

"He looked stressed."

"Exactly. What did you think?"

Meg caught her lower lip between her teeth. "Not sure. He deals with such difficult personalities all the time. Part of his job is to answer his phone 24/7."

"What did your gut tell you?"

Meg's focus returned to Enrique in the cart ahead. "That he was in trouble."

"Okay. We're on the same page. You don't mind if I hang on to my reservations for a while?"

Meg released a breath. "Okay. But for the record? You've already suspected my team. Now my friend—let me know when you've decided to investigate me. Okay?"

He laughed. "Touchy, aren't we?"

She briefly closed her eyes. "No. I understand you're clearing each option as you go. I'd do the same. I guess that's why you were called in. A fresh perspective catches what others don't."

Enrique pulled the golf cart into a circular drive. Another golf cart was already at the door, where the bellhop was waiting with their bags. Tico steered the car behind Enrique's cart. "Looks like we're ready to roll."

Enrique was out of the cart, waiting for them. "Come in. I'll show you the layout."

Tico slipped a twenty into the bellhop's palm as he took their bags inside. "Thanks, man." He turned to view the house across the street. The place was three times the size of theirs. Lights blazed throughout the sprawling residence. A stucco wall surrounded the house. A tall saguaro cactus with those beefy, upraised arms and needle-sharp spines guarded the arched entry. The glow of lights and music rose from the landscaped backyard, which looked expensive in the rose-colored illumination. "Ripley's?"

Enrique nodded. "Yes. They've had a nonstop

party for two days now. Looks like it's slowing down."

"Okay, show us around. I'd like to get to work."

ONE BEDROOM. MEG was mortified. The place was opulent but tiny. One bedroom posed an immediate awkward moment she'd been hoping not to confront on this sting. She turned to Enrique. "One bedroom was the best you could do?"

Enrique looked pained. "You wanted to be close to the Ripleys. This is the closest I have. I figured you two would work out the particulars."

Meg wanted to slap the grin off Tico's face. Instead, she checked out the bedroom. The king-size canopy bed made of chunky, hand-carved wood was breathtaking. It was a bed clearly intended for recreation. She'd feel adrift sleeping alone in that enormous field of silk.

She was curious to see what Tico thought but forced herself to keep looking around the room. Sitting close to him in the car when he looked so hot and smelled so good was grating enough on her libido. One glance from him now and her cheeks would flare with inappropriate thoughts.

The en suite bath area was separated by a half wall and glass. Shutters over the glass stood open, revealing a huge tub with a circular shower for two behind it. No way in hell was she going to share this room with Butler.

Harry had put both their bags in the bedroom

before leaving. A fair assumption, but wrong on all counts.

"We'll figure this out later," she said.

Butler had been standing close behind her. He'd whistled softly at the opulence, clearly impressed. His attention slid from the bedroom to the over-stuffed cowhide couch in the living room and back to the bed once more.

As Meg brushed past him, he said, "We'll flip a coin to see who gets the bedroom."

Enrique's raised brow mirrored Meg's surprise. "That isn't very gentlemanly of you, Detective," she said.

Tico didn't even look abashed. "You probably own a bed like this, Meg. I've never seen anything like it. Would you deny a guy the chance of a lifetime?"

Enrique headed for the door. Meg didn't blame him at all. "You have my number if you need to reach me."

Meg waved. "Of course. Thank you. We'll catch up soon."

The door clicked shut with a note of finality. She turned to face Butler in the small area between the kitchen and the living room.

He had a coin in his hand. "Heads or tails?"

She folded her arms across her chest. "You're kidding."

"Come on. Humor me."

"Heads."

He flipped the coin, caught it and slapped it on the back of his hand. Grinning, he said. "Tails. I win."

She been gearing up to tell him what a jerk he was but knew what response she'd get. *Hey, we're equals on the job. No difference just because you're a woman.* Yet Tico's earlier flirting had her thinking more like a woman and less like a detective.

He laughed. "You're actually flustered."

She lifted her chin a notch higher. "No, I'm not." Damn she hated how great his hair looked falling on his shoulders, standing there holding that coin as if it had magic powers or something.

"The bed is yours, Meg. Did you think I was really going to make you sleep on the cow over there?" He thumbed to the couch covered in black-and-white cowhide. "I was just having some fun."

He tossed the coin in the air, and with speed she didn't know she had, Meg swiped it in midair.

Admiration lit his dark eyes. "Nice."

She shoved the coin in her pocket. "I'll keep this for our next toss."

Amusement filling his voice, Tico upturned two glasses on the bar. "So, Amelia. Why don't we make some drinks and drop in on our neighbors?"

Meg took a moment to freshen up while Tico played bartender. She opened her suitcase, feeling the adrenaline starting to surge through her body the way it did every time she was about to do undercover work. Amelia Diaz was a spoiled, educated, well-traveled heiress who was bored out of her mind with life. The last thing she'd be carrying was a gun holstered beneath her bra. The press of the leather and the weight of the gun against her skin would help keep her focused on the invasion into the Ripleys' house. Especially when faking her role with Tico.

Her belly was in knots because the idea of Tico as her bad-boy lover was beginning to appeal to her. She pressed a hand against the gun one more time for reassurance. Sure, chemistry bubbled between them—more than she'd felt in a long time—but they were here for a purpose. He'd be gone when this investigation was over.

She ran a brush through her hair one more time and decided to change her conservative earrings for large, gold hoops. She'd smudged smoky colors on her eyelids, dabbed a pale pink gloss on her lips. It was a little more makeup than she used to wear, but the pampered woman she could have been stared back at her from the mirror. *Ugh!* Guess she'd play the part. Heaven knew she'd practiced the role. Plastering a bored look on her face, she headed back to the living room.

Tico handed her a crystal tumbler of clear liquid over ice with a twist of lime. "Water disguised as vodka on the rocks." He motioned to the door. "Shall we?"

Once they stepped foot outside, they'd be in character. It had never bothered her before. Now she started to chew her lip, then saw mischief light Tico's eyes. He was actually enjoying himself. She shook her head. "You're too much...Mick."

He lifted her hand, appraising her outfit. "Nay, nay, Amelia. *You* are too much. I can't wait to play your lover boy."

She laughed, despite her pounding heart. It bugged her that the intense reaction wasn't because of their assignment. No. It was him. Plain and simple. She couldn't deny she was going to enjoy this role more than she wanted to admit. "Okay, lover boy. One warning."

He opened the door. "Yes?"

"Touch my ass and you're a dead man."

A grin played his lips. "You're a cruel woman, Amelia Diaz."

When they stepped into the night, Tico swung a possessive arm around her waist, pulling her close as they walked down the drive. He nuzzled her neck. "Man, you smell great."

The feel of Tico's arm around her wreaked havoc with her senses. It was unnerving to have his face so close. She actually felt an impulse to kiss those lips. She pulled her attention away from his mouth and focused on the scar on his jaw. "Someday you'll have to tell me how you got that scar."

His arm tightened around her waist. "I was a kid."

"Really? Not a gang fight or something?"

He ran the hand holding his glass across his

mouth. "More like some jerk crack addict at my parents' house. He was having a bad moment on his high, and I got in his way. My face broke the glass coffee table."

"Oh." Anger rose like bile in the back of her throat. She swallowed a mouthful of water. Damn. A tequila shot would be better. No wonder he'd become a drug buster. He'd seen the worst of that dark underworld. Her heart swelled with understanding for this man who'd learned to live aloof just to stay safe. This assignment would be a picnic compared to fending off her reactions to Tico. Every time she learned something else about him, her regard for him grew. That wasn't what she'd wanted when he rode into town a few short days ago.

Unable to stop herself, she slipped an arm around his waist and squeezed him back. "You've made quite a name for yourself since then. You're okay."

"If you want to prove it, keep your arm there all night."

"Ha!"

She slid her arm back, her pulse pounding. Holy smokes. They'd only just begun, but he felt so right, so comfortable with his arm around her. She changed her focus to their destination. There were four cars in the driveway. Enrique must have been right about the two-day party winding down.

"There's not much of a crowd left."

Tico shrugged. "We don't need a crowd. Let's get inside."

She pressed the doorbell. Blew out a breath. "Showtime."

After what seemed a long wait, footsteps approached from inside just as Meg was getting ready to ring the bell again. The door opened, releasing a surprising surge of rock music and the scent of weed.

"Wouldn't you know I sent the maid to bed just when I need the door answered?"

Katrina Ripley was more beautiful in person than she was in her pictures. She swayed on her high heels as if she'd been partying for a while, then quickly caught herself. Her mane of blond hair, angelic face and sky-blue eyes had been plastered on magazine covers, sides of buses and billboards for the past two years. Strutting practically naked across television screens in lingerie commercials had boosted her fame. Usually seen smiling, the model had small frown lines between her brows as she looked at them.

"Do I know you?"

Tico gave Meg's waist a small squeeze. "Nope. We just moved in across the street. I'm Mick Sanchez. This is Amelia Diaz."

Her frown disappeared. She clapped her hands together. "Don't tell me. You're the couple from Washington."

Tico's grin widened. "Right. Enrique suggested

we introduce ourselves. Hope we're not coming over too late."

Katrina rewarded him with her million-dollar smile and opened the door wider. "Of course not! Enrique told me about you two. Come in. We're by the pool." She glanced at the drinks in their hands. "Brought your own. Good thinking."

Meg stepped in first, offering her hand. From her slurred words, it was pretty clear that Katrina had been partying. This would make getting into the group so much easier. "You know, for all the times I've seen you in the media, I never heard your voice. You have a lovely accent."

Katrina returned the handshake. "You are very pretty."

Not expecting a compliment in return, Meg warmed to the woman. "Coming from you, that's high praise."

Tico kissed the back of Katrina's hand. "A pleasure to meet you."

Katrina stood a head and shoulders taller than both of them. Her mile-long legs started in a pair of strappy red stilettos and ended in yellow hot pants belted low on her curvy hips. A red sleeveless shirt showing tons of cleavage was tied above her navel, exposing her taut belly. A complete bombshell with her gorgeous blue eyes, perfect lips and blond hair tumbling down her back, Katrina looked like someone who could use a bodyguard. Her attention dropped to Tico's snake tattoo. The small smile that curved the corner of her mouth told it all. She'd known men like him.

A little hum rose in her throat. "If you are as dangerous as Enrique suggests, maybe I could offer you a job."

Tico raised his eyebrows in mock surprise. "Me? I'm gentle as a kitten." He laid a heart-stopping gaze on Meg. "Ask Amelia. No one knows me better than she does."

Time to perform. Meg ran a salon-manicured fingernail along Tico's jaw. "And we'll keep it that way. Won't we, lover?"

Meg felt obliged to establish Tico as her territory since Katrina had begun flirting already. But her immediate impulse was to shake some sense into the woman. Did someone as beautiful as Katrina need attention so badly that she flirted with men on first contact? Meg was confident in her own appearance, but standing next to Katrina definitely challenged her femininity.

When Tico grabbed her face with both hands and planted a long, hard kiss on her lips, she practically lost her footing. The electricity that ran from him to her unleashed a reaction she had never felt. His kiss felt so dangerous, so right, that he had her shamelessly pressing her body against him in front of Katrina Ripley, but she didn't even care who saw. In her mind, she chanted, *It's all for the job.*

His mouth, hot, salty and soft, dared her to kiss him back, and for the life of her, it was all she wanted to do. Time seemed to slow. She kissed him back with gentle, wanton kisses that had him sliding his hand along her neck, into her hair. When Katrina started to chuckle, reason finally forced Meg to pull away. She was supposed to be used to his touch, not floored by it. She planted the heel of her boot on the toe of his and stepped hard.

God help her, she didn't want him to know the fire he'd just ignited inside her.

He grinned at her wide-eyed reaction. He whispered, "There's nobody but you for me, babe. Don't you forget it."

Katrina grinned. "Well done, Mick. I know what it feels like to have women hit on Josh all the time. As long as my husband knows who keeps his bed warm, I can handle it."

Trying to reclaim her equilibrium, Meg pursed her lips. "I'd probably kill anyone who tried to take him away from me."

Katrina's brows shot up. "Seriously, now?"

Meg laid a proprietary hand on Tico's chest. With the challenge of seduction filling his eyes, Tico looked so sensually dangerous Meg thought her knees would buckle. Instead, she grinned. "After all, where would I find another lover like you, eh, Mickey?"

His face grew stone-cold serious. "You never will, babe."

Katrina laughed. Her sweet German accent

sounded innocent and playful. "Oh, I'm going to like you two."

Tico sipped his drink, his calm, cool self once more. "Enrique seemed to think we'd have a lot in common. I like having him act as social manager. Makes it easier. I don't hang around with just anyone."

Katrina waved away Tico's concern. "Enrique is wonderful like that. I trust everything he does for me."

"Oh, yeah?"

A scowl crossed her face. "We had a two-day marathon here that got a little out of hand. We're down to a few of my friends now, and they're all good, but the night of the concert we had some trouble."

Katrina led them through the spacious living room with eclectic furniture similar to the decor at their hacienda. Candelabras burned everywhere. A white Steinway piano and a slew of guitars occupied the far corner of the room.

Meg shot Tico a meaningful look behind Katrina's back. Getting her to talk while she was intoxicated would be much easier than when sober. "What kind of trouble?"

The fashion model stopped next to the French doors leading to the patio. The backyard was surprisingly deep. Katrina glanced at the group of people seated on a small island in the middle of the pool. Leaning toward them, she lowered her voice. "We had a lot of friends of friends here after the show. I didn't know many of the people. One girl was way too drunk and way too chummy with Josh. I asked her to leave. Her friends got rowdy." She snapped her fingers. "I called Enrique, and within minutes, they were gone."

"Better than the police when you don't have a bodyguard," Tico said.

She sipped her drink. "I'll tell you a secret. Enrique has gotten me out of quite a few tight spots. Speeding tickets. One night I drove a bit too tipsy and was stopped. One call to Enrique, and I don't know who he knows, but he saved me from being arrested for a DUI. The nice policeman escorted me home instead. But I'm sure you know all of Enrique's fine talents, no?"

"Enrique's the man," Tico said. He gave Meg a glance as if to say, *See? Your friend has sway with people he shouldn't.*

Meg ignored him and said, "Love Enrique."

Katrina motioned to the curtained cabana, where the remainder of the party sat around the bar and in lounge chairs. A wagon-wheel candelabra overhead held gaslights that flickered in the dark. It took no time to spot Josh Ripley, a tall, imposing guy with frizzy blond hair. He wore a black Harley-Davidson shirt, unbuttoned with the sleeves cut off, faded jeans and black cowboy boots with metal tips. Holding court at the bar, he watched them approach with curiosity. Meg wasn't a fan, but

fame had a way of making a person seem imposing whether they wanted to be or not. Josh looked
as if he'd prefer not to be. Meg liked that. His attention slid from Tico and lingered on Meg. She
didn't like that.

"Who do we have here, love?"

Katrina beamed at Josh. "New neighbors. Just
arrived. Enrique told them to come by. Mick,
Amelia, meet my husband, Josh. These are our
friends...."

Introductions went around. Josh pulled out the
chair near his. "I'd offer you a drink, but I see I
don't have to."

Meg figured the seat had been Katrina's. She
was relieved when Tico pulled out the chair next
to it. "Sit here, beautiful. That way I can keep my
hands on you."

Meg kissed his cheek and took the seat. Tico
stood possessively close to her, slipping an arm
around her shoulder, making it hard for Meg to
concentrate on anything else. Even now, the press
of his kiss on her mouth still lingered. If that was
an undercover kiss, what would a truly passionate
one feel like?

Meg didn't miss Katrina sending Tico a grateful
smile for redirecting Meg and slid into the chair
near her husband. Josh curled his arm around the
back of Katrina's chair.

"So, what brings you two to the Quarry?"

Tico swirled the ice in his glass. "We needed some time away. Life in D.C. gets complicated."

"Daddy was also coming into town with the new wife and bratty kids." Meg wrinkled her nose. "If I'm not there, I don't have to be rude, now do I?"

Katrina laughed. "They'll never find you here."

"They don't even know this place exists. I figured two months here should give Daddy enough time to enjoy the summer. It's perfect."

Tico nuzzled Meg's hair. "Best part about this place."

Meg's palms grew warm with Tico so close. Perspiration trickled between her breasts. She forced her attention to her host. Josh was sipping scotch, the half-empty bottle on the bar. Close up, those deep blue eyes looked bloodshot, but he seemed clearheaded and relaxed. He favored his friends with a mischievous grin. "We come here to unwind, but everyone follows us."

Josh's drummer and his girlfriend shared a chaise longue. The girlfriend laughed. "Well, stop telling us what time to be at the jet and we'll stop coming."

"Then, who'd fly the damned plane, girl?"

"Oh, yeah. There's that."

Katrina nodded to the woman. "Isabel is our pilot."

Tico smiled at Isabel. "Nice."

"Anytime you need a lift, let Josh know," Isabel said.

Josh laughed. "See? There she goes. Sharing my jet with everyone."

Tico held up a hand. "No worries. I'm a two-feet-on-the-ground type of guy. Flying isn't for me."

"Yeah? How do you get around?"

Tico gestured to the emblem on Josh's shirt. "Harley." He caressed Meg's cheek with the back of his hand. "Would have ridden cross-country to get here, but Amelia wouldn't have it. Too impatient."

Meg agreed. "I'll take my jet anytime, thank you."

Katrina laughed. "Not me. I'll take my Jaguar instead of a Harley or a jet. A classic XKE. Cherry-red. A gift from Josh for Valentine's day."

Josh shook his head, grinning. "Women. They love their cars." He thumbed toward the house. "I have a Fat Boy. I've done a ton of custom work. Come on. I'll show you. It's in the garage next to Katrina's Jag."

# CHAPTER TEN

A COUPLE OF hours after midnight, Tico led Meg by the hand from the Ripleys' hacienda. Meg didn't speak until they heard Katrina shut the door behind them.

"You can let go of my hand now."

He squeezed it harder. "Nope."

"Why not?"

"Someone could be watching." Uncertainty filled his eyes. He hesitated, then said, "Besides, I like the way your hand feels."

She sucked in a breath. He was flirting, and from his look, he meant what he said. Feeling awkward as a schoolgirl, she teased him in return. "Well, aren't you one smooth dude, Mick Sanchez?"

He let go of her hand, putting distance between them. His face grew stern. Wow. He was more sensitive than he let on.

"You're right. Just doing my job. It's all for show."

Without warning, he stepped in, brushed her lips ever so gently with his mouth, sending tingles down to her toes. Before she could respond, he stepped away and headed for the hacienda. He turned, held out a hand for her. His voice low, he said, "Come on, girl. Let's get inside. I'd say we played our characters perfectly. No one knew otherwise."

Her fingertips flew to her lips. That kiss could have been a caress to her entire body. Every single inch. She watched Tico holding out a hand to her, willing her feet to move. She'd just learned that she had no control when it came to Tico, and he'd let her know there was no corralling him. And they'd only been on the sting a few hours.

Business as usual, Tico opened the door for her. Once he shut the door behind them, he slid off his jacket, as if nothing had happened. Tossing the garment on the chair by the couch, he went to the bar and poured a scotch on the rocks and pulled a cigar from his pocket.

"I'm headed out back to wind down. Care to join me and compare notes?"

Tico was so damned cool. His smile was the same as it had been since the day they'd met. Reality hit like a brick. Of course! Tico's flirting tonight was nothing but an act. Meanwhile Meg had been turned on by his every move. How humiliating.

Her gut reaction was to go off by herself. Regroup. She needed to get a handle on what this guy was doing to her libido. Second reaction? If he were any other detective, she'd already be jotting down notes and making plans for tomorrow.

She swallowed her embarrassment. Hell, Tico

had no idea what she'd been feeling. He no doubt took her responses to his flirting tonight as her cover and nothing more. Maybe she'd misread the look in his eye when they were outside. It had been a long night.

Meg motioned to his cigar. "Do you have another one of those?"

"Sure do." Reaching into a duffel bag on the chair, he pulled out a small black box. He cracked the sealed locks to reveal an insulated cigar case. "I take cigar smoking seriously."

He tossed her a stubby cigar.

"What's this?"

"It's for beginners."

"Really?"

He pointed to the choices. "This blend is owned by a buddy of mine. Catelli. Nice flavor. The short cigar will last about twenty minutes. The larger ones smoke longer. What are you in the mood for? A shorty? Or a long, slow smoke?"

She laughed, relieved he was joking with her again. "Oh, I don't know. After tonight's escapade, I think I'll try this big boy." She reached for the biggest cigar in the case.

"That's a Gran Toro. You've got balls for a girl." Tico pulled a cutter from his pocket. "Here, let me cut it and light it for you."

"Thanks."

He motioned to the bar. "Drink?"

"Is there brandy?"

He pulled a snifter from the glass cabinet. "If there's a snifter, there must be brandy." The bottle was easily located in the cabinet below the bar.

Tico led her outside to two chaise longues facing the pool. The pool lights were on, and the soft blue glow was the perfect backdrop for the late hour.

Meg watched Tico light her cigar. "So, what was the most interesting piece of information you heard tonight?"

He blew out a stream of smoke, checked the lit end. Satisfied, he handed it to Meg. "Don't inhale. You'll puke for sure. Take slow, easy puffs. You just want to taste it."

She grinned. "You're a pro."

He lit his own cigar. "To answer your question, I'll just say that you might want to trust my hunches."

"Excuse me?"

"The most interesting bit of information. Enrique. I know he's worked here for years. Knows the ropes. But helping residents escape law enforcement? Getting Katrina a police escort home instead of a DUI? Really? Who does he know or pay to get such favors?"

Meg had come to the same conclusion and had filed it in the back of her mind. She didn't want to think Enrique might have someone in the P.D. on payroll, and if he did, where did he get the funds? Could she really be too close to the people in her town to see the truth? She looked at Tico to find him watching her.

She sighed. "I'm beginning to see why you were brought in. The possibility that Enrique might be crooked turns my stomach." She swirled her drink, watching the amber liquid. "This town is so small, and we all know each other. Enrique could be talking to anyone in the P.D." Tico's face relaxed as he watched her, taking a slow drag of his cigar. She was about to sip her brandy, but paused with the glass in midair. "You already think you know who it is. Don't you?"

"Yes."

"Who?"

"Going on instinct alone? I'd say Mitchell."

"Why?"

His focus shifted to the cigar in his hand before taking another puff. "Mitchell is his go-to man for complaints. Maybe it's more than that."

"I can tell you don't like Mitchell," Meg said.

He nodded. "You're right. I don't. I didn't like the way he reacted when Eric announced Melissa Collins was missing. The rest of you were disgusted— he didn't even blink."

"No kidding."

He shrugged. "I was watching. You were reacting as you should in a crowd you trust. Unfortunately, I don't trust anyone."

His last sentence stung. "We can't go to Eric

with a gut feeling, Tico. It would look like petty griping. We'll need proof before we say anything."

He toasted her with his glass before sipping. "Let's keep this between us for now. We have bigger fish to fry than some fixed traffic tickets."

"But we can't overlook it either, Tico. If he's paying someone for favors, that's illegal."

"I know that, Meg. But the bigger issue is that if I'm right and Mitchell's willing to break the law in this way, he might also be willing to do something more extreme. It's possible he could be the contact person for the Carlito cartel."

Meg settled back on the chaise longue. "It's hard to imagine one of my team betraying the rest of us."

"I understand. Believe me. You don't want to point a finger like that unless you're dead certain. Once that accusation is made, it's hell for that person to win people's trust again, even if proven innocent. No one ever looks at them the same way again."

Another confidence shared. "You're referring to you and your late partner?"

"Yeah. As much as I think Mitchell is an irritating ass, let's not jump to any conclusions until we have hard evidence. No one, not even Mitchell, deserves a bad rap."

Meg smiled. "You're something else."

He puffed a cloud of smoke, making it rise like a veil between them. "So I've been told."

"Let's get more details from Katrina about what happened between her and Melissa Collins. She made the incident sound less messy than Melissa's friends did."

"We should talk with her friends again, too."

Meg nodded. "I can have Bill do that while you and I spend our time getting to know our neighbors better."

Tico grinned. "I like Josh. Bit of a punk, but riding a Harley doesn't make him bad."

"Coming from a gang leader. That's rich."

"I didn't like the way he watched you when we walked up."

"Oh, yeah. I think Katrina has her hands full with him."

"As far as the Harley goes, maybe the four of us can go for a desert run."

"How would you explain suddenly having your Harley?"

He shrugged. "We borrowed one from a friend."

She took a moment to take a long, slow drag of her cigar, slowly blowing out the smoke. Tico suspended his own cigar inches from his mouth as he watched her.

"Woman, you make that look like foreplay. Keep it up and I'll forget what I was talking about."

"Perfect."

"What do you mean?"

"This cigar. It's perfect. I've never smoked anything so tasty."

He laughed. "Now, tell me you like to ride Harleys, and I'll become hopelessly infatuated with you."

Meg's breath caught in her throat. She took another puff of the cigar to calm her reaction. As much as she loved hearing it, she had to stop this madness if they were going to get the job done.

"Tico, show's over. No more flirting. Let's get back to business."

He didn't answer, making her chest tighten with guilt. She'd snagged his attention and was surprised at how much she was enjoying it, but her satisfaction was at his expense because she wasn't planning on acting on any of his advances. Then again, was he truly attracted to her, or was he playing her again as he did so well?

TICO SIPPED HIS scotch before setting it on the table between them. Did Meg not know how unbelievable she looked lounging in that skirt while smoking that cigar?

Damn, he couldn't concentrate. He'd invited her outside a little longer because he couldn't bear to end this night of pretending to be her lover. Every time he'd touched her at the Ripleys', he'd wanted to make it real. Standing close to Meg tonight, his hand on her back, knowing she wasn't really his, had been sheer torture. He wanted to touch her more. Everywhere. He'd love to hold her in his arms right this very minute, run his hands through that gorgeous hair, smell her perfume.

He reached for his drink. Where were these thoughts coming from? Watching her stretch out on the chaise longue with her skirt daringly high and her smooth, tanned legs begging for him to explore them didn't help. Or was it her dark hair curling over her shoulders? God knew, he'd had his fingers tangled in those locks plenty of times earlier. Thick, soft silk. Sleeping in the same house tonight was going to be hell. It had been too long since he'd felt something for a woman. And now that he'd tasted her kiss, how would he ever be the same? Damn. Was he falling in love?

*Love?*

What the…? He practically choked on the sip of scotch he'd taken.

"You okay?"

"Fine. Went down the wrong pipe." He had to stop thinking like a romantic fool. Where would it get him to tangle with Meg on the job? Nowhere. There was nothing in Adobe Creek for him except this investigation. Once the case was closed, he'd be gone faster than the dust could settle. *Keep it light, fella. This woman is out of reach.*

"Okay, in a couple of days we can show up with my Harley. You'll ride with me. Right?"

She studied the ash of her cigar. "Never been on a motorcycle."

"What?" He turned to face her. "Really?"

"I have a horse. Why would I want to ride a bike?"

He shook his head. That made no sense. "Two different rides. I can promise you."

She tapped a finger to her chin. "Tell you what. You learn to ride a horse properly and I'll go for a ride on your bike."

"I have a Harley. Why would I want to ride a horse?"

"Because a horse is alive."

He laughed. "You saw me on horseback. Are you trying to kill me?"

Her smile revealed her beautiful white teeth. "You'll probably do that all by yourself."

"Hey! Low blow."

She shrugged. "Like the offer, or leave it."

"Let me consider my options for a while."

"Fine." She slid her boots off and padded barefoot to the pool and sat on the edge, dangling her feet in the water. "My feet are hot."

*As is the rest of you.* He had an image of her peeling off her clothes and sliding into the water. His mouth went dry. "I don't know how you locals handle the heat, day in and day out."

She lazily splashed the water with one foot. "You get used to it."

"Did you bring your bikini?"

She drew on her cigar a little more, the smoke curling around her head. "Of course."

"Well, I didn't." Suddenly all he wanted to do

was joke around with her. He couldn't resist. "Want to swim?"

Her eyes narrowed. "Now?"

He stood and emptied his pockets onto the chaise longue. Kicked off his boots and pulled off his shirt. He didn't miss interest sparking in her eyes at the sight of his bare chest. "I think it's a great idea."

Still wearing his pants, he stalked over to where she sat and dove over her head into the deep end. He worked his way across the pool before rising to the surface. The water felt great. He surfaced to see her standing on the steps. *Please, let her follow him in.* His hopes sank when she turned away.

"Where you going?"

She walked back to the table, leaving wet footprints on the tiles. She laid the cigar in the ashtray. "Maybe you were right. I should have smoked a small one. I'm off to bed."

He frowned. "Why? What'd I do?"

She grinned. "Everything, Detective, and nothing at all. First one up in the morning makes coffee." Carrying her boots in the crook of her arm, her brandy in one hand, she waved with the other. "Thanks for the smoke. I'll leave bedding on the cow couch for you. Don't get the hide wet."

He swam to the steps in a few easy strokes, watching her walk away, hips swaying, dark waves falling down her back. A chuckle rose in his throat. He should have known better than to think she'd give him any attention. "Damn, she's good."

She'd won this round. He tried to force himself not to care. He couldn't. She might be out of reach, but he'd never let that stop him in the past. Watching her disappear into the kitchen, he decided then and there to take a chance on letting himself fall for a woman again. He hadn't had ties to anyone in such a long time that the thought had him diving underwater once more. He had to sober up—and he wasn't even drunk.

MEG WOKE UP EXHAUSTED, the aroma of coffee teasing her senses. The clock next to the bed said eight, and she moaned in frustration. Although she'd been desperate for sleep last night, she'd tossed and turned for hours in that big, comfortable bed. Tico had done a number on her between that thunderclap kiss she hadn't seen coming and his disarmingly goofy side when he jumped into the pool half-dressed. She never quite knew what to expect from him.

On one hand, he had a hot sensuality that she'd suspected existed but hadn't quite grasped until that kiss left her gasping for breath. She'd liked it. Way too much. She'd been plagued by thoughts of him climbing into her bed last night, his hair down, those muscled pecs and shoulders flexing as he reached for her....

Whether it was the leftover adrenaline or Tico's effect on her, Meg had shamelessly ended up pleasuring herself, facedown on her pillow so Tico wouldn't hear. Given that he'd had a starring role in her fantasies last night, how would she be able to face him this morning?

She padded to the bathroom, regretting the dark rings under her eyes. She needed more rest to be sharp for today. But the coffee smelled too good to resist. Maybe if she got into character now she'd be able to overcome the embarrassment she felt over her growing interest in Tico. Amelia Diaz wouldn't blink an eye over fantasizing about a bad boy like Tico Butler. Heck, she'd seduce him first chance she got.

Meg inhaled deeply to absorb that thought, liked it and grinned. She turned the shower to hot. Reaching into her suitcase, she pulled out a tight-fitting low-cut denim dress. She'd leave the buttons of the dress undone from her thighs down. The dress paired with jeweled sandals and her hair piled on her head should do the trick for the day.

She peeled off her nightshirt and stepped into the shower. Amelia would have some more fun at Mick Sanchez's expense today. Heck, the sting wasn't going to last forever—she might as well enjoy herself.

The living room was empty when Meg came out of the bedroom. With no bedding in sight, she would never have known Tico had slept in there. The curtains had been thrown open, and sun poured through the wall of windows. She followed her nose to the kitchen and the coffeemaker. Tico sat at the bar on the veranda just beside the door.

He waved. "You're up earlier than I expected."

She gestured to the couch. "You're so neat. Looks like you didn't sleep at all."

"Maybe I had too much fun last night to settle down."

Had their kiss left him as restless as she'd been? She wasn't going to jump to any conclusions. To steady her reaction, she took her time adding sugar and cream to her coffee. "Yeah. What a performance we put on last night."

A slow smile curled his lips. "I enjoyed your performance."

She sipped her coffee. At some point in this conversation, she would either draw the line between them or ratchet the relationship up a notch. Seeing him sitting there barefoot, in a T-shirt and jeans, looking as comfortable as if they'd always spent mornings together, had her swallowing hard. Tico Butler was too damned sexy for his own good.

Tico watched her approach. "Nice outfit. Did you get that in Tucson, too?"

"Sure did."

"Do you wear clothes like that often?"

She sat across from him. The unbuttoned part of the dress fell open. She didn't miss Tico's appreciative gaze on her legs. "Once upon a time."

"But not since you became a detective?"

She shrugged. "I haven't had a reason."

He put his mug down. Staring at her, he said nothing, but the heat in his look made her aware of a small bead of perspiration trickling between her breasts. She sat back, letting her focus move to the sun-drenched cacti garden around the pool. The day would be brutally hot, but nothing like how scorching it could get right here at this table— if she let it.

He tilted his head, still watching her, those dark eyes questioning.

"What?"

"I could give you a reason, Meg."

Zing. His words were exactly what she wanted to hear. She could step over that line, but…

"Listen, Tico."

"Wait. I know what you're going to say. Let me speak first."

"Okay." Her breathing slowed while her mind prepared for the professional letdown. She'd allow him to give her the speech instead of delivering it herself. She swallowed a mouthful of too-hot coffee because she knew she didn't want to hear him say the words.

Tico leaned forward in his seat. "Meg, knowing I'd have to kiss you at some point as part of our cover intrigued me. I've worked with female partners before, and we had a hoot impersonating our characters. Got the job done. Arrested the criminals."

Oh, yeah. Here came the letdown. She put her mug on the table. "Me, too."

Distress filled his face, as if he was embarrassed. "The problem here is that I've been attracted to your mouth since you first told me off. I couldn't wait for the chance to kiss you. And when I did last night?" He shook his head, frowning. "I could have died on the spot. If I can't kiss you again, and soon, I don't know how I'll get through the rest of this investigation."

She wanted to fall on her knees and thank her angels for letting him speak first. If she'd been the one to invite him to cross the line, she would have put it the same way.

She pursed her lips. "I'd say we have an even bigger problem, Detective."

He looked deflated. "What's that?"

"If I walk over and crawl into your lap the way I've been aching to do since you fell off that damned horse, how do we keep this quiet?"

He stood, took the few steps to her side, letting that easy grin work across his mouth. Moving exquisitely slow, he slid his fingers across her collarbone and along her neck until he cradled the back of her head. "I know one way, Detective."

Meg let her head fall back into his touch. His hair fell like a curtain on either side of his face as he closed in on her mouth. He smelled of soap, fresh air, Tico. Inches from her lips Meg touched a fingertip to his mouth, stopping him. "What's that, Mick?"

"Oh, this is all me, darlin'. Not Mick. And I want to make you mine. If neither of us talks, no one will know. What do you say? No talking. Just touching."

A tingle shot down her spine at the idea of his hands all over her. She searched his eyes and saw soul-deep satisfaction. Tico Butler was smooth. Very smooth. With a look. With words. Right now, she didn't care if this was seduction. She wanted him. She parted her lips intending to capture this man with her kiss.

The hot pressure of their mouths together and the groan rising in his throat were all she needed to spur her on. When his free hand slid to her belly, reason began to fall away. He kissed her softly at first, his lips brushing, tasting, nipping. She began wondering who was capturing whom when he pressed harder against her mouth, his tongue commanding her senses, his body tightening with want. His hand on her belly moved to the small of her back, lifting her out of the chair and fitting her against him.

He broke the kiss, taking a moment to look at her. Oh, God. His hands caressed her sides, then up and down her back, cupping the curve of her behind, before resting at her waist. She wrapped her arms around his neck, wanting more. He held her tighter, and she never felt safer in her life.

"Ah, Meg. You feel so right in my arms."

She kissed him, whispering against his lips. "But this is so very wrong."

He shook his head. "No, it's not. No one could have stopped this moment from coming. I had a feeling this would happen when I first saw your profile picture."

"Really?"

Mischief filled his eyes. "Yeah. I was sure you'd be as stubborn as the horse I rode. Wasn't too far off!"

"Hey!" She tried to pull away to punch his arm, but he tightened his hold.

"Kiss me again, Meg."

As if she could stop herself. He felt so strong. Smelled so good. Tasted even better. She kissed him again, feeling giddy that this man she'd vowed to run out of town was now turning her world on end. She giggled against his lips.

He pulled away. "What?"

She pressed fingertips to her mouth, realizing that this intimacy with him was making her nervous. "And I thought you were so tough."

He cupped her face with his hands. "Hey, no talking. Remember? What if the neighbors hear? It'll make the tabloids."

She laughed and then saw the flex of muscle in his jaw. He was kidding, yet vulnerability radiated from him. She could feel his need as clearly as she could feel the hot desert air invading the veranda.

Tico was just as nervous about taking this step as she was.

She sucked in a ragged breath. "You talked first."

He brushed a curl from her forehead. "Then shush. Let me kiss you…here." He brushed his lips on her cheek. "And here." Along her jaw. "And here." Down her neck, his hands possessing her hips, holding her close against him. He pulled his face from her neck long enough to seek her mouth. "No more talking, woman. Kiss me. And don't stop."

She didn't need another invitation. She returned his kisses with the same fire he'd ignited. She fisted his T-shirt when she thought her knees would buckle, still immersed in the kiss. His reaction was intense. He finally relinquished his hold to work on her clothing. He paused at the top button of her dress, snapping it open with two fingers.

A sigh escaped his lips. "You are so very beautiful, Detective."

She snagged the hem of his T-shirt and pushed it up his chest. Unable to resist, she lowered her head to trail kisses along his abdomen. She brushed a hand across the bulge behind his zipper and moaned softly. Then she kissed her way up his stomach and across his pecs, stopping to nibble on his collarbone.

All the while Tico's fingers continued to undo buttons. One. Then another. And another. As he revealed more of her skin, his fingers explored. His warm palm flattened against the black lace of her bra, cupping a full breast. He sucked in breath as he beheld the soft mounds above the cups.

"Amazing." He shook his head in sheer admiration.

Meg pulled his shirt over his head, taking in the smooth plane of his chest, his washboard abs and the line of hair running from his navel into his jeans. She splayed her fingers on his stomach. "Yes. You are."

Tico whistled softly when her dress, now fully open, revealed her gym-honed body clad in matching bra and panties. He lifted one side of her panties to inspect the tan line no wider than a string on her hip. He smiled. His hand skimmed her belly rising to her bra, moving the strap aside. Meg grinned when she realized what he was doing.

He whispered, "No tan line on the top. You sunbathe topless."

"So?"

"I think I just came."

She threw her head back, laughing. He dove in and kissed her neck, pulling her half-naked body against his. The heat of his skin practically seared her soul.

"My God, you feel good," she said, nipping at his earlobe.

He maneuvered her through the kitchen door,

stopping just long enough to press her against a cabinet for more kisses.

"You haven't felt anything yet, love."

Breathless, she managed to say, "Promise?"

He began moving her toward the bedroom. "Never been more serious in my life." To prove it, he slid his hand between her thighs, caressing the warmth he found there. "Ah, God, Meg. You're white-hot."

Meg couldn't resist. She cupped his erection, feeling the thickness through his pants. She needed those jeans off. "It's you, Tico. You're turning me on," she panted. "Don't stop. Please."

He lifted her up, and she wrapped her legs around his waist as he headed for the bedroom. Meg held on for dear life, burying her hands in his hair to capture his mouth. "Hurry!" she whispered.

With Meg in his arms, he fell on the still-unmade bed. She started unfastening the waistband of his jeans when her cell phone rang.

Recognizing the ring, she stopped cold.

"Don't pay any attention to it, darlin'," he said.

"It's Dad. That's his ringtone."

As if on cue, Tico's phone began buzzing on the kitchen counter. Meg fought the passionate haze filling her mind. She laid her forearm over her eyes. "Something is up. They're trying to reach us both."

Tico rolled off the bed. He headed out of the room for his phone. "Damn!"

Meg reached for hers on the nightstand. She cleared her throat before answering. "Dad. Good morning."

# CHAPTER ELEVEN

Tico watched as Meg shifted the Ferrari into gear and started down the driveway. Twenty minutes had passed since their phone calls. Eric Longwood had called Tico. After hearing the news, the two of them had scrambled to get on the road as fast as possible. Melissa Collins had been found at dawn this morning—dead and buried in a shallow grave. Since Meg and Tico were undercover as jet-setters, they couldn't go to the crime scene. They could, however, be guests of the mayor's and attend a brunch at his ranch.

Things were getting hotter in Adobe Creek, and Don Francisco's blood pressure was rising. The team would meet at Rio Plata Ranch since the crime scene had been secured. At Barbara's insistence, wives were invited to make the brunch look as natural as possible.

As they passed the spa, Tico and Meg both looked toward the parking lot. Enrique's car was there along with several others. "Looks like Sunday morning is a busy time," Meg said.

"And Enrique is front and center." They both turned their attention back to her driving.

"Why does going to brunch sound so wrong when we're dealing with a young woman's death?" Tico asked.

She patted his hand. "Welcome to life with Don Francisco. Things aren't always conventional. Besides, from what he told me on the phone, he believes we're being watched. Eric didn't want to blow our cover when we're just starting."

Meg had changed into what she called ranch clothes. She looked stunning in tight jeans, a turquoise embroidered Mexican tunic and boots. Bangle bracelets jingled on her wrist, and silver hoops gleamed in her ears. Her dark hair fell in waves on her shoulders. Tico reached over, toying with a tendril. "So, your father heard that we're doing the investigation together and isn't happy, eh?"

"You heard me arguing with him?"

"It was hard not to. You sounded pretty angry."

Worry crossed her brow. "He'll try to stop me."

She'd downshifted to wait while the Quarry gates opened to let them out. He intertwined his fingers with hers over the stick shift. "No, he won't."

"How do you figure that?"

He released her hand so she could bring the car up to road speed. "I just explained to Eric about the leads we found last night. We have to stay in the Quarry until all our hunches are cleared."

She looked at him gratefully. "And you'll explain why we have to finish as a team?"

"Precisely. There's no real danger at the moment.

I can't imagine your father would want to ruin the investigation he spearheaded."

"I wouldn't abandon the case anyway, you know."

"For the record, I wouldn't want to work without you."

After a moment, Meg said, "We'll beef up surveillance when we need it. That should make him feel better."

"Do you have a problem facing him now?"

"Nope." Meg punched the pedal, shifting into fourth gear, taking the remote road to the ranch at over ninety miles per hour. The Ferrari's engine thrummed. Meg handled the car the way Tico wanted her to handle him—smoothly, skillfully and with satisfaction on her face. "Dad thinks he's tough, but he forgets I'm far more stubborn than he is. I was born for this case. He can't stop me."

"I've got your back, Detective."

She raised a brow. "Really?"

"Yeah. And when I get the chance, I'll get your front and every inch of beautiful skin I can lay my hands on."

A noticeable shiver ran through her body as she chuckled. "I'm getting a visual, but you have to stop talking like that."

He exhaled. "Not likely. I'm all charged up. Your father and his grim news ruined what was going to be one of the best moments of my life."

Meg pursed her lips. "*One* of the best?"

He stifled a grin. "Can't be the best until I've had it."

She took the curve in the road more quickly than necessary. Tico had to brace himself for the turn. She was toying with him. Saying nothing, he simply straightened when the turn stopped.

She shot him a teasing look. "Maybe you lost your chance, cowboy."

He unbuckled his seat belt, reached over and nuzzled his face against her neck. She smelled like powder and roses and everything he'd ever wanted in his life. The thought made him swallow hard. Inhaling one more time, he kissed the pulse point below her ear. "We'll see about that, sweetheart."

She elbowed him away. "Hey. Stop now. I'm trying to drive."

He turned his attention back to the road. When had spending time in Meg's company gone from difficult to the most comfortable feeling he'd ever known? He wasn't quite sure what had turned Meg's head in his direction, but after almost having her naked under him this morning, he wasn't going to lose her now.

"What would you say if I told you that you're my fantasy, Meg? You have an unstoppable body, you're smart, dangerous, and your kisses drive me wild."

Color rose on her cheeks. "I'd say I had no idea you were such a comedian."

Comedian? He was being sincere, but she was

turning his words into a joke. Was she trying to undo what they'd started? He'd lighten up, but not for long. An hour ago her legs had been wrapped around his waist, her breasts pressed against his chest. That wasn't something he could forget. But he'd give her quarter for now, if only because they were headed for her parents' house.

He pointed at her. "I wasn't being funny. Funny was when I arrived in the sheriff outfit on horseback. You didn't laugh."

"I was too pissed at you to think you were funny."

"The other guys laughed."

"And that pissed me off something fierce, too."

He slapped his leg. "You like me!"

She turned onto the road dividing the Rio Plata Ranch from the Judumi tribe. "Oh, shut up, Detective."

That stunned him into a momentary silence. He tapped her cheek. "Hey. What's happening here? An hour ago you were completely interested in my attention."

Silence. Small frown lines creased her brow. "Meg?"

She sighed. "You scare the devil out of me."

He sat back in the seat. "Do you really mean that?"

She downshifted, slowing the car. "You're making me feel things I've never felt, and I don't know what to do about it."

"So you'd rather stop?"

"Neither of us is the commitment type."

He laughed. "Well, I'm not here forever, Meg. We both know that. Neither of us has ever stepped over the line with a colleague. Am I right?"

She nodded once. "Yes."

"So, there must be something between us that we both feel is too strong to ignore."

She nodded once more. "Yes."

"Well, honey, how about you think about that for a while instead of giving up on us before we've even started? Let's talk again after your father has finished with us."

She smiled. "There you go with your jokes again."

"Will you give me a chance?"

She looked out at the barren land spreading around them. "Okay. Do you mind if we go slowly? Can I set the pace?"

"Sure, baby. No pressure." He nodded, watching her closely. She was actually nervous. He'd give her all the time she needed, but he knew as sure as the sun burned in the sky that she felt the same attraction for him. She'd shown her hand this morning.

"These are Judumi lands, you know," she said, still looking out the window.

An unexpected tug pulled at his heart. He'd already figured that much but didn't want to ask. "Looks dry."

"You'd be surprised at the amount of life that

exists in a desert." She pointed to the mountains a few miles away. "Tribal lands include the mountain range. Your people care for their holdings in alignment with nature, the same as they have for over a hundred years."

He was already feeling raw that Meg had cooled on him. Now she wanted talk about his father's tribe? He really didn't want to go there.

"*My people?* Easy does it, girl."

She shrugged. "You have family here."

"What? I thought my grandparents were dead."

"Nope. You have an aunt, a grandmother and a cousin living here."

"My dad had a sister?"

"Dawn. She's really sweet."

His insides grew cold. His chest tightened. "So, where was this sweet Dawn when I needed help?" Damn, he hated the angry kid he heard in his words.

"She probably didn't know you needed help. Your dad turned away from everyone." Tico could hear the concern in her voice.

"The tribe kicked him out."

Meg compressed her lips. "He was feeding cocaine to kids, Tico. Trying to get them hooked. The tribe tried to help him recover. Instead, he chose to disappear."

Tico felt as though a lead weight had just been dropped on his heart. "I heard a different story."

"Of course you did."

"You have no idea what I lived with," he said softly.

She laid a hand on his shoulder. "I'm beginning to get the picture, my friend. And you know what?"

"What?"

She pulled the car over just before the turn into Rio Plata Ranch. Removing her sunglasses, she unbuckled her seat belt, leaned over and grabbed his face with both hands so he'd have to look her in the eye. "I've…never…been…more impressed… by a man…ever."

She kissed him long, hard and sweet until, unable to resist her touch any longer, he buried his hand in her hair and kissed her back, ratcheting up the heat in the car. Oh, yeah. Meg had magic. Fire. Juju. Casting spells. He was snared for good.

Coming up for air, Tico said, "You call this going slowly?"

She laughed. "I guess I've decided."

He shook his head. "Be sure, girl. Don't start something you don't want to finish. I want you worse than I've wanted anything in my life."

Meg searched his face for a moment. From what he could read in her expression, he'd say he'd just scared the shit out of her.

Swallowing hard, she said, "I've thought over your suggestion. Against my better judgment, I'm incredibly attracted to you. If we keep this affair quiet between us, with no strings attached, I'd like to explore what we have here."

Another guy might have jumped all over this agreement. But for someone who'd always kept women at arm's length, Tico felt Meg's conditions like a punch to the gut. "Your offer sounds ruthless. I'm not sure I can handle it."

She tapped a finger to his lips. "What? A tough gang leader like you can't handle gratuitous sex?"

He ran a hand along the inside of her thigh and felt a tremor go through her. Damn, she was hot. "Oh, I can handle free sex, sweetheart. I'm thinking more about you. Don't want to break your heart."

She fell silent, concern darkening her eyes. "What if I'm willing to take that chance?"

Maybe she was, but was he? Meg Flores was the single most fascinating woman he'd ever met. If he made love with her once, could he let her go? He already knew the answer. No. Sex with Meg would shatter the walls of his carefully protected life. He felt it deep inside. Yet, somewhere in his lonely world, he needed her touch. Now. Before he became a coldhearted bastard for the rest of his life.

"Speechless, Butler?"

"Thinking this through."

"Wow. You have to think?"

"Not anymore." He pushed a lock of hair behind her ear. "I'm taking you up on your terms, beautiful." Cupping the back of her head, he pulled her in for one more kiss. "Just don't say I didn't warn you." He caressed her face, letting his desire show in his eyes. "I can't wait to get you naked again as soon as possible."

She shifted the car into gear, kicking up dust in their wake. "Then let's get this meeting finished—fast."

Bill Mewith and his wife pulled in behind them as they drove up to the ranch house. Tico was surprised no other cars were there. Meg parked the Ferrari near the front door. Bill parked his truck in the shade of a bottlebrush tree. Meg waved to his wife. Tico exited the car and came around to meet her. He almost took Meg's hand, but stopped himself.

She shoved her hands in her pockets. "I saw that."

He lowered his voice. "I want my hands all over you. This is going to be rough."

She whispered quickly, "If one person guesses, it's over, Tico. I've worked too hard on my career to have a fling ruin everything."

He stopped. "Fling? You're just going to use me and drop me after you've had your fun?"

She snorted back a laugh. "Sounds like you've heard that line before."

He tried to look disappointed. "Yeah. I wanted to try it out to see how it feels."

"And?"

"Not too good on the old self-esteem."

She headed for her friends. "So banish that remark from the records, eh? Besides, we now have a murder case to crack."

Bill's eyebrows rose at the banter between Meg and Tico as he led his wife across the driveway. He hugged Meg and shook Tico's hand. "Let me introduce my wife, Dove."

Dove's mouth dropped open briefly before she smiled. "A pleasure to meet you, Tico. Bill has told me all about you."

Meg wound her arm through Dove's. "I've missed you, my friend! Let's go inside. It's been way too long since we've had a girls' night. We'll have to get together when things calm down again."

As Meg led Dove out of earshot, Bill snagged Tico's sleeve. "This isn't a good development. Don Francisco is going to be irritable."

Tico faced Bill. "Meg and I did some investigating last night. We have a few thoughts to go over with you. I'm as anxious to get this case closed as you are."

Bill motioned toward Meg opening the front door for Dove. "I take it you two have found common ground."

*If one person guesses, it's over, Tico.* He knew better than to share the enthusiasm bubbling up inside him over Meg's willingness to become his lover, despite the turn of events for the worse in the investigation. "Yeah, well, I used all my charm to get her to work with me."

Bill looked skeptical. "Charm. Right."

"More like bribery." Tico leaned in to whisper, "Don Francisco threw her under the bus. She realized she was better off working with me than having him sabotage her job."

Bill let out a low whistle. "He would do it, too."

Tico shook his head. "Not on my watch. She's talented. He's being a fool." He held up a finger. "But don't quote me. I'll deny it."

Bill opened the door to the house and motioned for Tico to enter. "Can't wait to hear about your leads."

"We might want to talk separately first."

Bill frowned. "Meg, too?"

"Of course."

"Okay, then. Oh, and Tico?"

"Yes?"

"We need to make plans."

"For?"

"I can't tell you."

"Then why should I go?"

Bill stopped inside the door. "Because you are Judumi."

"No, I'm a New Yorker."

"I already got that. We'll talk later. Let's get this farce of a luncheon over so we can get back to work."

THE HOUSE WAS COOL, as usual, with the enticing smell of herbs and simmering meat rising on the air. Through the open living area, Meg could see her parents sitting outside beneath the pergola. She let Bill lead Dove outside and held up a finger to stop Tico. "Remember, Detective. Strictly business."

"Got it." He whispered, "If my hand ends up on your ass, just ignore me."

"Be sure not to use your shooting hand because I will break it." She plastered a smile on her face. "Don't blow the chance to get laid, cowboy. I'm serious."

"Yes, ma'am."

Ana and her mother were busy at the stove filling platters and bowls. Ana's eyes lit up when she spotted Tico.

*"Hola, Señorita Flores, y Señor Butler!"*

Interesting how Ana hadn't forgotten his name. But then, Tico probably had that effect on most women. Meg waved briefly. "We'll be outside."

Tico and Meg joined the group. Barbara hugged Dove like a daughter. Don Francisco and Bill shook hands, then her father turned to greet Tico.

Meg wound an arm around Dove's petite shoulders. "Tico, I want you to know two things about Dove. First, we've been friends since we could walk and share all of our secrets."

Tico gave Meg a look as if questioning whether she'd tell Dove about them, but she wouldn't. She frowned slightly in response. Disappointment flashed in his eyes.

Tico turned to Dove. "Wow. You two are lucky." He cocked a brow. "And the second point you want to make?"

Meg grinned. "Dove is the daughter of the Judumi chief, so that makes her a true-life princess."

Dove blushed. "Stop, Meg. You don't have to tell every new person I meet."

"I've never met a princess," Tico said. "Should I bow or kiss your hand or something?" He wondered if her father was the chief he'd written to for help as a young boy.

Dove laughed. "Neither, please." She held one hand to her mouth. "Oh, brother. You look so familiar."

Bill slapped Tico on the back. "My wife recognizes a Judumi when she meets one."

Surprise filled Dove's eyes. "Come now, Bill. He looks like Marcus Antiman. Only older."

Was Meg coming to know Tico so well that she sensed him withdraw from the conversation though he hadn't moved? She wanted to touch his arm in reassurance but didn't dare.

"Marcus is the cousin I mentioned to you in the car, Tico."

Bill held up a hand. "I noticed the similarity when we met, but Tico doesn't want to know, so I said nothing."

Barbara Flores looped an arm through Tico's. "I think we all noticed, my dear."

Tico took a step back. "Really? Is this some conspiracy or something?"

"Of course not, Tico. We were respecting your privacy." Barbara's smile brightened. "Would you like to meet your family?"

Ana approached with a tray of drinks. Tico snagged an iced tea. "They're relatives, not family. Family cares. Relatives simply share the same blood."

Dove shook her head. Her sweet voice soothed. "Oh, you don't understand the way of the Judumi."

"I'm from New York, Dove. I certainly don't."

MEG FELT ANXIOUS to rescue Tico from this uncomfortable conversation. She figured if Dove or her mother pressed the issue any further, Tico would become rude. Then again, that might end the meeting sooner and the two of them could get down to business.

She banished the thought when she caught her father watching her look at Tico. No way she'd let him catch a whiff of their new relationship. She smiled. "So, Papá. Are we expecting anyone else for, ah…brunch?"

"Eric left messages with the team. Didn't hear back from Mitchell or Jose."

That got Tico's attention, much to Meg's relief. "Are you comfortable discussing the latest development with the ladies here?"

Barbara led Tico to a chair next to hers. "Why

don't we sit so you detectives can finish this gruesome discussion before we lose our appetites and no one eats Nita's cooking."

Don Francisco remained standing. Tico sat next to Barbara. Meg took a seat opposite him, so Don Francisco's attention switched from one to the other. "What evidence did you two find strong enough to plant yourselves up at the Quarry?"

"I already explained on the phone, Dad." Meg let her impatience come through in her voice. Her father was harping on the issue because she'd initiated the surveillance without notifying him, and he didn't like being the last to know. But she wouldn't permit her father to bully her in front of her team members and friends. She cast a meaningful glance at Bill, needing his support here.

Years of exposure to the mayor's disposition had Bill speaking up, as she'd hoped. "With all due respect, Don Francisco, this new homicide supports their hunch. Melissa Collins was last seen in the Quarry. The shallow grave we found on the edge of the corridor is just north of the Quarry Mountains."

Barbara shook her head. "I heard the girl's mother practically had a breakdown at the news."

Bill continued, "No one would have found the body if the shadow wolves hadn't investigated the circling buzzards."

Tico's attention turned to Bill. "Your tribesmen?"

Bill nodded. "They are constantly patroling the

reservation." He looked at the mayor. "Don Francisco, an autopsy is being done, but given the number of needle marks, we think she was drugged for transportation, then dumped when she overdosed. I wouldn't normally say anything now in front of civilians, but the story has already been picked up by the local paper."

Meg's chest tightened, and she felt her cheeks grow hot. "Worse is that if the other missing women were abducted by the same group, they're now gone." Meg looked at Tico and was so angry, she actually had to fight back tears. "We're too late."

A movement at the kitchen door caught her eye. Mitchell Blake emerged carrying a lunch roll, already half-devoured. "Sorry for the delay. I came as soon as I got your message." He thumbed back toward the kitchen. "Brunch looks terrific."

He greeted his hosts. Kissing Barbara on the cheek, he said, "Jose asked me to tell you that his wife isn't feeling too well this morning. They know you'd understand."

Barbara gestured to a seat. "Of course. Please join us."

Don Francisco returned to the conversation Blake had interrupted. "Meg, if you believe we've lost the other women, then we tie up the loose ends here and let the feds chase down the leads outside our jurisdiction."

"No!" Tico and Meg spoke at the same time.

Don Francisco favored Tico with an irritated look. "You can continue the investigations from the station."

Meg wanted to laugh out loud at the way her father looked at Tico. After insisting she adjust her team to work under Tico, her father now didn't want him alone with her. "So, my new team leader becomes a bad boy overnight because he's alone with me?"

Mitchell Blake laughed.

She turned on him. "What's so funny?"

"I thought he was a Wonder Boy."

"That's my point. The last time I had this discussion with my father, Tico was the answer to a prayer."

"That's enough, Meg," Don Francisco said.

Tico shot Meg a quelling look. "Sir, we don't have a problem here. We can conduct business from the police department, if you wish. The only thing is that we uncovered a lead or two that would best be followed if we just had a little more time undercover."

Don Francisco crossed his arms. His concentration lingered on both of them for longer than Meg was comfortable with. "Explain."

Meg and Tico exchanged glances. Meg met her father's expectant gaze calmly. "We'd prefer not to, Dad."

Mitchell Blake leaned forward. "Do tell. What's your hunch?"

No one noticed Tico's nod of dissent, except Meg. She agreed. The less said, the better. After she and Tico had discussed the possibility of someone on the inside smoothing legal problems for Enrique's clients, they'd concluded that anyone on the team or at the department could be a suspect.

If her father insisted on pulling the plug on their cover at the Quarry, she and Tico would fill Bill in later about their concerns regarding Katrina Ripley's story. For the time being, the others didn't have to know, unless their help was needed.

Meg exhaled. "We got a different perspective on the night Melissa disappeared. We want to compare notes." She looked at Bill. "Meanwhile, Bill, you and Jose should speak with Melissa's friends once more. Find out who was talking to whom and what was said. Then find the people they spoke with and see what they know. Also, question any hired help working the party. Someone must have seen Melissa leave that hacienda."

Mitchell nodded. "Good idea. I say do the follow-up, but it sounds to me like a dead end."

"Why?"

"I'll bet you a hundred bucks all of these women were taken by a smuggling group moving through town. If fingerprints were wiped from Melissa's vehicle, the perp is someone the feds already know. The group will be moving fast and not slowing down. Mark my words. The next abduction will happen in another town farther along the border."

He shook his head. "Best thing we can do is alert the local towns and stake out every airport in a fifty-mile radius."

"If the women have been taken across the border, they're lost," Tico said.

Meg jumped out of her chair and began pacing. "I'm not giving up. There's a lead here somewhere, and I don't care how long it takes. I'm going to find it."

"Local taxpayers will be glad their money is being put to good use," Mitchell said.

Meg turned on him. "Are you saying I'm wasting money?"

Mitchell opened his palms. "You know what, Meg? The truth hurts, but we lost this one. How about we spend more energy educating our citizens about human trafficking, teaching abduction precautions and encouraging folks to report anything suspicious as it happens?"

Meg wanted to spit. Mitchell's willingness to throw in the towel disgusted her. "Since you're the expert, why don't you do that job? The local library will surely find time for you." She poked a finger in his chest. "I want to catch these bastards. I'll work until the job is finished."

Barbara tugged on the hem of her tunic. "Calm down now, Meg. This is a volatile subject. It upsets us all. We need clear heads, not tempers." She shot an apologetic glance to Mitchell.

Tico stood. "Don Francisco, you hired me to

do a job. Meg and I need a few more days in the Quarry. We'll finish following the lead we have. If nothing comes of it, we'll do whatever you ask."

Ana interrupted the discussion. "Brunch is served, *Señora.*"

Relief filled Barbara's face. "Good. Let's hammer the rest of this out later." She stood. "Shall we?"

Mitchell offered Barbara his arm and led her through the kitchen to the dining room. Bill escorted Dove. He sent Meg a commiserating glance letting her know he was on board with anything she and Tico wanted to do. As always, she could depend on her friend.

Following Meg, Tico quietly said to her father, "Two days are all we need, sir."

"Two days to get the job done?" Don Francisco stopped, rested a hand on Tico's shoulder. Speaking low enough not to be heard by most people, but within Meg's earshot, he said, "You can have your two days. But know this—I hired you for a job. Don't touch my daughter."

## CHAPTER TWELVE

MEG PUNCHED THE Ferrari up to eighty miles an hour within seconds of leaving the ranch. As the desert passed in a blur, the set of her jaw said it all. She was pissed at her father. Brunch had been uncomfortable as hell watching her shoot daggers at him for the rest of the afternoon.

When Meg had cornered Don Francisco in the dining room after everyone had taken seats at the table on the veranda, Tico had preferred to join the others rather than get involved. Now he wanted to know.

"What did you say to your father when I left you guys in the dining room?"

"Do you really want to know?"

"Of course."

"I told him that I was a professional and that it was insulting for him to think I'd act otherwise. My job requires me to work closely with men *and* women when working undercover. I suggested that if my professional conduct didn't suit him, I'd be happy to find another police deparment elsewhere that would welcome my expertise."

"An idle threat?"

A look of incredulity filled her face. "Really? You'd ask me that question?"

He shrugged. "You love this place."

"I don't love my father's attitude. He's driven by an overprotective nature based on fear." She slapped the steering wheel with her hand. "I understand his motives, Tico. I truly do. But there comes a point where he's going to have to let go or lose me. I'm not his pet. Or a tool for him to use at will. Sorry. Not going to happen. We have a job to do, and I intend to see it through."

Tico crossed his arms. "And the little tangle we had this morning? How did you fit that into your speech?"

She grew quiet. "My personal life is none of his business."

"The mayor's observation puts a damper on our enthusiasm. Wouldn't you say?"

"Maybe for you, but I'm not speeding for nothing. I was hoping we could pick up where we left off. Pronto."

He laughed. "Oh, now you want to do me to spite your father? That's not making me feel all warm and fuzzy, Meg."

Meg jammed on the brakes, stopping the car in the middle of the deserted street, a cloud of dust and tire smoke pluming in the air. She faced him, tears brimming in her eyes.

"Maybe I want to *do you* despite my father, not

in spite of him. I've never been as attracted to any man as I am to you. My father's interference doesn't change that fact. Should I let him stop us before we even figure out what this is?" She laid a hand on her heart. "I'd like to explore what we have, Tico. If you don't, that's fine. But tell me now."

Tico felt his heart wrench as he watched a single tear run down Meg's cheek. God, she was beautiful. He slowly shook his head. "Fling, my ass. You've fallen for me."

Another tear fell. "So, what if I have? I'm scared out of my wits. I'm not used to wanting someone like I want you."

Tico had had so many women come and go in his life. Jackie had been the love of his life, and he'd mourned her deeply after she'd been killed. But the feelings he'd had as a young man in his twenties were so different from what he was feeling now at nearly forty.

This powerful, hard-ass detective with bedroom eyes and the sweetest smile he'd ever seen had worked her way into his heart in such a short time. He'd spent way too long as a loner to let her get away, especially now that she'd offered herself to him. She was going to trust him—if only for a little while. Trust wasn't something he'd been willing to share with anyone since Jackie. But he'd craved Meg since seeing her profile picture, and he wasn't going to wait another minute. He wanted her over and over again and knew he would for a long, long time.

Admitting that simple fact was a revelation. He was ready to take the plunge. "And to think I was worried you would fall for me. You just flattened me with a tear."

He reached over and wiped away the tear with his thumb. "I have three words for you."

She swiped her cheeks with the back of her hand, watching him as if he was about to break her heart. "What are they?"

He pointed out the window toward the Quarry, a grin breaking on his face. "That way. Now!"

They drove in silence. Tico took care not to distract Meg from her driving, er, speeding. He kept a proprietary hand on her thigh, however, unwilling to break the link between them. Meg's cell phone rang. She looked at the console where it lay. "Can you check that for me?"

Tico looked at the caller ID. "Penny."

"Can you put it on speakerphone?" When he hit the speaker button, Meg said, "Hey, girl. I'm driving a Ferrari. You're on speakerphone. Tico is with me."

"Well, hey, hey, kids. Are we playing nicely with the new toy?"

"Doing about ninety-five. How are you?"

"Great. Enrique's assistant manager quit. He asked me to apply for the position."

Tico and Meg exchanged glances. She'd be a great informant. "That's a big step, Pen. Congratulations."

"I'm just lucky she didn't leave a couple of months ago, before I was up to speed. I'm in the right place at the right time."

"You certainly are," Tico added, grinning at Meg.

"What are you two up to now?"

Meg swallowed a laugh. "Headed back to the Quarry for some undercover work."

Penny laughed. "Oh, yeah. I'll bet you are. Well, Bruno misses you, sweetie. Call me when you can!"

"See you in a few days."

"Be good."

Meg grinned again. "As always, sweetheart. Bye!"

Meg and Tico spoke little for the rest of the ride back. Given the looks they kept sending each other, no words were required.

THEY PULLED UP to the hacienda, barely making their way into the driveway for all the cars parked along the street. Tico lowered the window of the Ferrari and immediately the pulse of rock music hammered the air from behind the Ripleys' hacienda. Tico punched the portable garage door opener. Meg pulled the car in and watched as he clicked the button to close the door behind them.

He reached over, cupped her face with his hand and kissed her soulfully. When he broke the kiss, she sighed against his mouth.

Meg's phone rang. Tico laughed. "So, every time we kiss, your phone will ring?"

"Doesn't matter now. We should probably get our butts across the street and see what else we can learn." Checking the caller ID, Meg cocked a brow and displayed the phone screen. "Well, look at this. Katrina Ripley."

"She has your number?"

"Gave it to her last night." She tapped the speakerphone button. "Hey, Katrina!"

"Hi, Amelia. Did I just see you two pull in?"

"Yes, indeed."

Katrina sounded excited. "Well, climb into your swimsuit and come on over. We're having a barbecue before we leave tomorrow."

Tico frowned. Meg said, "You're leaving? We just got into town."

"Josh wants to record a couple of songs in L.A. He gets restless, you know. But we'll be back soon." She paused to sip her drink, the tinkling of ice coming through the line. "So, will you come over?"

Tico nodded emphatically.

"Sure! Give us a few minutes to get changed. What can we bring?"

Katrina laughed. "You're so neighborly! Nothing, of course. We have it all. See you!"

She ended the call.

Tico was out of the car and opening Meg's door before she could take a breath. He rested his attention on her legs as she stepped out.

A grin tugged at her mouth. "What's your rush, cowboy?"

He held out a hand. "I'm not wasting another minute."

"For what?"

He closed the car door and tugged her toward the house. "To see Amelia in a bikini. Hurry up. Let's do this."

As MICK SANCHEZ, Tico watched Meg walk along the far end of the pool from where he sat with Josh, his drummer and two other guys. Thirty or more people milled around, swimming or hanging out on the gazebo island suspended above the pool. Some were tossing ice cubes at the swimmers or chatting as best they could over the music blasting from the speakers. A few of the Ripleys' friends manned grills with steaks and barbecued chickens, while caterers worked the crowd with drinks and finger foods.

Tico couldn't take his eyes off Meg, er, Amelia. In typical Meg fashion, she didn't wear a traditional bikini. Instead, she wore a hot-pink one-piece that looked like a bikini from behind, while from the front, a narrow strip of fabric connected the cleavage-revealing top to the tiny bottom. That suit had him wanting to slide his hand beneath that tiny strip covering her belly. As she walked, the tiny ties curving along her hips begged to be released. Oh, yeah. He was just the guy for the job, and it wouldn't be long before he'd get his chance. In the meantime, he enjoyed the hell out of watching how nicely that bikini bottom cupped her beautiful ass.

As Amelia, Meg had a sultry walk, slow enough to look deliberate but with an energy that could only be natural. She walked like a sleek, sexy predator any man would welcome the chance to tame. Dark tortoiseshell sunglasses shielded her eyes. Those full lips glistened with pale gloss. Her hair fell in waves over her shoulders and down her back. She'd kept the silver bangles on her right wrist. He imagined he could hear them jangling from where he sat. Meg headed for Katrina on the chaise longues lined up in the sun by the edge of the deck. It took every ounce of Tico's control for him to stay in his seat and not follow her.

"You look like you can't get enough of that," Josh said, watching him with amusement.

"Damned straight, brother." Tico sipped from his bottle of water. "A man doesn't get too many chances at a woman like Amelia."

"She's quite the looker."

Tico peered over the top of his sunglasses to

where Katrina sat. Meg took the lounge next to hers, and the two women greeted each other with kisses on both cheeks. Meg was a class act, acknowledging the friends Katrina introduced. It made Tico want Meg even more, especially because he now knew what her body felt like against his. He hadn't been lying when he'd answered Josh. He wasn't about to lose this opportunity with Meg. He didn't know where their relationship was headed, but he knew damned well he wanted to start. Right away.

Watching Josh's beautiful wife hold court while her husband ignored her sent up a red flag in Tico's mind. Now more than ever, he wanted to know what made this rock star tick. "I'm sure you understand that possessive feeling with a beautiful wife like Katrina."

"Oh, she's amazing, I can tell you that," Josh said. "But in my business, beautiful women throw themselves at me all the time." He sipped his scotch and grinned. "Unfortunately, I am a weak man."

Tico's hand fisted involuntarily. This guy was a prick. The kind of man who felt entitled to break rules and the heart of the woman who loved him. And Tico had thought he liked this guy. Did Katrina know her husband was a player? And if she did, was she okay with it? Did she fool around, as well?

"I've been there, brother, but like I said, a woman

like Amelia doesn't happen often. I'm happy to stay put."

Josh raised his glass. "All power to you, buddy. At least I don't have to worry about you chasing my wife."

A frown creased his brow. "Sounds like you two have some unique challenges."

The drummer laughed. "Sometimes it's better than a circus. We've been talking about starting a reality TV show with these two."

"Oh, yeah?"

Josh shot his friend a quelling glance. "Yeah, well, it's not pretty when Kat and I start arguing. Definitely not for prime time." He pointed a finger at his bandmate and stood. "And we're going to keep it that way, Kyle. I need a swim."

Tico followed him. "Not a bad idea." After all, once in the pool, he could make his way to the other side and see how good Meg looked in her bikini while stretched out on a lounge chair.

WHEN THE MEN STOOD, Meg couldn't take her eyes off Tico. While Josh was taller and lanky, and lightly tanned from weeks around the pool, Tico's body was perfectly proportioned, corded from training but not overblown. His charcoal-colored bathing trunks sat on his hips with the white waistband resting against his dark skin like a neon stripe accentuating his fitness. She could taste his kisses and feel his hands on her all over again. Meg already knew the texture of his skin. Her fingertips tingled to touch him again.

The women around her seemed to be as interested in Tico as she was. One redhead said, "Wow. Who brought the Indian? I'd powwow with him anytime."

A slow smile curved Meg's lips as she imagined cooling the babe off full blast with a fire hose, and not only for her racist comment. Meg's immediate possessive reaction took her by surprise. But she caught herself. And honestly, she couldn't blame the young hussy for having the good taste to be interested in Tico. All the same, she'd put an end to that interest right now.

"Sugar, you'd have to go through me to *powwow* with Mick. He's mine." Oh, God. She loved saying that. If only it were true.

"Oh, honey, I mean no harm," the redhead said, stretching lazily on the lounge. "I simply was admiring the scenery."

Meg sipped the iced tea she'd been served. "Can't fault you there."

Tico turned toward Meg, and she held her breath when he shot a grin her way. Still wearing his sunglasses, he waded down the steps, acknowledging the people he passed along the edge, and broke into a breaststroke in her direction. Josh caught up with him and swam alongside, the two men chatting as they came closer.

"Oh, I know what my baby wants," Katrina said, cooing.

The redhead said, "Well, if it's what I think it is, I hope you have enough to go around."

Katrina laughed. "Of course I do, sweetie."

She opened a beautiful Chinese lacquered box on the table between her and Meg. Meg could have arrested her hostess on the spot. Carefully arranged like cigarettes in a case were about twenty joints, the pungent smell of the marijuana rising between them. Below them was a line of eight small, stubby brown vials about an inch high. Katrina took one of the vials and tossed it playfully to her friend. "You girls work on that one for a while."

She smiled at Meg. "We keep the drugs rated PG around here. Pot and cocaine. Which would you prefer—or both?"

Tico and Josh had arrived. Meg used the line her team always used in these circumstances. "Coke is our favorite candy, but Mick and I can't indulge." She shrugged, making sure she looked disappointed. Sharing a look with Tico, she continued to embellish the lie, knowing he'd go along. "We don't tell folks, but Mick and I met in rehab. We've been straight for over a year. Don't want to blow it now. But help yourselves. We don't mind at all."

The redhead was already indulging. She inhaled the first spoon of coke, then licked her lips before dipping the tiny spoon back into the vial for the other nostril. Meg couldn't get over how such a pretty woman could suddenly look so ugly sticking a spoon up her nose.

Josh pulled himself out of the pool and sat on Katrina's lounge chair. His wife handed him a vial.

"I hope we're not tempting you two. I would feel awful," Katrina said, not looking the least bit remorseful.

Tico joined Meg on her lounge, running a proprietary hand up and down her thigh, which made goose bumps rise on her skin. He grinned at her to be sure she understood he'd noticed. Tico was so damned sensual. The touch of his strong hands did incredible things to her insides.

Tico turned his attention back to Katrina. "Amelia is my only temptation these days. Don't worry at all. Enjoy yourself."

Not asking twice, Katrina spooned herself a dose of coke as Josh opened his vial. Whether to avoid staring as the rock star and his wife snorted their drugs or simply using the moment as an excuse, Tico reached over and planted a long, soft kiss on Meg's mouth, his wet hair dripping cool water on her chest.

She wanted him so very badly; she had to consciously remind herself to breathe.

He whispered against her lips, "Did I tell you how beautiful you look in this swimsuit?"

Meg laughed, deep and throaty. She needed to get a handle on her emotions here and not let her role take over her good sense. "And have I told you how fine you look in yours?"

Katrina frowned. "Hey, Josh. We don't talk to each other that way anymore."

He buried his hand in her hair. Moving in, he kissed her soundly. "You're right, Kat. Want to start now?"

She caressed Josh's face. "Sure. But coke makes you horny. How about a little romancing the wife before we disappear for the afternoon?"

The redhead capped her coke vial and sighed with satisfaction. "Katrina, you always serve the best shit."

Katrina laughed. "Oh, yeah. My hot spa manager never lets me down."

Tico's hand hesitated on Meg's leg for a split second. In response, Meg laid her hand on his. Oh, yes. She'd heard. Enrique not only made sure Katrina stayed clear of trouble; he was her drug dealer, too. Tico leaned down and kissed Meg's bended knee. "How about a swim, love? The water is great."

She twisted her hair into a makeshift bun. "I could cool off."

Tico slid into the water first, then turned to reach for Meg as if they'd done this routine a hundred times. She didn't mind a bit as he eased her slowly down his body, and she couldn't do otherwise without drawing suspicion. She could test out her desires for him and flirt mercilessly all in the line of work.

Damn, she loved her job.

She smiled at Tico, glad her sunglasses hid the emotion rising in her eyes. "Oh, the water is wonderful."

The desert heat seemed less oppressive once in the pool, even though the scorching sun burned the top of her head, her neck and her shoulders. She dipped beneath the water up to her chin. Tico pulled her closer. Milking the moment for her own satisfaction, she wrapped her arms around his neck and her legs around his waist, letting him hold her.

"Oh, baby," Tico whispered. "Keep up the good work, and I won't be able to get out of the pool."

She grinned. "Just doing my job."

Tico turned slowly in the water, the warm liquid swirling around them. He cupped her ass. "Well, then, I wouldn't want you to upstage me, my precious." He dipped his head, trailing tiny kisses along her collarbone and up her neck. "How am I doing?"

A purr rose in Meg's throat. She squeezed her legs tighter, pressing her crotch against his stomach. "Oh, my. What's your name again?"

He laughed. "You are a rare one, Amelia."

Ah, she was rapidly willing to believe he meant what he said. Lord above, after all her bellyaching against Tico's arrival, Bill and the others were going to have a field day if they ever found out that she and Tico had become an item. Right about now, she couldn't care less. Not with her skin against his, that grin on his face and the hunger she could feel through every pore in his body.

Tico brought his mouth to her ear. "Now I know how your friend affords his watch and designer clothes."

Meg tapped the clenched muscle in his jaw, smiling for show, and leaned forward to whisper in return. "I'm so disappointed in him. The news will kill his mother." She nibbled his earlobe for effect. Damn, though, it was making her insides tighten. He felt so good against her.

Tico kissed her gently. "For a smart guy, he's a fool."

Meg sighed. Feeling bolder, she gathered a fistful of Tico's hair, surprised at how silky soft if felt between her fingers. "I've never brought a friend down. It's a pretty low moment for me."

Tico chuckled.

"What's so funny?"

"This conversation managed to get my body under control, after all."

"Does this mean we need to get out of the pool?" She was startled at the disappointment in her own voice.

Tico swirled them around in the water again. "Look for yourself, honey. Our hosts are stepping away."

Meg looked over Tico's shoulder in time to see

Josh and Katrina entering the master suite from the pool deck. She chuckled. "And to think they didn't even say goodbye."

Tico smiled. "I wouldn't waste a minute either if I was getting you into the sack."

Meg untangled herself from her partner. "Well, then, last one out of the pool takes their clothes off first."

Tico laughed. "I can't resist a challenge." Lightning fast, he grabbed her leg, dunking her under the water as he lunged past her, swimming for the edge of the pool.

Sputtering and grasping for her sunglasses, Meg surfaced to see Tico standing on the deck with both arms in the air. With a shit-eating grin on his face, he beckoned her over. "Come on, baby. You lost. No towel for you!"

Meg waded to the edge where Tico stood. "Help me up, honey."

When he offered her a hand, Meg caught him off balance and tugged hard.

"Hey!" Tico fell into the pool.

"Gotta go!" Meg climbed out, grabbed her things and scurried to the side-yard gate. She glimpsed Tico climbing out to the sound of laughter from the others watching. She called to him, "Double or nothing. I'll race you home."

Hearing more laughter behind her, she unlocked the front door of their hacienda and turned. Tico emerged from the Ripleys' side yard with a trail of onlookers egging him on. She was having more fun with Tico than she'd ever had with anyone else in her life. He was a practical joker and could give as well as he could take. This was going to be good.

She sat on the steps, still dripping wet and grinning, ready for him. He wasn't going to get the best of her. He arrived, standing before her, doing everything he could to seem vexed. "Are you having fun at my expense?"

Grinning, she said, "Hey, I said double or nothing. You lose." She grabbed each leg of his swimming trunks and pulled, pantsing him. As the crowd roared over his bare butt, she bolted into the house with Tico hot on her trail, slamming the door closed behind him.

She didn't get halfway through the living room before Tico tackled her. They landed on the couch.

"Double or nothing, my ass," Tico said, his voice husky.

Meg laughed. "Your ass is lovely."

"Now it's my turn to see yours." He pulled the strings on her bottom, releasing the hot-pink fabric from her skin. Turning her over, he smacked her playfully on the behind.

"Ouch. Hey!"

"Showing my parts to the neighbors can't go unpunished."

Holding her down with one hand, he untied the string from the top, unlacing the crisscrossed ties. "This is going to take some undoing."

Breathless, Meg urged, "Hurry, Tico. I want you so badly."

He stopped untying her top and turned her around. "Really?"

She met the fire in his eyes, his chest heaving with want. She shook her head. "I have never felt like this with anyone. I'm lost here."

"Oh, no, baby. You're right where you belong." A sigh escaped his lips. His focus roamed her half-naked body, setting her on fire as if he touched her. When he trailed fingertips along her stomach, playing with the circle of her navel, shivers rippled through her. He splayed his palms over her belly, then feathered them down, toying with the soft curls between her legs, caressing her liquid heat. "Sweet Meg. I've wanted to make love with you all day."

She wriggled the rest of her suit over her head. Her hair spilled on the couch, her breathing coming in gasps as she arched against his hand. She whispered, "Well then..." Her eyes opened wide. "Wait!"

He was leaning over her, his body intoxicating. "What, honey?"

"Condoms." She was breathless. "I brought some."

"Ah, yes. It just so happens..."

Sliding between her legs, he lowered himself down, achingly slow, teasing the skin of her inner thighs with the length of him. Feeling his hardness against her skin made her restless, running her hands up and down his arms, pulling him closer.

"Oh, God. I want you, Tico."

"I want you, too, Meg." He stretched his body over hers, reaching for his satchel at the end of the oversize couch. "No need to get up, darlin'. I have some right here."

Pulling the packets from the case, he opened one, rolled the sheath over himself as she watched. He smiled at her, and her heart skipped a beat. "Want to play now?"

She reached for him. "In the very worst way."

He kissed her softly, brushing his lips along her mouth, down her neck. Breathing in her scent, he sighed into that soft place just above her collarbone. He pressed kisses there, then along her chest, before dipping his head to the rising mound of one breast, nibbling the nipple, then gently pulling the hardened nub into his mouth until Meg inhaled a ragged breath.

"Tico…"

"Shh, sweetheart. You are so very beautiful. Let me explore."

He kissed her other breast, using his tongue to toy with the waiting nipple, licking and suckling the pink bud while his hands possessed her stomach, hips, sliding beneath her to cup her ass and draw her closer to him.

Unwilling to endure another minute of waiting, Meg grabbed his face with both hands, pulling him to her. She kissed him hard. Between the near miss this morning, their foreplay in the pool and the tussle inside the door, her need was explosive. "Please. Don't make me beg."

He rubbed his hardness against her opening. "You feel so good."

She arched up to meet him, the weight of him causing pressure. Wanting more, she rocked against him, electricity shooting through her. She was about to burst. "Please, Tico. Now!"

He entered her, shuddering as he buried himself inside her warmth, letting his body possess her.

"Ah, Meg!"

Meg wrapped her arms around his neck, her legs around his waist, mindlessly arching to take him in as deeply as she could, over and over again.

He slowed. Withdrew. Looked into her eyes. "You are amazing," he whispered.

"Come back…" She ached for him.

Holding himself over her, he teased her with his tip, making Meg crazy with want.

"Tico!"

"Yes, Meg." With one deep thrust, he buried himself inside her. Pulled out. Drove in. Over and over in a slow, steady rhythm. Watching her, branding her with his need and urging her on. He shuddered again. "Ah, Meg. I knew it would be like this."

"I never thought we could be…" She lost her train of thought as she used her inside muscles to pull on him, her body pulsing against his size. Her orgasm began to rise like an aching, igniting flood. Moving more and more quickly, she clung to him. "It's been so long. I'm going to embarrass myself."

Tico was intent on her, a slow grin tugging his lips. "It's okay, baby. There's always more."

He increased his thrusts until she cried out, her hips arching with the shattering reaction. Tico covered her mouth with his, kissing her senseless. Together they tumbled off the couch and onto the carpet, just missing the coffee table. Neither noticed. Meg bucked and arched and ground out her orgasm, panting for breath.

Tico held her until she calmed. She sensed him waiting, felt the tension in his body. Still hard inside her, he rolled over on the carpet, pulling her on top of him. "Ride me, darlin'. Let's see if you can do that again."

Regaining her equilibrium, Meg took a deep, soulful breath. She pushed her hair off her face, absorbing the man she'd fought against and now straddled, wanting more. A shiver of anticipation ran up her spine at the knowledge of how generous a lover Tico was. Exploring his chest and abdomen with sensuous strokes, she murmured, "I knew I liked you, Detective."

A soft chuckle escaped his throat. His hands caressed her thighs as he captured her gaze. "No, beautiful. You didn't know you liked me till…now."

Meg gasped with arousal when he began moving once more, this time in slow gyrations. She matched his movements, until she began rising and falling on him, slowly at first, then more quickly as the sensation began mounting inside her again. His hands explored her belly, trailed up to capture her breasts as she moved, fondling her, watching her face. His attention moved from her mouth, down her neck, to her breasts, before finally resting where their bodies joined in rhythm.

"You are unbelievably sexy, Meg," he whispered. "I could watch you move every waking minute of my day."

Seeing Tico beneath her, his strong body responding to hers, his hands wreaking havoc on her skin, encouraging her to take as much of him as she desired, had her reacting to this Judumi man in a way she'd never known. The intensity of his dark, emotional eyes tugged at her heart as he filled her, moved with her, egging her on to orgasm again. The snake tattoo on his right wrist, with its mouth open, fangs bared, where he gripped her hips, seemed dangerous as he lifted himself to meet her, his brow creasing with the intensity of his pleasure.

"Meg!"

A wave of ecstasy began to build in her core. "I'm going to come again. I can feel it," she said breathlessly, speeding up her movements. "Come with me, sweetheart."

Crying out his name, Meg threw her head back

as another orgasm rocked her body, more intense than the first. Her quaking insides triggered Tico's own release. He succumbed, climaxing with a deep, guttural moan, Meg arching and spreading wider above him to take him completely as his orgasm filled her.

She collapsed on top of him, inhaling his warm masculine scent and feeling as if her world had finally been put to rights. Tico's heart pounded against her skin, her heart echoing in return. She exhaled a breath in wonder, one mind-blowing fact rising crystal clear in her mind. She'd just given herself to the lover she'd been seeking all of her life.

What was she going to do now?

## CHAPTER THIRTEEN

MORNING DAWNED, POURING sunlight through the
windows and flooding the bed with golden rays.
The warmth on Tico's face nudged him awake.
While he was disoriented for a moment, the feel of
Meg's skin reminded him that he was in her bed,
with her delectable body entwined with his.

If heaven existed on earth, he'd finally found it.

She stirred against him, his arm wrapped possessively around her. A small rumbling noise rose
from Meg's belly. Yeah. They'd made love all
through the night and never stopped for dinner.
Between the living room floor, the tub and tan-
gling the silk sheets, they deserved a breakfast of
champions this morning.

Sensing a change in Meg's breathing, he looked
down and was amazed at the affection he saw in
her sleepy eyes. Meg looked like a drowsy angel.
Her dark hair spilled over his arm while those liquid brown eyes searched his.

He tapped her kiss-swollen mouth with a finger.
"Morning, beautiful."

She stretched lazily. "What time is it?"

He turned on his side to face her, body to body. "The sun just rose. Can't you feel it?"

She smiled. "Guess we were too busy to close the curtains last night."

Her warm, soft skin was turning him on again. He pressed against her, her breasts, her belly, her thighs. "There's something to be said for going to bed early."

"Well, sleeping didn't last very long."

He grinned. "We can sleep when we're dead, sweetheart. Do you want breakfast?"

She reached down under the covers. "I think you have breakfast right here."

She lifted her face for his kiss. "Looks like we have a problem."

He kissed her softly. "What's that?"

"Now that I've had you, I don't think I'll be able to keep my hands off you."

Her hand was doing wonderful things. "So... don't resist."

"As if I could," she said, feathering kisses along his neck, working downward along his chest, across his abdomen.

Anticipation had him rock solid. He caressed the small of her back as she moved, his hands gripping her waist as she licked and teased her way down his body.

"Oh, Meg."

Then she stopped talking, and he stopped thinking. Only the feel of her mouth on him, the press of her breasts against his thighs, elevated the power of touch to a whole new level. There was no room for thought. Only sensation, friction, silk, fireworks and the pressure of resisting release. They rolled in the sheets, exploring each other, their sighs from intimate touch filling the room until the morning sun slowly moved across the floor.

Meg was magical. Unquenchable. She was sunlight, wind, rain and fire. The hot, warm feel of her had him turning her on her back, stroking her with his hands, enjoying her mouth when she found her way once more to his erection and sucked, purring pleasure until he couldn't wait any longer. He had to be inside her. He reached for his last condom, Meg's knowing hands stroking him and making him want her more.

Stretching her arms over her head, he entered her without hesitation, without question. Meg responded by crying out and rocking against him. Her well-toned body knew precisely how to make him lose his mind. He covered her mouth with his, kissing her deeply, tenderly, swallowing her cries with moans of his own. Sensing her climax approaching, Tico abandoned his restraint, and they came together. Shuddering. Panting. Sighing in each other's arms, as Tico collapsed on top of her. There was nowhere else he needed to be. Ever again.

They both dozed, Tico on top, her body his pil

low, Meg's arms holding him close. After a while, Meg stirred. "Tico?"

He rolled off her. Meg's sleepy grin made his chest tighten. "You hungry now?"

She chuckled. "I could eat." She caressed his jaw with her fingertips. "Thank you."

He leaned on one elbow, savoring the flush of satisfaction on her skin. "For?"

"Making me feel beautiful."

He laid a hand across her belly. "Your beauty drives me wild, Meg. I do nothing."

She traced a finger on the rattler's head of his tattoo. "I expected more."

Tico frowned. "More sex?"

She laughed. "No. More tattoos. I didn't think you'd just have one."

He brushed hair from her cheek. "I'm not a fan of ink."

She lifted his hand and inspected the underside of his arm where the snake wrapped around. "Oh, no? This looks like it took a bit of time."

"Enough to make me realize I only needed one."

"Do you regret getting this tattoo?"

"No."

She tilted her head. "Why?"

"It means something to me."

"What?"

He puffed out a breath. "You have to understand, Meg. I had no support as a kid. Every day I survived on the streets came from me, not from any kind of outside help." His fingers flexed on her belly. "This snake took on new importance after Jackie was murdered. Shooting her killer didn't stop my rage. I only had myself to rely on to not go off the deep end. So, this tattoo."

She shook her head in wonder. "A rattlesnake tat got you through."

"In a way. The meaning behind the rattler drove me to focus on what I wanted from life once that cop gave me a second chance. I'm grateful to have her inked on my arm."

"Her?"

He shrugged. "Yeah. Women are mysterious, powerful. They have shifting moods, can heal, protect, nurture, renew." His heart squeezed remembering the past. "I needed those qualities to stop my anger. I'm not proud of things I've done," he said, his voice lowering to a whisper.

Meg's gaze softened, making his heart pound. "I've never told anyone," he said.

She pulled him to her and wrapped her arms around him once more. "You sound more like a Judumi man than some of the men born and raised in the tribe."

"That doesn't thrill me to hear."

She pulled back to look him in the eye. "Get to know Bill Mewith better, Tico. He's a fine example of a gentle but strong warrior." She tapped the scar on his jaw. "You may find you have more pride in your heritage than you know."

He watched her, not sure how to respond. She and her family seemed insistent that he should learn more about the Judumi. They'd brought the topic up three times now. She wanted him to trust her—with his heart and mind. He'd stopped trusting people a long, long time ago. Could he take that one critical step with her?

He wasn't ready to promise anything. "I'll think about it."

They faced each other in silence for a while until Meg said, "Have you been in love, Tico?"

He gave her a guarded look. "After Jackie died, I never let any woman get close again. Too dangerous."

Meg grew still. "Another reason no one should know about us."

"I know."

Meg pushed his silky black hair behind his back and rested her hand on the smooth muscle of his shoulder. "Don't take this the wrong way, okay?"

He hesitated. "You're dumping me already?"

She laughed. "As if I could." She wagged a finger at him. "I'm not finished with you yet, Tico Butler."

He slapped a hand to his heart. "Thank you, God."

She kissed him before settling back. "But, listen."

"I'm a captive audience." He teased her, but his insides tensed. He knew what she was thinking. He was thinking the same thing, but he didn't want to acknowledge it yet. She was too damned wonderful to ruin the moment.

She sighed. "I don't want us…our relationship getting out of hand."

There it was. "Like me falling head over heels for you?"

She winced. "I'm going to say something I can't believe I'd admit out loud."

"Yeah? Is this going to be good?"

She frowned. "Don't tease."

He pulled her against him. "Tell me."

Meg buried her face in his neck. "I feel so strange. I'm more comfortable now as your lover than I was as the angry woman who felt threatened by your arrival."

He kissed her forehead. "That's good, Meg. Real good."

She shook her head. "No. It's not."

He leaned back to look at her. "If you think I'm going to try to hold your hand at a team meeting, you can relax. I'm not that stupid."

"It doesn't matter. Everyone will know. Why do you think my father spoke to you?" She tapped his chest, then hers. "You. Me. We create energy people can feel."

"So?"

"When we shared animosity, we were safe. But attraction? Come on. You think we can fool people?"

"Hell, yes. We're undercover agents. We excel at deception."

A grin chased away her frown. "So I can continue to get annoyed and yell at you in public?"

He laughed. "If we can have makeup sex in the parking garage when no one's looking. Sure!"

She pushed him away. "Not funny."

He captured her chin with his hand. He grew serious. "Baby, I understand. I have no desire to put either of us in danger. We have no idea who our enemies are yet. If we keep our attachment under wraps, we can't be used against each other. Is that what you're trying to say?"

"Yes. And no."

"What's the no?"

She looked pained.

"What is it, Meg?"

She watched him for a moment before her gaze moved to the sheets. She smoothed an invisible wrinkle as she spoke. "Don't get too attached, okay?"

Her words hit him like a two-by-four. She'd just used the same line on him that he'd used over and over again with women who'd come and gone in his life. Hearing it from Meg practically knocked the breath from his lungs.

He cleared his throat, so he could lie more easily. "Not a problem, darlin'. The sex is amazing, but I'm clear on no commitment." At least, he used to be before her. Why did this promise feel like acid in his gut?

Apparently satisfied, she slid from the bed, her dark hair falling in waves down her back. "When is your birthday?"

"Late October. Why?"

His attention devoured every curve of her body, lingering on the tanned, curvy hips gracing that sweet, sculpted ass.

She turned, recognized the appreciation in his look and grinned. "Your tattoo. Did you also know that most Native American shamans are born under the sign of the snake?"

Unable to believe that this exquisite woman who had just spent the entire waking night making love with him now expected him not to fall for her, he blew out another breath. "And?"

"Late October to mid-November is the sign of the snake. You're more Judumi than you think." She padded naked toward the bathroom. "I'm taking a shower. Care to join me?"

THE RIPLEYS HAD been gone a week already. After five days of hanging out by the pool, using the spa facilities and meeting just about anyone worth meeting, Meg and Tico hadn't uncovered any other leads at the Quarry.

Eric had agreed that it was okay for them to discreetly attend a team meeting this morning. They'd returned to their respective dwellings at Rio Plata

Ranch last night and arrived separately at the station. This would be their first time with the team since becoming lovers. Meg felt as if she was putting on the performance of a lifetime. So far so good.

Meg and Tico had walked in, talking business. Tico chose a seat by Eric Longwood, and Meg filled a cup of coffee before taking the chair between Bill and Jose. No sign of Mitchell yet.

Meg wanted to laugh. Outwardly feigning disinterest toward Tico was easy, but inside? She fought the urge to watch his every move. In one week this New York ex–gang leader had awakened a passion greater than she'd ever known. She hadn't been kidding when she told Tico she couldn't keep her hands off him.

Without even looking, Meg was aware of his posture as he sat there in deep conversation with Eric, the strength of his hands palms-down on the table, his straight black hair falling down the back of his denim jacket. Meg's senses were on full alert. She felt like a wolf on the prowl. She'd never been in love, but if this was what love felt like, she was falling hard. And fast. And she didn't like the overwhelming rush of emotion one bit.

She sipped her coffee, reminding herself that she'd dedicated her days to law enforcement. In her line of work, being emotionally attached to someone posed danger of the highest order. Plain and simple. Never mind her feelings, she had to think about their safety, and the safety of the team should anyone find out. Emotional ties were an easy target for their enemies, especially powerful ones like the Mexican cartel. Their primary objective was to locate and recover the abducted women. Mooning over Tico wasn't helping her or the lost women in the least.

She looked around the table. Surely the team could feel the emotional tether binding her to her lover, but no one seemed to notice. And even though Tico hadn't looked at her once, Meg knew damn well that he was as aware of her as she was of him.

They had agreed before the meeting that Tico would fill Eric in on their latest suspicion. While Tico quietly spoke to their chief, Meg glanced at her team. Jose looked tired. She turned her attention on him.

"Jose? Any sign of the baby?"

He shook his head. "Not yet, Meg, but Julia isn't sleeping well. Not good when she'll need all her strength for delivery. Not to mention caring for a newborn when the time comes."

"You let me know if there's anything I can do." She patted his arm, feeling his anxiety. "You two will be fine."

Before Jose could answer, Mitchell Blake burst through the open door, carrying an eight-by-ten photo. "Sorry I'm late. Received this image and had to show you our tax dollars hard at work."

He tossed the photo on the table. Meg practically choked. Bill and Jose looked at Meg, eyes wide.

Bill, as straight-faced as possible while laughter tugged at his mouth, asked, "So. How'd the stake-out at the pool party go on Sunday?"

Meg grabbed for the photo, but Tico reached it first. There, in all his bare-assed glory, stood Tico with his bathing trunks down at the perfect angle from the back to show Meg, with her sunglasses on, hands gripping his lowered trunks and laughing up at him.

"Gotta love today's technology," Mitchell said, chuckling. "Cell phones. Internet fan sites. I hope the mayor doesn't get wind of this one."

Meg narrowed her eyes at Mitchell. No doubt, he'd already emailed the snapshot to her father.

Tico tossed the photo back on the table with disregard. "After Meg's little prank at my expense, I can guarantee you that not a single person at the Ripleys' has any doubt about us. If the mayor has a problem, he can talk to me. I was the naked one." He thumbed his chest. "If anyone should object, it's me, and I don't. I thought your team leader acted with finesse."

Bill hooted.

Meg's face heated with a blush. Damn it all!

Eric shook his head. "Did you two have to be *so effective?*"

Meg sighed, truly embarrassed. "My fault, Chief. I couldn't walk away from a perfect opportunity to treat our new team member in the manner he deserves."

The guys roared with laughter.

Not the chief. "Okay, let's not give this photo too much attention, and if we're lucky, it'll go away." He pushed the picture toward Meg with a finger. "Make this disappear. I never want to see it again."

Meg slid the photo into her folder. "Yes, sir." If she had her way, she'd frame the shot and hang the photo by her front door.

Eric continued, "Listen up, everyone. Aside from the circus show, Tico and Meg have stumbled on something that doesn't sit well with me." Eric looked pointedly at Mitchell. "You're not going to like the news, Blake."

Mitchell sat back in his chair. "What are you talking about?"

Eric indicated to Tico. "Care to inform everyone?"

When Mitchell looked concerned, Meg wanted to feel sympathy for her old mentor, but after this photo stunt, she was glad he was about to look stupid for being the department representative to a drug dealer and not knowing it. This news would kill his credibility as a consultant. She almost wished Tico would delay the information to make Blake squirm more.

Tico cleared his throat. "As you can imagine, our young rock star and his wife are drug abusers. Cocaine and marijuana. Katrina was doing coke with her friends and commented that her 'handsome spa manager' supplied her with the best drugs." Tico looked at Blake. "The only spa manager at the Quarry is your contact, Enrique Comodin."

Mitchell slapped the table. "No shit? The little bastard."

Meg added, "And he was our contact for our cover at the spa. Not good."

"Was he at the pool party?" Bill asked.

Meg shook her head. "No."

"Well, several of Melissa Collins's friends reported seeing Melissa talking with a man who fits Comodin's description," Bill said.

Tico frowned. "Didn't Katrina call Enrique after the confrontation to clear out her unwanted guests?"

"Yes," Bill said. "But witnesses placed Comodin at the party as one of Katrina's guests before the trouble started. He'd brought a bottle of expensive tequila and was doling out shots."

"Did your witnesses see Melissa drinking with him?"

Bill nodded. "Yes. According to her friends, Melissa was too drunk to drive. They confirmed that Katrina slapped her for sitting on Josh Ripley's lap. Again, witnesses confirmed that Ripley invited Melissa's attention, and Katrina discovered the flirting. Melissa left the group in tears. Thinking she'd gone to the bathroom, two girlfriends looked for her, but she'd already left."

"And Comodin?" Tico was frowning.

"At the time, he wasn't present. That's when Katrina called him on her cell phone to remove Melissa's friends."

"He was on the premises?" Mitchell asked.

Bill shrugged. "He had to be if he showed up so fast. Maybe inside the house? Ripley and the trouble crowd were at the bar over the pool."

Tico sighed. "So, now we know Comodin deals drugs. The question I want answered is if he's tied to the cartel, or just a two-bit punk supplying his rich clientele at whim."

"Looks like Enrique needs babysitting," Bill said.

Eric nodded. "I think that's a good idea. I want a court order to tap and ping his phone. Let's find out who he contacts and where he goes."

Mitchell headed for the coffeepot. "You know, I'd like to be the one watching this clown. He's played me for a fool and I don't like it."

Eric looked at Mitchell long and hard. "Damn straight, Mitchell. I'll get the paperwork for you. I want this lead brought to a close as fast as possible."

Meg sensed Tico watching her. She looked at him. He frowned. With that one look she understood what wasn't sitting right with this scenario. While any of them would have been willing to tail Enrique, and Mitchell was best suited to be the tail, something in his tone raised a red flag. He sounded angry at being duped, but the undertone was desperate. They were relying on instinct here, but sometimes that's all they needed. Katrina had already told them about Enrique saving her from illegal tight spots. Mitchell could very well want to track Enrique to cover his own ass in helping him with those tight spots. The next question they needed to ask was if Mitchell was willing to bend the law, had he known about the drug dealing, as well?

And if he had, could he be involved in more? And were she and Tico jumping to conclusions because they had no other leads?

Meg's blood ran cold. The man was innocent until proven guilty. They'd simply have to pay closer attention to detail. She glanced at Bill. He was watching her. From years of working together, Meg knew Bill wanted to share her thoughts. She'd get Bill and Tico together for lunch and hash over this new possibility. Given his wife's near-term pregnancy, she wouldn't involve Jose unless they really needed him.

Eric pointed at her. "What happens now at the Quarry?"

"The Ripleys are gone. We can go back if you want and nose around to see what Enrique does."

Her phone rang. She glanced at the caller ID, and her stomach churned. "Oh, great. My father." She looked at Mitchell, who turned his back to the group to fix his coffee. "I wonder if he just happened to get a copy of that photo."

Mitchell ignored her and stirred sugar into his coffee.

Eric shook his head. "Maybe you'll be leaving the Quarry sooner than you thought."

MEG LED TICO and Bill into the cantina on the edge of town. They had a lot to talk about and needed privacy. After the disciplinary phone call from the mayor about the photo, Tico and Meg had left the meeting poised for battle with Mitchell Blake. He'd been after Meg's hide ever since she'd taken his position, which made no sense since he had chosen to retire.

The same Mexican woman with the white peasant top and flowery skirt who'd served Meg and Tico several days ago led them to a table under the window. Much to Meg's amusement, the woman smiled broadly at Tico, then at Bill.

Meg took a seat. "So, why is Mitchell gunning for me?"

Tico sat next to Bill, so both men would face Meg. "I have my suspicions."

"Like?"

Bill interrupted. "Wait, let me take a guess. Mitchell has some kind of link to what's happening at the Quarry and wants to discredit you from the investigation. Or worse yet, keep you from finding facts."

Tico agreed. "Again, it's only suspicion, but throwing the photo on the table for a joke with the team is one thing, but sending it to Don Francisco?" Tico shook his head. "Deliberate sabotage."

"What now?" Bill asked.

Meg scanned the menu. "Eric yanking us from the Quarry to placate my father wasn't so bad since the Ripleys left. We can work from home on the leads we have, but damn Mitchell Blake for sending Dad that photo."

"If Comodin and Blake are working together, our cover was blown before we got there," Tico said. "They were playing us for fools."

"Maybe, but they were keeping an eye on your progress to cover their tracks," Bill said. "If, in fact, they're actually involved. Then again, unless Josh and Katrina Ripley were pretending, they had no idea who you were."

Meg shook her head. "I don't think they knew. Katrina wouldn't have pulled out her drugs if she did."

Bill tapped the table. "Why would Enrique have introduced you to them so easily if he knew you might find out he's a drug dealer?"

"Maybe he had no choice. Or, better yet, *Mitchell* had no choice because the investigation headed in that direction."

"And maybe he's cooperating because if he becomes an informant on the cartel, he could avoid jail time."

"And very possibly end up dead," Meg added. "The cartel doesn't take lightly to traitors."

"Mitchell may have helped get us into the Quarry quickly, but he also had us removed just as quickly with that photo. Maybe Enrique thought Katrina would have been more discreet, and he and Mitchell panicked when they found out she'd talked," Tico said. "More reason to think we're onto something here."

Bill said, "Enrique's mother will be devastated when she learns her son is rotten."

Meg smiled sadly at her friend. "I said the same."

"What if we're wrong?" Tico said.

"You mean about Mitchell? Maybe. We don't have enough evidence to nail him. But Enrique has been identified as a drug dealer," Bill said.

Meg put down the menu. "After Mitchell's stunt this morning, I'm hoping he's guilty. I'd like to kick his butt from here to jail."

Bill sat back in his chair. "You know, if Mitchell is working for the cartel, that would explain why none of our stings produced anything. He warned our targets before we arrived."

"That would explain all the dead ends to our leads, too," Meg said. She snapped her fingers. "And why he retired but signed back on as a consultant. He made it look like he was just enhancing his retirement pay, but maybe he came back on board to stay informed."

"Do we go to Eric with our hunch?" Bill asked.

Tico frowned. "Not yet. Let's not make waves until we can produce a tsunami to wash that creep right off the map."

"Agreed." Meg appreciated Tico's willingness to support her. She looked at her watch. "Changing the subject, I wonder how Jose and Julia are doing."

Bill laughed. "Did you see his face when Julia called and said she was having the baby?" Jose had received the call just as the meeting was breaking up.

Tico chuckled. "Ran out of there like his pants were on fire!"

Laughing, Bill checked out the menu. "So, what's good here?"

"The *chile relleños* are great." Meg and Tico smirked. They'd answered together.

TICO HAD PARTED company with Meg and Bill and just arrived at his cabin when his phone rang. "Butler here."

"Tico. Bill Mewith."

"What's up, Bill? Miss me already?"

"Very funny. What are you doing in twenty minutes?"

"I planned to go over files. Otherwise, nothing."

"Ride over to the reservation. Remember those plans I wanted to make with you? I think it's time."

Tico opened the door into his cabin. He liked the raw wood planks on the walls and floor. The Spartan furnishings. The colorful blanket on the wrought-iron bed. He shook his head. "Sorry, Bill. I won't come to the reservation. Nothing personal."

Bill was silent for a moment. "Do you know where the reservation meets Rio Plata Ranch?"

"Yes."

"Meet me there."

Curiosity goaded Tico more than anything. He poured himself a glass of water from the fridge. "Okay. Twenty minutes."

Fifteen minutes later, Tico slowed his Harley as he approached the meeting place. He parked the bike. Bill was nowhere in sight.

This point where the boundaries of the properties met was like a nowhere land all the way to the distant mountain range. He couldn't see any buildings on the reservation. Nor was the ranch visible from this low area along what Tico had learned was an arroyo, which was nothing more than a dry riverbed that flooded occasionally from rain in the mountains.

He kicked a few rocks with the tip of his boot. Watched a lizard scamper into underbrush and crouched down by a low beavertail cactus to inspect its thick skin and curved, spiny needles. Prickly, indeed. He stood when he heard the timbre of horses' hooves, rising from a vibration beneath his feet to the thundering noise of approach. From the sound, more than one horse headed his way.

He left the arroyo and stepped closer to his bike. Within seconds, Bill rose up over a low hill on the reservation side. He was bareback on a horse and led another one by the bridle running beside him. Tico watched, amazed at how naturally the man and horses moved together.

They came to a stop a few feet away. Dust swirled around the horses' feet. The horses' scents filled Tico's nostrils. He breathed deep. He'd always loved the earthy smell of horses.

Bill laughed. "You should see your face."

"Your arrival was very impressive."

Bill slid off his mount. "Good." He wore moccasin boots instead of sturdy cowboy ones. He handed Tico the bridle of the free horse. "This is Baron. I'm going to teach you to ride bareback."

"What?"

"For your best interest, I believe time has come for you to learn how to ride a horse. Properly."

"Why?"

Surprise filled the Judumi's eyes. "Are you kidding me? Do you know what you looked like when you rode into town?"

Tico grinned. "I *wanted* to look like a fool."

"You did, brother. I can promise you. But if you want to keep the attention of your new partner, I suggest you change that image as fast as you can."

"For my partner?"

Bill gave him a hard look. "Okay, let's view the scenario this way. Since the investigation has slowed and you're stuck in Adobe Creek for a while, I figured it's time you learn how a Judumi warrior rides."

# CHAPTER FOURTEEN

MEG TURNED HER pickup into the long drive to Rio Plata Ranch, country music blaring on the radio. Dove and Penny sat elbow to elbow on the bench seat alongside her, singing to the latest man-done-me-wrong song. They'd been to Jose and Julia's to see the baby for a second time now that the new parents were down to a routine.

Jose, Jr. had been born four weeks ago and was doing fine. For most of the ride back, Pen and Dove had been pumping Meg for information about Tico. Her close friends were right to suspect she and Tico were carrying on, because they were.

Meg's world moved from one swirling minute to another, waiting for a chance to be alone with Tico while they followed dead-end lead after dead-end lead on a case that was running out of time. After several weeks, the team had to concede that the women were no longer in the area. That grim fact didn't stop them all from posting missing-persons notices throughout the country and into Mexico, investigating each and every clue. But with all leads going cold, it was more and more difficult to stay optimistic with the families of the missing women.

Taking a day off to spend with friends was an excellent antidote to work. It took strength to carry on a normal life with the grim sadness that surrounded them. These past weeks had been a mixture of frustration from the unsolved case and amazing stolen moments with Tico. But, for everyone's sake, Meg and Tico worked hard to keep their trysts under wraps. Meg wasn't about to give up her secret now. Thank goodness the girls' favorite song had come on to distract them from prodding her further.

She'd love nothing more than to share her excitement over being Tico's lover. She had dark smudges under her eyes from working overtime on the abductions, but she didn't regret the sleep she lost with Tico. Enrique was under surveillance since suspicion had been raised about his possible drug dealing, but, so far, there were no grounds for arrest. If he was selling drugs, he was stealthy. There wasn't a trace to be found other than Katrina's poolside slipup. Meanwhile, Meg and Tico met at his cabin in the wee hours almost every night when the rest of the ranch slept.

The first night there, Tico had whispered, *We can sleep when we die, Meg.* And to this day, four weeks later, she couldn't agree more. Meg didn't want to miss a single moment of his company. And he seemed to be just as enthusiastic about keeping hers.

The song ended. Not missing a beat, Pen nudged

her friend. "So, come on, Meg. Tell the truth. You've gone soft on Tico."

Rolling her eyes in frustration, she said, "Why do you say that? We're *working* together."

Pen gave her a knowing look. "I haven't heard one obscenity attached to his name since you came home from the Quarry." She grinned at Dove. "Right, Dove? Tell her."

"Tell me what?"

Dove ducked her head. "Bill seems to think you two…um…work very well together."

Meg laughed. "So?"

"Oh, never mind. You don't have to tell us if you don't want to."

"There's nothing to tell!"

Dove and Penny exchanged glances. "Riiight."

Pen added, "I'm sure Whisper gets all those midnight runs because she's restless."

Meg almost choked. She could have sworn Pen had been sleeping the nights she snuck away. "No. *I'm* restless. Whisper always welcomes a run."

Up ahead a small dust cloud rose along the road inside the Rio Plata fence. Meg pushed her sunglasses onto the bridge of her nose. "Who's that?"

Dove focused on the sight. "Looks like a rider."

"And he's riding fast," Pen added.

"It's not one of my parents. They're in town."

As they drove closer, Meg gasped. She'd recognize that black hair anywhere. "Oh, my God. It's Tico!"

"I thought he didn't know how to ride," Pen said.

"He doesn't...didn't."

Meg slowed the truck as Tico approached. He was riding a horse Meg didn't recognize, and they were tearing up the desert. Leaning close to the horse, Tico's form was perfect. Meg jammed on the brakes. He was bareback! And shirtless. And wearing moccasin boots over his jeans!

His hair flying behind him, his hands lightly gripping the horse's mane, Tico glanced their way, grinned and kept riding.

"He's riding like a Judumi!" Meg said, her voice in awe.

Dove grinned. "Bill's been taking him out. That's his brother's horse."

Meg looked at her friend, stunned. "You knew and you didn't tell me?"

Dove looked ahead, all innocence. "Well, if you're not involved with him, why would it matter?"

Meg wagged a finger at her friend. "Oh, you're good. But not that good. I have nothing to say." Yet she turned to watch Tico ride away through the rear window.

Dove let out a sigh. "Okay. Well, I have something to say."

Meg looked at her. "Is everything okay?"

A small grin tugged at her lips. She dipped into her purse and pulled out a package. Meg's eyes grew wide.

"Is that what I think it is?"

Dove smiled. "A pregnancy test."

"Are you pregnant?"

"I'm not sure."

"Well?" Pen grew impatient. "Why haven't you checked?"

"Please. With Bill's mother living with us? She's very helpful, but sticks her nose into everything. If I do this test at my house, she'll know and she'll tell Bill before I can." She frowned. "She means well, but I want to be the one to tell my husband whether or not he's going to be a father."

Meg pulled the truck back onto the road. "We'll be at my place in five minutes. Care to check there?"

Dove placed the package back into her purse. "I thought you'd never ask."

The women laughed. Pen wrapped an arm around Dove. "God, I love my friends."

Meg reached over and kissed Dove on the cheek. "Me, too. Don't know what I'd do without you two."

She drove on, the image of Tico stuck in her mind, making her pulse race faster. Oh, he had a lot of explaining to do.

TWENTY MINUTES LATER, Meg and Penny sat on Meg's bed while Dove occupied herself in the bathroom. Pen sprawled on her back, arms over her head, and sighed. "Someday that will be me in there."

"You want kids that badly?"

"Come on, Meg. Don't we all?"

"Oh, no. We've had this conversation before." Meg lowered her voice. "You two can do whatever you want. I'll be happy for you, have your baby showers, but I'm not playing in that sandbox."

"That's okay with me, Meg." Pen gave her a sly look. "But maybe if you were in love you'd feel differently."

The image of Tico bareback on the horse rose in her mind, one more time. Would she ever want to have his baby? Would she be okay with a little Tico tugging at her hem? She pushed the thought out of her mind as if pushing a boulder over a cliff. She didn't even want to consider the option.

"Being in love has nothing to do with wanting kids. I'm just not the mothering kind, Pen. I'm sorry you don't like the idea, but it's true."

Dove came out of the bathroom. "I have to let the tester sit for a few minutes." She sat on the bed between the women. "I heard what you said, Meg."

Meg laid a hand on her friend's arm. "My choice doesn't mean I'm not happy for you. I think the fact that you might be having a baby is wonderful. You and Bill will be amazing parents." She shrugged. "Motherhood just isn't for me."

Dove smoothed her skirt over her knees. "Your career takes up so much of your life, I'd be amazed if you even had time to get pregnant."

Meg laughed. "I do prefer to work. Much easier than raising children."

Pen sat up. "Want do you want? A boy or a girl?"

Dove chewed her lower lip. "A girl would be so much fun, but when Bill and I talk about children, he always talks about a son."

Pen rolled her eyes. "Men and their egos."

Dove shrugged. "A boy would be nice. He could be the big brother for the next child—maybe a sister."

Meg slapped her forehead. "You're already thinking about two? Heaven help you!"

Dove looked surprised. "Who said I was stopping at two?"

Pen's phone rang. She checked the caller ID. "Oh! I was hoping he'd call."

"Who?" Dove asked.

"Anthony. We've dated twice." She punched the button. "Hello?"

Meg watched her friend chat up her latest conquest and make a date for that night. When Pen hung up, Meg laughed. "You're not making him work too hard if you accept a date with four hours' notice."

"He's worth being spontaneous for."

"How did you meet him?"

"At the spa. He has joint ownership of one of the haciendas." She looked sheepish. "I'm breaking the rules. If Enrique finds out, I could lose my job."

"He's worth that, too?"

Pen shrugged. "Right now he is. Besides, Enrique's so busy these days, he has me running the place. I don't think he'd let me go."

Dove returned to the bathroom. The silence between the women stretched out. Meg thought over Pen's information about Enrique. She'd share this tidbit with Tico when she saw him.

Dove came back, her hand to her throat.

"Dove?"

She held out the tester. "I have to go home. I'm going to be a momma!"

Meg jumped up and down on her bed. "Oh! How wonderful!" She jumped off, joining Pen in hugging Dove. Poignant moments like these with her friends were what made life precious. "When are you going to tell Bill?"

She gave the women a shy look. "I think I'll tell him tonight while making love."

Penny laughed. "Perfect! Ruin the moment."

"No! We've been trying to have a baby for months. He'll be thrilled."

"Sounds very romantic," Meg said.

Penny swung an arm around Meg's waist. "So, Dove is going to get lucky tonight. I'm going to get lucky tonight. How about you, Meg?"

Not again with the probing. "Me? Oh, a nice soak in the tub. A glass of wine. A good book. Best date ever."

Pen headed for her room. "Well, I'm not planning to come home tonight, so be sure to lock yourself in. There's a dangerous city slicker lurking out there on the ranch."

MEG TEXTED PENNY around midnight to make sure she wasn't returning until morning. When Pen responded, too busy to come home, and signed with half a dozen red hearts, Meg texted Tico, confirming it was safe for him to come over.

When she heard him approaching the house on horseback, her pulse quickened. She sauntered out the bedroom door onto the veranda and watched him ride up. The full moon made him look ethereal in the silvery light. A Judumi on horseback had an exotic appeal. The tribe was so in tune with the elements that it seemed as if the earth responded to their every breath. She could feel Tico's passion all the way from where she stood. Did he know how much he looked like his people? Meg unconsciously smoothed her form-hugging sheath along her belly in anticipation. Her New York nemesis was rapidly becoming her Judumi dream-come-true.

She slipped her sandals on outside her door. Bruno came with her, sniffed the air, then decided to head back inside to his little cushion without even barking. Even Bruno didn't mind that Tico had arrived. Grinning, Meg met her lover at the split rail fence. The desert air curled around them, mingling with the earthy scent of the horse. Tico hadn't ridden far, but he'd ridden fast. The horse followed easily when Tico led her by the bridle with one hand and captured Meg's waist with the other.

His gaze roamed over Meg in the sheer black sheath. His obvious appreciation of her body sent a flutter through her core.

A dangerous grin tugged at his mouth. "You're going to walk me to the stable half naked?"

He wore jeans and his moccasin boots. An unbuttoned faded denim shirt lay open against his tanned chest, making her fingers itch to touch him.

"I have something to say that can't wait."

His gaze traveled from her mouth to where her hair rested on her breasts. His grin widened. "Nice."

Ignoring him, she gestured to the horse. "How? When?"

His hand moved to her shoulder. He toyed with her hair as they walked. "You mean riding?"

"Bareback, no less. Why didn't you tell me?"

"Do you like it?"

A tingle ran through her. "Oh, yeah. You have no idea how hot you looked riding this afternoon.'

He cupped the back of her neck with his hand, drawing her mouth to his. "Bill has been teaching me. I learned for you."

She pulled back to see him better in the moonlight. "Why?"

"Because we have a deal."

She pushed the stable door open. Whisper whinnied when the Appaloosa entered with them. The horses had been raised together. They'd enjoy each other's company.

Meg turned on a dim light by the door. "We do?"

"Remember? If I learn to ride a horse, you'll ride with me on my Harley. I can't wait to take you up the Pacific coast."

Tico led his horse into the stall next to Whisper. Meg watched, amazed at how easily Tico handled the animal. "Do you like horses now?"

He shrugged. "Never disliked them until I met Diablo."

The horse nudged him with her nose. When he pulled a sugar cube from his pocket and fed it to her, Meg practically fell over in surprise.

Whisper reached over, nudging Tico. She wanted one, too. He pulled out another sugar cube. At Meg's silence, he looked at her. "What?"

"You're a natural with animals."

He grinned. "Yeah. How about that?"

She nestled underneath his arm once more. "How Judumi of you."

The muscles in his arm stiffened. "Did you have to say that?"

She laid a hand on his bare chest. "Is being Judumi so terrible?"

He slowly shook his head. "I'm starting to wonder. Bill is a nice guy."

"Most of the Judumi tribe is kind, honorable and

trusting." She laid her head on his shoulder. "You lived a bad experience."

A ceiling fan above their heads cooled the heated air stealing in from the open doors at the ends of the stable. Tico stared up at the turning blades for a long time. When he spoke, his hand tightened on her shoulder. "Sometimes, when my dad wasn't stoned out of his mind, he would tell me stories about living here. Like the few times he took me riding."

Meg kept still. She didn't want to distract Tico from his thoughts. He looked at her. "I was proud to be Judumi in those moments."

"I'm glad."

He blew out a breath. "I feel like I missed so much."

"The tribe is here. You can introduce yourself whenever you wish."

He led her toward the door. "Bill said the same."

"Okay. So you know."

Lacing his fingers with hers, they walked in silence toward Meg's bedroom door. "I still have so many prejudices."

She kissed his shoulder. The clean smell of laundry detergent clung to his shirt. "I hear time is the great healer."

He laughed, but said nothing.

"Why do you laugh?"

Pulling her to him, he pressed her against the

door to her bedroom. "If I remember correctly, I don't have much time. I'll be run out of town after this case is solved."

The heat of his bare chest against her flimsy cover sent a tremor right down to her toes. She tapped his chin. "Keep this up, and I'll tie you to my bed. You won't go anywhere."

He nuzzled her neck. "Sounds like far more fun." He started running his hands over her hips but stopped. He stepped back and held up his hands. "Horse. Where can I wash before manhandling you?"

She pointed to her bathroom. "Help yourself. Can I get you something to drink?"

"Water. A big glass. Get yourself one, too. We'll need to stay hydrated."

"Mmm. I'm beginning to think you coming over is a better idea than I thought."

He patted her behind. "I've been fantasizing about doing you in your bedroom." He looked around. "No frills. No lace. All woman without the fluff. Nice."

She crooked a finger for him to come closer. "I have a secret."

He raised a brow. "What's that?"

Pressing her lips to his, she whispered, "You are the first man to see my bedroom."

"No kidding?"

She pushed him toward the bathroom. "Go wash."

TICO HEADED FOR the bathroom thinking, *And I'll be the* only *man to see your bedroom, chica.* He stopped short. Whoa. Why so possessive?

He caught his reflection in the mirror and gawked. He'd never recognize the guy in the mirror as the same man who'd ridden out from New York City six weeks ago. A slave to his job, he'd seldom taken free time to start new friendships the way he had with Bill. The detective's instruction and their laughs over the bruises he'd earned falling while learning to ride bareback had carved out some great moments for Tico.

Now, his olive skin browned up from the sun, he wore his hair down far more than he ever did in New York. And, much to his astonishment, he liked his friendship with a goddamn Judumi.

Amazing how his world was changing. The more time he spent riding the horse, the more he wanted Meg on the back of his Harley. He felt free on his bike. He wanted to share the experience with her. Sort of a biker's version of the stories his father used to tell about riding ponies with pretty girls.

While teaching him to ride, Bill had questioned Tico about Meg, but Tico refused to fall for the questions. Bill was a good interrogator. If Tico hadn't understood the strategy, he would have been spilling his guts. Laughing, Tico had said, "Quit pretending you want to be my best friend, and tell me why you're asking all these questions."

Bill had grinned. "First, I *am* your friend. Second, I've known Meg my entire life."

"I know."

"I can tell when she likes someone. And she didn't like you when you arrived."

"And now she does?"

"You tell me."

Tico had stood face-to-face with his Judumi counterpart, looked him straight in the eye and said, "Ask me anything you want to know, but don't ask me about Meg."

Bill had taken the hint and proceeded to drill Tico about his past, his worldview, even wanted to know Tico's version of what had happened to his late partner. After Tico had satisfied all his questions, Bill had eased into the Meg arena once more. Instead of answering, Tico had turned the tables by asking Bill about his life, his marriage, his job. Then about Meg, but he'd kept the questions circumspect. His fascination with her had only escalated over these past weeks. They hadn't had one argument. They'd talked endlessly about everything—except the direction their relationship was going.

Tico loved the bond that was growing between them. He'd never known anything like it before. If he and Meg hadn't promised each other to keep their romance under wraps, he'd blab his feelings for her to Bill. He liked Bill that much. But he and Meg didn't have the luxury of taking their relationship public. Danger was no joke in their line of business.

Tico washed his hands, the aroma of lemon soap rising from the bubbles. So Meg. Drying his hands, he soaked in her style, liking the terra-cotta tiles on the floor, the fuzzy white area rugs, the matching wall tiles. The deep sunken tub big enough for two. Oh, yeah. They'd make use of that before the night was over.

He placed the hand towel on the rack, but it slipped off and fell to the floor next to the wastebasket. He bent to retrieve it—and stopped.

A home pregnancy test lay faceup in the empty container. From where he stood he could read the digital response as clear as day. *Pregnant.*

## *CHAPTER FIFTEEN*

MEG RETURNED WITH a pitcher of water and two glasses on a tray. Her silhouette against the background light revealed every curve of her body. Tico's body tightened in response. They had used condoms every time they'd made love. Those weren't foolproof, but they'd been careful. And since he'd been with her practically every waking hour, he was confident she wasn't seeing anyone else. How could she be pregnant?

And if she was? Tico leaned up against the sink, heart starting to do a double thump against his chest. Okay. If she *was* pregnant? He had to know how he felt about this before talking to Meg.

Being a father had never been an option in the past. The women he'd dated weren't mother material. He'd chosen unattachable women on purpose. Nothing permanent had ever seemed possible for him. Not until Meg had he even considered the possibility.

Could he commit to this woman? Support her? Stay in Adobe Creek? He watched her pour water into glasses. Yeah. He could handle a steady dose

of Meg Flores. Could he raise a kid? Nurture a
child when he'd never been nurtured himself? In
their line of work, the reality of safety would be
a huge issue. With Meg as his child's mother, he
suddenly realized he'd give the responsibility every
ounce of energy and protection he possessed.

Holy shit. The truth floored him. He ran a hand
over his face. So, he'd be willing to go the distance
and be the father of Meg's baby. But was Meg willing? He was jumping the gun. He needed to know
what was going on. Only one way to find out.

He returned to the bedroom, pulled her into his
arms. "I like the idea, Meg. Never thought I would,
but with you…I know we can make it work."

She leaned back, confusion creasing her brow.
"What are you talking about?"

He took her hand, led her to the bathroom.

"What, Tico?"

He pointed to the trash basket. "Is there something you want to tell me?"

Meg looked into the basket. Looked again. Then
burst out laughing.

An uncomfortable mixture of relief and confusion had Tico frowning. He felt strangely insulted.
He released her hand. "You're laughing?"

"That pregnancy test belongs to Dove Mewith."

"What is Dove's pregnancy test doing in your
bathroom?" His voice went up a notch, betraying
his stress.

"She needed privacy from her mother-in-law."

Meg's eyes grew wide. "Oh, that must have been an awful moment for you, thinking I was pregnant. I'm so sorry!"

His hands fell to his sides. He didn't want to admit that the discovery had had the opposite effect. For him, it had been the revelation of a lifetime, but for Meg the possibility was awful. It was a serious blow to his pride. Now he wanted to know what she thought of a future for them. They had yet to have this discussion, and he didn't like the amusement in her eyes.

"So, tell me. What if you were pregnant?"

She folded her arms across her chest, sobering. "Don't worry. I'd never let it happen."

"Why not?"

"Marriage? Kids? Not for me."

"Ever?"

"Would you want that?"

How could he tell her that the idea of her carrying his baby had stirred him like never before? He shook his head. "Never really considered it." He leaned against the sink and crossed his arms, mirroring her stance. "Until this very moment. The thought of having a family with you struck a chord I never knew existed. I like the idea. I'm almost disappointed you're not pregnant."

Meg took a step back. "You're kidding."

He frowned again. "Is that so bad?"

"This isn't personal, but please, understand, Tico. I'm never. Getting. Pregnant."

At the determined look in her eyes, he whistled softly. "Wow. That's harsh."

She shrugged. "If you don't like it, we're probably done."

Just like that? He got a windfall insight into his deep-seated desires, expressed them, and because Meg didn't like them, she tossed an ultimatum? Up to this very moment their romance had been exciting, provocative and so damned easy. One comment about a possible future together and they were done?

He couldn't keep the shock from his voice. "So, what's been going on here between us for all these weeks?"

Meg stared at him. Her mouth opened. Closed. She said nothing.

"What, Meg? Just enjoying a little fling with the clown from the big city?"

Palms up, she left the bathroom. "I don't know what *this* is between us, Tico, but I know marriage and children have nothing to do with it."

He didn't move. Meg had logic on her side. He'd never wanted marriage or kids, either. Meg was expressing the exact feelings he'd had for years, yet her negative reaction tied his stomach in knots.

He found her sitting in the dark on a chaise longue by the pool. He sat in the chair next to hers. "Most couples have this conversation a little more amicably."

"Tico…"

"What, Meg?"

"My feelings for you happened so fast. Run so deep."

"That's good. Makes me feel a little better."

She sat up. "I'm not mother material. Kids. Diapers. Schools. Staying tied to a house. My skin itches thinking about it. I want to catch bad guys. Go to shooting ranges. Not worry about someone I love getting hurt because of me."

"What about Bill? Jose? They're willing to take the chance."

She swung around to face him, planting her feet on the ground, looking wild and sexy and innocent seated there in that sheer black gown with her hair tumbling around her shoulders and angst creasing her brow. "They didn't grow up with a father reciting the horror of losing loved ones, or the dangers of not being able to defend oneself. I'm better off exactly as I am."

Tico felt as though his heart was being squeezed in his chest. "I know those feelings. Believed them, too, right up until…"

She looked devastated. "The pregnancy test."

He nodded. "Yeah. Something inside me shifted when I imagined us having a baby. All of a sudden I knew I wanted that more than anything."

Her voice grew soft. "You are so different from the man I expected you to be."

"Yeah, well. Something's happening to me." He reached for her and gently guided her into his lap.

"And if I'm thinking about having a family with you, then I need to know where I stand."

She closed her eyes. "Tico." Her voice sounded pained.

"Are you going to break up with me?"

She looked at him, and he saw the answer in her eyes. "I told you not to get too attached."

"I don't understand, Meg. One minute you tell me you have feelings for me like you've never known, and the next, you tell me to back off."

She wrapped her arms around his neck. "We have something exciting here, but look at the way we're hiding. How can we build anything real and lasting when we don't even want anyone to know about us?"

"Wait. That doesn't have to be forever. Didn't we decide it was better to keep our attachment under wraps until this assignment is closed?"

"Yes."

"Then what is it? Your father?"

She laughed. "Oh, no. My father has no say over my personal life."

"Well, then what about Penny? Bill? Dove? I, for one, get the impression that your friends like the idea and would keep our secret."

"They're your friends now, too."

He shook his head. "That would be nice to think, but truth is I have no place here."

He grew silent. Holy shit. That was it. How could he have been so stupid? He'd been right at the beginning. She was having a fling with the bad boy from the big city. Nothing serious. Nothing she'd want to bring home to Mom and Dad.

"Tico?"

He let his hurt show in his face. "What an ass I've been. I understand now."

She looked confused. "Understand what?"

"When the job is done, I'm gone. You'll be finished. You're surprised you've grown fond of me, but I'm still not enough. You really have nothing more to offer." He unwound her arms from his neck and stood.

"That's not true!"

"No? If I stayed in Adobe Creek, you'd what? Eventually let me move in, but no marriage? You'd call the shots, and I'd have no say?"

When she didn't answer, he shook his head. "I see why you told me not to get too attached." He started to walk away, then turned. "Just for the record, Detective. You are the closest I've come to falling in love since Jackie." He looked away because he didn't want to see pity rise in her eyes. When he looked at her again, he didn't bother to hide his anger. "No. I'm wrong. I don't think I even felt for Jackie what I feel for you. Thanks for stopping me before I made a complete fool of myself."

"Tico!"

He held up his hands to halt her. "No. I should be grateful. You awakened something in me I never thought existed. Now I know I want a family, Meg.

A wife. Kids. Maybe I'll even retire from this rat race someday and do something good for me. My family. Can you say the same?"

She didn't speak. Just stared at him, her eyes pleading.

"Well?"

Finally, she shook her head. "No. I can't."

"Yeah. That's what I thought. I'll see myself out."

MEG STOOD IN the dark, listening to Tico ride away, his anger pounding in the horse's hoofbeats. After a few moments she could see him in the moonlight as he followed the shores of the lake. He rode low on the horse, his hair flying behind him. So Judumi. She watched until he disappeared around the trees by the cabins.

She blinked away tears. Her chest heaved with unreleased pressure. She wanted to scream into the night. *What the hell happened?* Just once she'd like to say, *I don't want to get married. I don't want to have kids,* and hear, *That's fine, Meg.* Why did everyone she love want to change her mind?

Tico had misunderstood her silence. Inside, she'd been battling her own emotions, wanting to give herself completely to this man—for the first time in her life—yet also struggling with the fears and opinions that had brought her to this point. He couldn't just hit her with his question and expect an immediate answer. She needed time to think. Instead, he'd pulled her, and she'd pushed him. Away. Better safe than sorry.

Then why did she feel so devastated?

She wrapped her arms around herself, regretting Tico's absence. The night air seemed cooler without him. She'd become used to their day-in, day-out interactions. Why did he have to ruin everything by putting her on the spot?

How would she handle seeing him at the next team meeting? She had to laugh at her own question. It would be no different from every other meeting. They'd been playing it cool since becoming lovers. She wouldn't have to change a thing.

A wave of exhaustion overcame her. Her brain felt numb. She didn't want to think anymore tonight. She retraced her steps into the bedroom, secured the door and climbed into bed. She lay there, her body still hungry for Tico, even though she'd driven him away. She pulled a pillow across her face to block out the hurt, knowing a sleepless night lay ahead.

BAD DREAMS AND coyote calls in the foothills made for fitful sleeping. Despite her distress, Meg finally fell asleep around dawn and would still have been sleeping now if Eric Longwood hadn't called to gather the team at the office. There'd been a new development in the case, and he wanted them all assembled by ten.

She was fixing her second cup of coffee when

Penny burst through the front door. Bruno had been sullen all morning since Penny hadn't come home, and now he danced around her feet until she scooped him up. "Bruno, my sweet puppy." She gushed and cooed all over him, kissing him between the ears and letting him lick her face.

"Morning, sunshine! I'm late for work." Penny kissed her on the cheek.

Meg wiped her cheek. "Ugh. You have dog slobber on you."

Penny put Bruno on the floor and topped off the food dish that Meg had already filled.

Penny reached for a travel mug and slid it across the counter, where Meg was stirring cream into her coffee. "Can you pour me one of those? I have to hurry."

"Sure."

Penny looked back at Meg as she headed for her room. "You don't look so good. Bad night?"

Meg waved away her concern. "Didn't sleep well."

Pen laughed. "I didn't sleep much, either!"

Within fifteen minutes, Penny appeared again, dressed in her usual camisole and peasant skirt. A chunky turquoise necklace adorned her neck. "I hate working Saturdays, but I get my best tips. Besides, Enrique is giving me hands-on manager training at noon."

Meg handed her the travel mug. "I have a team

meeting this morning, too. Let's have dinner later? I want to hear all about your date and your job."

Meg wanted desperately to ask Penny to keep her eyes open for any suspicious behavior at the spa but didn't want her actively involved in anything dangerous. Besides, Penny was a smart woman. If she saw something fishy, she'd let Meg know.

"Great idea." Pen scooped Bruno up one more time and kissed him on the head before she headed for the door. "I get off work around six. Call me later!"

Meg carried her coffee mug around while she collected her stuff after Penny departed. She felt empty inside. Keeping her relationship with Tico a secret had seemed a good idea, but now she also couldn't share her misery with anyone. Time to go.

For the first time in her career, she didn't feel that familiar excitement about the job. Yes, a fresh development was positive news. But discussing it with Tico sitting an arm's length away? Watching him talk? Knowing she'd never feel his touch again? She drained her mug and headed for her truck.

Sheer torture.

Damn. *Was she in love?*

Heading down the drive she passed her parents' house. Her father stood outside talking to Tico, who straddled his motorcycle. They seemed to be having a serious discussion. Both looked up as she drove by. Her father waved, then frowned as she kept going. Under normal circumstances, she would have stopped to say good morning, but she wasn't ready to face Tico. Especially not in front of her father. She'd rather face her ex-boyfriend with the team around her. She'd already gotten used to that drill. Damn. She was a real-life chickenshit.

TICO ENTERED THE meeting as Eric was explaining that Mitchell would be late coming back from the spa. Eric had been waiting at the head of the table when Meg arrived. Bill and Jose came in together behind Tico.

Meg glanced at Bill, wondering if Dove had broken the news. His grin said it all. She smiled back at him from across the table. When she glanced at Tico, he looked away. She understood. He'd read their nonverbal exchange and could have responded, yet chose not to. He'd already removed himself from their circle.

Eric started the meeting. "The feds busted another drug train last night. Heroin and cocaine."

"Where?" Bill asked.

"Just inside the border. Four big-wheeled pickup trucks. They were headed toward Adobe Creek."

"Again," Bill said. "Not good. That means the traffickers are still hanging around."

Eric nodded. "Exactly. I should wait for Mitchell to get here, but I'll say this now. Under surveillance, Enrique seems clean. We see that most of his movements stay around the Quarry. I expected as much since he lives there. I can't justify tapping his phone too much longer."

"What if we send in someone he doesn't know?" Tico suggested. "I can have an agent from New York here in a day. Enrique socializes with the residents enough that one new client could be irresistible for a drug deal."

Eric nodded. "If we can't come up with a solution by the end of this meeting, I'll file that request."

Meg clicked her pen. Open. Closed. Open. Closed. "Did anyone from the drug train have useful information?"

"There you go, jumping to my next subject," Eric said. "Always one step ahead of me."

She didn't even feel like smiling. "Sorry, Chief."

"The officers confiscated cell phones from two men traveling with the group. I'm not happy to report that the text messages on those phones contained photos of the three of you." He motioned to Tico, Meg and Bill.

"I guess we got under someone's skin," Tico said.

"The photos had cash amounts attached to them. The cartel has put a bounty on your heads. These men weren't here for running drugs. You three are now a top priority for protection 24/7."

Meg gave Eric a hard look. "My father doesn't need to know about this, Chief."

"He already does," Tico said.

This quiet statement forced Meg to look at him.

He was watching her, cool as could be. Her simmering emotions caused her to swallow hard. Anyone watching would have thought her reaction was because of stress over this news. Tico would know differently and that upset her. She wished she could be as self-possessed as he was. She let irritation lace her voice. "Is that what you two were talking about this morning?"

"I was convincing him not to pull you off the case. He's concerned, to say the least."

She shook her head. "When is he *not* concerned? We've heard worse."

That wasn't true, though. This was the first time they'd ever received proof of a contract. The idea was daunting, but not enough to stop any of them from continuing the investigation.

"I'm asking each of you to carry a weapon at all times and wear vests," Eric said.

"In this heat?" Bill voiced what they all were thinking. They now had lightweight, state-of-the-art bulletproof vests, but they were still hot.

"You have a better idea?" Eric asked.

Bill sat back in his chair. "Nope. I'll wear full body armor if you think it's a good idea."

Of course he would. He was going to be a daddy.

Meg's phone rang. Penny. Her friend had a knack for calling when she was in team meetings. She'd call her back later. Switching off the ringer, Meg put the phone facedown on the table.

Mitchell Blake walked into the room, his hair

windblown as if he'd been driving with the window open. He took a seat.

Meg ignored him. "Chief, how much was the bounty?"

Eric shook his head. "You don't want to know."

Mitchell looked up. "Bounty?"

Eric waved a hand. "I'll fill you in later."

"We must be getting close if they want to take us out so badly," Tico said.

Meg laughed. "Funny. We don't even know what we're getting close to." That lie was for Mitchell's benefit. For a long time, she hadn't quite understood why Mitchell was so antagonistic toward her, but now, with her suspicions, his actions made sense. By constantly discrediting her, he kept her distracted from the job. The clever bastard.

Eric said, "I want a couple of bugs planted in the Ripleys' house. Today. It would be better if Enrique doesn't know you've been there."

Bill nodded. "Done."

He indicated Tico and Meg. "I want you two back at the Quarry tonight. Josh and Katrina should return any day now. I want you in place when they do," Eric said.

"Fine," Meg answered. Her heart pounded double time. Alone with Tico again? She'd love to think they could reconcile, but from the set of his jaw, that seemed impossible.

She spoke again for Mitchell's sake, though she

meant every word. "Enrique is a friend of mine. I don't like that he's a suspect."

"Look," Mitchell said, "I just met with him. I was discreet, but I didn't get the sense that he's part of the human trafficking. So far, our only lead is that he's dealing drugs. Anyone can get blow or pot in a border town. If that's all we nail him with, then he can do his time and start over."

She gave him a grateful glance. "You're right. Drug dealing isn't as damning as kidnapping and murder. Since we're going in again, will you let Enrique know we're coming, or shall I call him?"

"I'll set it up right now." Mitchell drummed his fingers on the table. "Don't you think Daddy might object with you in such grave danger from the cartel?"

"*Shut up,* Mitchell."

Meg's mouth dropped open. It wasn't the venom in Tico's voice that shocked her, but Mitchell's massive mistake. They hadn't said anything to him about the cartel. He'd just walked in on the end of the discussion. She pushed to her feet as Tico reached over and knotted the man's shirtsleeve with his fist.

"Tico!"

He shot her a look that said he'd heard what she'd heard, but he said, "I'll handle this, Meg."

The fire in his eyes said it all. Tico was going to play the bastard into their hands. His reaction seemed a bit overblown, but she'd trust that Tico had a plan.

"I don't know why you think it's okay to harass the team leader, but it's getting real old, buddy. We're supposed to be working together here. Remember?"

Mitchell pulled his arm loose from Tico's grip. "Back off, Butler. A little banter never hurt anybody."

Tico poked a finger in Mitchell's direction. "That's not banter. It's a blatant attack, pal. I'm beginning to think *you* could be this team's problem."

"Enough, you two," Eric said. "There's plenty of pressure on this case without arguing. Let's get the job done." He stood. "That's all. Protect yourselves. Stay vigilant. Any developments at all, I want to hear them. Immediately."

"NICE MOVE," BILL said under his breath to Tico when they left the meeting.

Tico looked at Bill to gauge his sincerity. The admiration in his eyes showed him that Bill understood what Tico had been doing by getting tough with Mitchell. "Thanks."

They headed out. Tico was grateful for Bill's company. He felt torn up from watching Meg seated across the table from him. He didn't even want to think about the stakeout at the Ripleys' again tonight. That damned house was going to be full of memories of their lovemaking. He wasn't sure he could maintain the distance he'd drawn between them in such close quarters.

He heard Meg's footsteps catching up to them in the parking garage. Even the rhythm of her walk was imprinted on his heart. Damn. He was such a sap.

"Tico. Bill."

Both men turned to wait for her. She frowned at Tico. "You intentionally riled up Blake."

Tico shoved his hands in his pockets. "You know I did. I want to make things hotter for him. Throw him off balance."

"You're forcing his hand."

He shrugged. "I'm tired of waiting. I need him to make another mistake. We heard him slip about knowing the cartel set a bounty on us, but he could have learned about that from someone on the bust. It's close, but if he's guilty, I want to make him angry enough to come after us."

She nodded. "Good job. And thanks. I appreciated the defense."

Tico turned to walk away. "No thanks necessary."

"Wait. Do you guys want to get some lunch?"

Bill declined. "I'm heading home for lunch."

Tico shook his head. "Not hungry right now, but thanks."

She was acting as if nothing had happened between them last night. In his mind, it had been catastrophic. He'd walked away from a chance at happiness. Happiness that, until he'd met Meg, he hadn't believed existed. He'd learned enough over the years to accept the impossible. What he wanted from Meg was, by her own admission, impossible. No reason to torture himself any longer. There was no way he could go to lunch and pretend there wasn't anything between them. He could play the game in a business meeting, but that stretched his limits already. Seeing her at the Quarry tonight with no barriers between them would be bad enough.

"Okay, then," Meg said. "Shall I pick you up on the way to the Quarry?"

"I'll meet you there. I'd like to ride my Harley."

As if dismissing him, Meg laid a hand on Bill's arm. "Congratulations, Poppa."

He grinned. "I'm a happy man. I know my son will be healthy and strong."

"Your son? I've already bought pretty pink dresses."

Bill's face remained serious. "No son of mine will wear a pink dress, Meg. Did you keep the receipts?"

She laughed. "Don't worry. I won't buy anything frilly until we know for sure."

"You can buy him a pony, if you'd like."

She waved. "Give my regards to Dove."

Without acknowledging Tico, she moved away. What had he expected, a hot kiss on the mouth? He looked at Bill, keeping his poker face in place.

Bill clapped him on the shoulder. "You don't fool me with that not-hungry crap for a minute. Why don't you come home and have some lunch with Dove and me?"

Tico didn't want to think about what else Bill might not be fooled by. "To the reservation?"

Bill shrugged. "That's where I live. It's your turn to come to my place."

Tico felt as if his feet were rooted into the earth. He'd sworn never to step on Judumi lands. "No. I can't."

Bill goaded him. "What? You scared of a few Indians? We stopped scalping folks a long time ago."

Tico chuckled. "You must think I'm an idiot."

"No, my friend. I think you lived with a lot of pain."

The two men stared at each other. Tico couldn't help but wonder if he and Bill would have been friends growing up if his parents had lived a normal life in his father's community.

"Dove would welcome you. Just don't mind my mother. She asks a lot of questions."

Tico blew out a breath. "I swore I'd—"

Bill interrupted him. "I'll bet you swore a lot of things. But that was then, and this is now. Come on."

"I'll follow you." He couldn't believe he'd just agreed.

Bill shook his head. "I'll meet you at your place and drive you over. I don't want to give you the chance to change your mind." He pulled his keys from his jacket. "Besides, we need to talk."

At the ranch, Bill pulled up behind him in his pickup truck. Tico climbed into the passenger seat, his heart pounding.

Bill frowned. "Shit, man. You're sweating."

Tico wiped his brow with the back of his hand. "It was a hot ride."

"Sure." He put the truck into gear. "So, get real with me. Are you and Meg fighting, or did she dump you?"

Tico pulled his sunglasses out of his shirt pocket and slid them onto his nose. "What are you talking about?"

Bill looked at him and chuckled. "I've known Meg my whole life, as I told you. We even dated once when we were stupid enough to think it was a good idea." He thumbed his chest. "I know what a dump from Meg Flores looks and feels like."

Tico grew quiet. "I've never met anyone like her."

"I hear you, brother. And you know what?"

"What?"

"You'd be good for her."

Tico thought that over. "Well, you're wrong. I want to have a family with her—get married and all that—but she's made it very clear that that's the last thing she'll ever want."

Bill whistled softly. "Don Francisco did a number

on her and her brother on all counts in the family-raising department."

"What do you mean?"

"Meg's brother runs the family silver mine outside Mexico City. He lives and breathes his job. Never married. Travels all the time. They never see him."

Bill turned into the reservation, and Tico wiped his sweating palms on his jeans. He couldn't believe he'd agreed to come here. Yet he soaked up his surroundings like dry earth in a rainstorm.

Scrub trees dotted the vista. Cacti and desert sands spread as far as the eye could see. About a mile ahead of them lay the community of the Judumi tribe. Many of the houses were cookie-cutter, new sand-colored brick construction with A-line roofs and clean white garage doors. Farther in the distance lay the older communities. Low adobe ranches or newer ranch-style houses made of more sand-colored brick and white roofs.

Bill drove past the newer construction and headed for the heart of the community.

Bill continued, "Then we have Meg, who was raised by a father who never got over the abduction of his sisters."

Tico remembered this story. "So I've heard."

A dusty Ford Taurus passed them. Bill waved to the driver. "Did you know that Meg never rode a school bus? One of her parents always drove her and her brother to school. Drove them to all their friends' houses, when the rest of us were riding horses to get around. Never let them go anywhere alone until high school—and even then they had to call home when they arrived and when they were leaving."

"Wow. I always walked to school. Rain, snow or sunshine." Tico had hated the sense of abandonment. He'd learned to wait for kids from the neighborhood so he wouldn't have to walk alone.

"So it goes. And we react according to our upbringing, eh?"

"Which means?"

"I'm not surprised Meg chose a career in law enforcement. If she couldn't stop her father's grief, she was going to save everyone else from ever losing someone."

"Sounds like a lonely job."

"You can't convince me that you're still doing this job to keep your ass out of jail."

Tico grinned. "That's my story and I'm sticking to it."

The men grew silent. Tico watched Bill navigate the dirt road, dodging the occasional tumbleweed.

Bill said, "My guess? Don Francisco scared the piss out of Meg too badly for her to even consider marriage or kids. He probably never would have had his own if Barbara hadn't insisted."

"Okay. I can see that. But it's not my place to change Meg. I'd never force my choices on her."

Bill took an unexpected right-hand turn away from the community.

"Where we headed?"

"My brother and I built a compound by the foothills. We live close so we can share space with my mother."

Tico looked around. "Where did my father live?"

Bill gave him a hard look. "You really want to know?"

He'd come this far. Might as well see it all, despite the demons. "Yes."

Bill jammed on the brakes, backed the truck up to the corner and headed back toward the center of the community. "You'll laugh when I tell you the name of your father's neighborhood."

"Why?"

"Because you wear it on your body."

Tico held up his arm with the tattoo. "This?"

Bill took a few more turns and stopped in front of an old adobe hacienda with nothing behind it but miles of desert. "Welcome to Rattlesnake Point." He gestured to the worn but neat house before them. "That was your father's house. Your aunt and grandmother live here now."

A woman came to the door. She looked to be in her sixties. She was trim and wore jeans with a plaid shirt and cowboy boots. Her silvered black hair was plaited. She recognized Bill and stepped out of the house.

Tico watched the woman walk toward him. A

rush of memories flooded his mind. The woman had the same walk as his father, carried the same pride in her face, only she smiled where his father usually looked angry. Suddenly he was glad to be wearing his sunglasses. "My aunt?"

"Yes. Dawn. A good woman."

"For God's sake, Bill. Don't tell her who I am."

## *CHAPTER SIXTEEN*

DAWN APPROACHED THE TRUCK, saw Tico and slowed.

Under his breath, Bill said, "Oh, shit. I was afraid of this." He waved. "Hey, Dawn."

With her hand to her throat, the woman looked past Tico. "Bill?"

She looked again at Tico. "Are you bringing me the dead?" she asked, her voice low.

Tico's blood ran cold. His face grew hot. He hadn't felt this panicked since he was a kid. He sat there stupidly and stared at this woman with shock written all over her face.

Bill interrupted. "He doesn't want you to know who he is."

Dawn threw her head back and laughed. "How could I not recognize the spitting image of my brother?" She rested a hand on Tico's shoulder. "Tell me you are not Tico, and I will not believe you."

Tico cleared his throat. "I really shouldn't be here."

"I am so glad to finally meet you after all these years."

Tico shook his head. "This is very surreal for me. I never expected to come here."

Bill added, "The mayor hired Tico from New York to help with a delicate case. He's a little shell-shocked to be in Adobe Creek."

She frowned at Tico. "Your pa has been dead for years. Why didn't you come home?"

Tico's defenses went up faster than a rocket. "You're kidding me, right?"

She looked confused. "Of course not. We thought that once you grew up you'd find us."

Tico couldn't believe his ears. "Once I *grew up?* I needed you when I was a kid. I sent a letter to your chief begging for help after my mother died. Nobody—let me repeat, *nobody*—from the tribe came to help me."

Dawn blanched. "Oh, my goodness. You never knew, did you?"

"I knew I was alone for a very long time." Tico looked at Bill. "I need to go. This was a mistake."

"Wait!" Dawn said.

Tico took off his sunglasses. "Look, Dawn. It was a long time ago. It's okay. No one is to blame."

"Tico! We *came* to New York. Me. Your grandparents. We traveled together as a family to bring you here. We knew you needed support."

"You did?"

Tears filled Dawn's eyes. "You lived in a narrow brownstone building on a small street off Bay Parkway. Your grandmother kicked us out and told us never to come back. Said we were animals and not to be trusted with a child."

Tico's heart pounded. She knew where he'd lived. "Where was I?"

She looked lost. "At school, I think. Your granny wouldn't let us stay to talk to you."

"I never heard this."

A look of calm seemed to settle on her face. "But, look. You're here now. You've found your way. So none of her actions matter." She exhaled a long breath. "Please, come in. Your grandmother would love to meet you."

Tico's muscles were so tight, he wanted to jump out of his skin. Years and years of pent-up anger and conflicting emotions regarding his Judumi heritage gnawed at his gut. He didn't want to hurt this woman's feelings, but he needed air. Badly. "Maybe another time. I really have to go."

Dawn sighed. "We worried about you, Tico. We understood you were trapped. You were always welcome."

Why did it feel so hard to breathe? Thankfully, Bill put the truck into gear. "Thank you for telling me, Dawn. I'm glad to have met you."

"Don't be a stranger. Come back. Okay?"

He managed a smile. "Okay."

When she stepped away from the truck, Tico whispered, "Go, Bill. Go. Go. Go."

Tico glanced back, as Bill rounded the corner and saw Dawn still standing where they'd left her. He waved. She waved back. And then he understood. Tico may have been stuck with the drug induced monsters who were his parents, but Dawn had lost a brother, a sister-in-law and a nephew. It hammered home once again that the choices people made had a ripple effect on their loved ones whether they cared or not.

When Tico had consciously made bad choices, he suffered the consequences. That's why choosing to dedicate his life to fighting crime had been so meaningful. He'd finally made a *good* choice. Improved his life. He now had the freedom to get to know his Judumi relatives. But was that a choice he wanted to make?

He sighed. "That was rough."

"Sorry, brother. Now you see we weren't kidding at the mayor's place when we told you how much you resemble your father."

"A warning would have helped."

Bill chuckled. "Nah. I wanted to see how you'd handle Dawn. She's quite the community caregiver. The complete opposite to your father."

"You sound like you knew him."

Bill shook his head. "I didn't. He left before my time. My older brothers say he had a very compelling personality, but could be rotten when he felt like it. I remember them saying they never trusted him."

"Apt description."

Bill put a hand on Tico's shoulder. "Considering the odds, you're an okay guy."

Tico gave him a skeptical look. "You're not going to ask me on a date now, are you?"

"And piss off Dove, especially now that she's pregnant? Are you crazy?"

The two men laughed like cronies sharing a life-long joke. Tico realized he wished it were true. His focus shifted to the mountains in the distance. "How do you handle desert living?"

"You mean miles and miles of sand and scrub?"

"Pretty much."

Bill thought a moment. "Well, it's all I've known. You learn fast. No bare feet. Don't play with spiders, snakes or small funny-looking bugs with crab claws and curly tails."

"And the good part?"

Bill smiled. "The desert. She pulls you in. Shifts all the time. The sun plays colors across the sky and the views go on and on. A kid knows a freedom here that doesn't exist in a city. And then there's heritage."

Tico gave him a sideways look. "Heritage."

"Yeah, brother. We are ancient. We were here when the mountains were born."

"No way."

"Your bones hold memories of your forefathers Now that you've been in the desert, especially here don't you feel it?"

Tico thought about that. "Probably when I ride."

"You'll have to let me know how the city work

for you after you've spent a few more weeks and get acclimated."

"I may not be around that long."

Bill looked surprised. "No? What about Meg?"

"There's nothing left for me with Meg, Bill. She ended it. I'm out of here as soon as this case closes."

Bill turned on the road leading to his compound. "That's too bad."

"I see no other choice."

"Well, maybe. If you have no *cojones.* But never mind Meg. The real question is, are you man enough to meet my mother?"

MEG ARRIVED AT the Quarry around four to find Enrique had already gone for the day but had left an envelope with the house keys and a note wishing them luck.

Seated under the veranda by the pool, she could hear the music blasting from the Ripleys' backyard. They must have arrived earlier today because the limo was still parked out front. They probably brought friends who weren't staying the night.

Meg sipped her iced tea. Right now the Ripleys were the least of her problems. She'd already chewed one thumbnail down to the quick trying to figure out how she'd handle being alone with Tico. Not even twenty-four hours had passed, and she wished she could go back in time and keep her big mouth shut.

She sighed. Not that it mattered. If their romance had lasted any longer, the heartbreak would have been worse. There was never going to be a happy ending for the two of them. She'd have to get back on track with Tico as one of the team and get to work.

Piece of cake. *Not!* She'd worn this strappy red sundress to impress Tico. Sheesh. She was a fool if she thought she'd get over this love affair easily.

She checked her phone. Again. She and Penny were supposed to have dinner, but Pen hadn't answered her text. Then she remembered Penny had called this morning. Meg had gotten so caught up with the meeting, dealing with Tico and getting herself back out here that she'd forgotten to listen to Pen's message. Maybe she'd left a message to cancel.

She hit Play. Penny's voice sounded rushed. *"Oh, God, Meg. I'm leaving the spa right now. I overheard something pretty awful and I can't stay here any longer. Meet me at the house. You might want to bring Tico. Call me when you get this message."*

Meg sat up. Whoa! She hit the play button again. Pen definitely sounded agitated. Frightened. And now she wasn't answering her phone.

The throaty resonance of Harley-Davidson pipes rose from down the road. Tico. Arriving like the cavalry when she needed help. She headed out the front door and watched him pull into the driveway. He wore sunglasses, so she couldn't see the expression in his eyes, but there was no smile on his lips. His hair fell in a ponytail down his back. Black T-shirt. Jeans. Biker boots. He pushed his sunglasses to the top of his head. The look he sent her was stone cold. She wanted to cry.

Instead she held up her phone and walked over to him. "I think we have a crisis."

His brow creased as he frowned. "What do you mean?"

"Remember my phone call in the meeting this morning?"

"No."

"Of course you don't. I didn't answer. It was Penny."

"What's wrong?"

"Come inside. You need to hear her message."

Once inside, Meg hit the play button and put the phone in Tico's hand. Tico listened to the message. "Maybe she's at the house."

"I was there all afternoon. No sign of her since she blew through this morning before work. And she's not answering her phone."

"Did you check the spa?"

"Closed. Enrique left everything in an envelope at the registration desk."

"He left you a key to an expensive house in the open?"

Meg frowned. "Now that you mention it, yes. That's strange."

"Last time he stayed late waiting for us to arrive."

"Maybe Mitchell told him not to worry about it this time."

Meg suddenly felt numb. "Penny called from work. Maybe she saw something. If anything has happened to her..."

"What about her new boyfriend?"

"Some guy named Anthony. We were supposed to have dinner tonight, so I could get all the gossip."

"Where did she meet him?"

Meg paced the living room. "At the spa, if I remember correctly. He has a place at the Quarry."

"Was her car in the parking lot when you picked up the key?"

"No. There were a few people using the pool, but that's all."

Tico grew silent. He watched her pace from where he sat on the arm of the couch, arms crossed. Damn, she wished he'd move to a chair, or something. She couldn't think about the last time they'd been on that couch together right now.

She reached for her phone. "I'm calling Bill. Given her message and the situation, I'm freaked."

She continued pacing until Bill answered. "Hey. I have you on speakerphone."

"You at the Quarry?"

"Yes. I think we may have a problem. I can't find Penny."

"Since when?"

"This morning. We were supposed to meet for dinner, but I couldn't reach her. I just picked up a phone message she left me around ten-thirty. She sounded upset. Said she'd overheard something and wanted to meet. Her car isn't at the spa, and she never showed at the house this afternoon."

"Is Tico there yet?"

She glanced at Tico. The way he watched her made her knees weak. "He's here."

"You two check some of her hangouts. I'll get some uniforms to look around town for her car."

"Okay. She was dating a guy who lives here. We'll cruise the neighborhood for her car, too."

"Let's call each other in an hour."

"Perfect."

"Meg?"

"Yes?"

"Don't worry. We'll find her."

Meg disconnected. Closed her eyes to collect herself. "I don't like this."

Tico pushed off the couch. "As lovely as your dress is, how about changing into jeans? We'll take my bike. It gets around easier."

*He noticed.* She exhaled. "I guess it's time to hold up my end of the deal. You learned to ride a horse."

"Doesn't matter now. Let's get going. I'll meet you outside."

Meg headed for the bedroom. A flush of emotion almost brought her to tears. If anything happened to Pen because she hadn't nailed Enrique in time, Meg would never forgive herself. And damn it all, if she hadn't blown it with Tico, he'd be right behind her watching while she changed her clothes, making her feel sexy and wanton.... And oh, God, she didn't think she could handle his cooler attitude toward her.

The front door closed. She missed him already. Her tears blinded her as she rummaged through her suitcase for a T-shirt and jeans.

Before heading out to Tico, Meg dialed Penny's phone one more time. The call went directly to voice mail. Pen's phone was switched off.

Tico was finishing a call when she walked up. She pointed to the phone. "About Pen?"

"I updated Eric."

"Oh, God. Now my father will know."

"He'd find out eventually." He started the bike. "Climb on."

She laid a hand on his shoulder to swing into the seat behind him and felt his muscles tense under her palm. That little bit of contact sent a tremor through her. Her heart pounded, but she told herself it was simply because she'd never been on a bike before.

She settled into the seat. Much to her surprise, the seat had back support and fit her perfectly. She hadn't expected such comfort—and liked it. Tico's scent filled her senses, and she wanted to wrap her arms around his waist. Instead, she slid her hand off his shoulder and sat back. This wasn't a joyride.

"Where to first?" Tico spoke quietly.

"We don't have long before dark. Let's check the neighborhood for Pen's car. Vintage BMW. Powder-blue."

He chuckled. "Of course it is."

He backed the bike down the driveway. Meg looped her hair into a bun and secured it with a clip she'd tucked into her jeans pocket. She'd never ridden before yet felt as comfortable as if she'd been on the back of Tico's bike a hundred times. Not good.

Tico gestured to the limo in front of the Ripleys' hacienda. "Looks like they're back."

"Right on time. Maybe we'll finally get to close this case."

He revved the bike, headed to the top streets of the Quarry. "That would work. This town is too hot for my liking."

Low blow. She couldn't help herself. "Yeah. Takes a certain strength to handle a life like this."

He shook his head but said nothing. Let him think what he wanted. She'd lob back as much as he could deliver.

The upper perimeter of the Quarry stopped where the mountains became too steep to build on. Tico pulled to the side of the road.

"Wow. Check out this view."

Adobe Creek spread below them, then fanned out to the mountains on the other side of the valley.

Meg never ceased to be awed by the desert vistas. "Beautiful. I've never been up here." She turned to see how the sunlight played on the rising crags behind them. She did a double take. "Tico, look."

Curving along the side of one of the rises was a narrow path. The trail would have been invisible except for the way the lowering sun blasted the mountainside with golden light. It illuminated a patch of trail exposed by a scrub tree that had fallen and hung precariously over the edge.

Tico shaded his eyes for a better look. "Looks like a footpath."

"There are mine shafts dotting these hills. I'm pretty sure they've all been sealed for safety." She shrugged. "Like I said, I've never explored this side of the mountain. Dad always said it was too dangerous. Makes me think we should get horses and explore the area more."

"Are your antennae up on this one?"

She nodded. "Yeah. And my stomach just knotted up."

"Good sign. Let's check the other streets before it gets dark."

They threaded through the neighborhoods in silence. No sign of Penny's car. Tico headed for the Quarry gates. "Let's check the ranch."

They arrived at Meg's house as the sun dropped below the horizon, spilling breathtaking hues of magenta and gold onto the remaining clouds.

Tico brought the bike to a halt. "No car."

"This is not good news."

"Do you want to check in with Bill again?"

Meg pulled her phone from her boot. While she dialed, Tico's attention was taken by the sunset.

"One thing I can say. I've never seen sunsets like the desert has."

"My, my. A compliment."

Tico opened his mouth to answer, but was cut off when Bill answered on speakerphone. "Meg, any luck?"

"No sign of her at the Quarry. We just got to my house, and she's not here."

"Eric wants us all at the station in an hour."

"Okay. We're on our way. Thanks."

Her phone rang as soon as she disconnected with Bill. She looked at the caller ID, shook her head. "Hi, Mom."

"Sweetheart, did I just see you and Tico ride by?"

"Yes, Mom."

"Well, can you two come by? Your father and I would like to have a word with you."

"We have to go downtown. Eric…"

"We know, dear. We'd like to speak with you first."

Tico started the bike once more. "Wow. Does your mother have you wiretapped or something?"

"You should have tried growing up with them. Nothing was sacred."

"What do you think they want?" He gunned the bike toward the ranch house.

"I have an idea. I just hope I'm wrong."

TICO OPENED THE front door of the Flores house for Meg.

"We're in here, honey," Barbara Flores called. The foyer was lit, but the living area was dark since the sun had gone down. Meg led Tico toward the kitchen.

Barbara and Don Francisco were seated at the antique farm table in the kitchen. They were dressed casually, but both looked less than relaxed. Dishes from what must have been a hasty dinner lay stacked in the sink, and the air still held the strong aroma of roasted meat. It had been a long time since lunch, and Tico's stomach let him know. Meg heard the grumble and grinned at him.

"We can grab a burger on our way into town."

"Sounds good."

Tico didn't miss the way Don Francisco watched them. "Come here. Sit." He gestured to the seats at the table.

"We can't stay long, Dad. Eric called a meeting downtown."

"I know. That's why I want to talk with you. What's the news on Penny?"

"Nothing."

"I want to hear that voice message."

Meg pulled her phone from her boot, laid the device on the table, pushed Play.

Hearing Pen's voice sounding so strained sent a chill through Tico. She'd overheard something she shouldn't have and knew she had to get away. And given that she'd since disappeared, chances were someone else knew it, too. The longer she stayed missing, the worse the situation would be.

The message ended. The four of them sat, speechless. Barbara held a hand to her mouth. Outside the open doors to the veranda, the hum of bees swarming an evening primrose filtered into the silence.

Don Francisco pushed the phone toward Meg with a finger. "Your friend is in trouble."

Meg inhaled a deep breath. "I know."

"This is work of the cartel, Meg. Too close to home."

"Sir," Tico said.

Don Francisco silenced Tico with a glance. "Meg can work with Bill on surveillance, where no one will see her. I do not want her in the line of fire. Period."

"That's impossible, Dad. We've already established our cover. We're back at the Quarry as of tonight."

"Oh, Meg. I don't like it." Barbara shook her head.

"Your mother and I disapprove for obvious reasons." He pointed at Tico. "I hired you to do a job. I gave you a warning. From what I have seen between you two, you didn't listen."

There was no way Tico would let Don Francisco bully him. He and Meg might be finished, but Tico had proven himself with his work, and he deserved to be judged on that alone. "With all due respect, sir, your daughter and I…"

Meg pushed her chair back. "Dad! That's enough. You've made your point. I appreciate your concern, but there is no need. We have a job to do, and that's even more important now that Penny is involved." She stood. "Come on, Tico. We'll be late for the meeting. This discussion is over."

MEG AND TICO were the last ones to arrive for the meeting. Bill was frowning when they came in.

Tico sat next to Eric, Meg next to Bill. Across the table, Jose looked like a new father with dark circles under his eyes. Mitchell sat next to him doodling with his pen on a small pad.

"Sorry we're late. We were sidelined by my father," Meg said.

Eric sighed. "I know. He called after you left the ranch."

"What now?"

Eric gave her a soulful look. "You're off the case, Meg. Your dad pulled rank on me."

Meg blanched. "Impossible."

Eric opened his hands. "There's nothing I can do. I'm sorry."

"The puppet's strings got cut," Mitchell said under his breath. He continued doodling and glanced at Meg long enough to shoot her a satisfied grin.

A surge of disgust had Tico's fists balling, but he couldn't jump to Meg's rescue again. It would look too protective.

"Is that you or the Jack Daniel's talking, Mitchell?" Meg asked. Tico could tell she was about to blow her top. "I hope it's the booze because only a bona fide idiot would have the balls to speak to me that way."

"Meg!"

Meg looked at Eric. "What, Chief? What do you want me to do? Ignore his insults? I'd appreciate a little support here."

Eric rose to his feet. "Meg. Tico. In my office. I'd like to have a word with you."

# CHAPTER SEVENTEEN

ERIC SHUT THE door to his office. The anger rising in his eyes startled Meg. "Chief…"

"No, Meg. You don't understand. I'd like to rip the windpipe right out of that jackass's neck!"

Meg and Tico exchanged glances. Meg's jaw dropped. "Mitchell?"

Eric nodded. "Oh, yeah." He gestured to the two chairs in front of his desk. "Sit, please. This won't take long."

Tico leaned forward in his chair. "What's going on?"

"I had a late lunch with a couple of federal agents, who confirmed a suspicion I've had. Something surfaced from searching the drug train they stopped the other day."

"And?" Tico and Meg asked together.

"They found a key to a locker in that second-rate gym south of town."

"The one that nobody goes to anymore except amateur boxers?" Meg asked.

"Exactly."

"You're killing me, Eric. Get to the point." Tico was on the edge of the chair.

"Mitchell rented the locker."

Tico jumped to his feet. "A money drop. The bastard works for the cartel. That's why you couldn't solve any cases. He was tipping them off."

Meg couldn't believe her ears. So, they had been right. It was true. "You suspected Mitchell, too?"

"I saw where you two were going with your investigation." Eric gave them a hard look. "Even though you didn't think to fill me in."

Meg winced. "Are you arresting him?"

"Can't yet. Mitchell can argue that someone stole his key. The feds are tailing him. He's tapped. It's a matter of hours or days. If Penny has been caught in his net, I'm hoping this is how we nab him."

Meg lowered her voice. "Enrique?"

"The bugs we planted at the Ripleys' house show he was there all day."

"Mitchell knew we planted bugs there," Tico said. "Enrique probably used our ability to listen in to create an ironclad alibi."

Meg looked confused. "Enrique's golf cart wasn't at the house. Someone dropped him off? Picked him up?"

Tico laid a hand on Eric's desk. "I'm thinking Penny walked in on Mitchell and Enrique this morning, overheard something, so they took her."

"I agree," Eric said.

"Oh, God. You don't think they…"

Eric shook his head. "No. I don't think they'd kill her."

Tico snapped his fingers. "Of course not. They lost their drugs, so they'll collect a few more women to make up for it."

"That's what I'm thinking. We'll watch Mitchell while we search Adobe Creek. Penny is out there somewhere. The feds are starting at the outlying ranches and working their way in. Every inch of desert is being combed."

Tico frowned as something occurred to him. He looked around Eric's office. "Eric. Have you checked your office for taps?"

For the first time in the six weeks of this investigation, Eric smiled. "That's what I like about you, Butler. You think like a criminal."

Tico laughed. "I'll take that as a compliment."

"The entire police station has been swept." Eric lifted the receiver from the phone on his desk. "We found a device in my landline, in my car, under the table in the break room and in the restrooms." Eric gave Meg a pointed look. "We've checked Bill's and Jose's trucks. Bill's was bugged. So, don't say anything in your car or truck until we can sweep them."

Meg kicked Tico's ankle. They'd had some pretty intimate conversations in her car. Meg could see her own outrage reflected in Tico's eyes. She returned her attention to Eric. "Okay."

"And if you want to know why the mayor is so incensed, it's because they found a tap in *his* car."

Meg sat back in her chair. "Son of a bitch. Mitchell is screwed."

Tico shook his head. "If you've removed the bugs, Mitchell knows you're onto him."

"He'll know we're onto *something*. There were no prints on the bugs. We can't trace them to him."

Tico grinned. "But the temperature is rising. He might get desperate and do something to tip his hand."

"Exactly. Mitchell has a place in Costa Rica, but he can't go there to escape the law. We'd extradite him in a heartbeat. So, he's stuck in Adobe Creek until he covers his tracks."

"We'll nail him," Meg said.

"Fine, but stay cool. I'm not arresting him without concrete proof. I don't want to let him slip through our fingers because of half-baked accusations from either of you. I want to see that son of a bitch in jail for life." Eric looked at Meg. "Will you indulge me for a while longer before knocking Mitchell's teeth out?"

"Oh, I'm willing to wait, Chief."

He nodded. "Good. But you're still off the case."

"No!"

"I have no choice, Meg. I could kick up a fuss and tell the mayor that he can't interfere in police business, but I can't overlook the fact that the new missing person is Penny. *Your* roommate. This is all too close to home for you. You know that. I'm putting Tico in charge of the team."

The fact that Tico was taking over hit her like a brick to the head. Everything Meg had feared since Tico had ridden into town slammed down on her. She started to tremble with anger. "What am I supposed to do? Go home and wait?"

"You can sit in. Listen. Advise. But you're not going out anymore. You'll work from the sidelines or you'll go home."

The air grew thick with tension. Eric wasn't happy about taking her off the case, but with Penny involved, he didn't have a choice. Meg understood that, but her father had added extra pressure by meddling where he didn't belong—for the last time. Her father's life and career may have been dominated by fear, but she'd joined law enforcement to conquer that fear. What her father, Eric and Tico had clearly failed to understand was that if she were shoved behind a locked door, she'd escape through a window.

She felt Tico's stare and ignored him. He was team leader now. Acknowledging that fact reawakened all her original suspicions. She'd always believed that her father had brought Tico into the investigation to take her place once and for all. Suddenly, her greatest fears seemed to have come true. Could Tico and her father have had an arrangement? Could Tico possibly have lied to her all along?

Her gut didn't believe it. But her anger insisted that someone had to be blamed.

There was a knock on the door. Bill stuck his head in. "Sorry to interrupt. We have a new development."

Meg felt a surge of hope. "Penny?"

Bill shook his head. "Her car. A cruiser found it at the Amtrak station outside of town. They're checking for fingerprints now."

Eric stood. "Come on. I know this isn't easy for you, Meg, but I need your cooperation. We'll go back in there and finish this." He held the door open for her. "We can talk more later, but I want to get this show on the road."

"MEG!"

She'd left the meeting with Bill, and now Tico was catching up to them in the parking garage.

"Yes, Tico." Wound tight, Meg attempted to sound neutral but struggled to keep an even tone. She'd explode in a tirade if she didn't put some distance between her and this police station.

"Thought you might want a ride back to the ranch to help clear your head."

She would have liked that under other circumstances, but not now. "No, thanks. Bill will give me a ride. I want to fill him in on what's happening."

Tico's lips compressed with concern. "I'd like to be part of that conversation."

She gave him a sideways glance. "Is the team leader making a demand?"

Tico shot Bill an exasperated look. "Is she always this ornery when she doesn't get her way?"

Bill shrugged. "Don't know, brother. She *always* gets her way."

That was clearly meant to be funny, but at her irritable expression, neither man laughed.

"You can joke all you want, but my entire career was shot to hell. You know once I'm taken off an investigation, it'll be impossible to regain any authority. I'm pissed. Frustrated. Worried sick about my friend. Now my hands are tied, and you two want to banter about my situation. Thanks."

"Meg, we feel for you," Bill said.

She stalked away. "That's great, but it changes nothing. I'll borrow a cruiser from the precinct. See you two around."

"Hey, I thought you were going to fill me in," Bill said.

She didn't look back. "Don't know what I was thinking. The team leader will bring you up to speed." She turned and shrugged with upturned palms. "I'm off the case."

MEG CAME TO a screeching halt in front of her parents' house. The drive from town had given her too much time to stew. Her folks were probably settling down for the night, but by her reckoning, her timing was perfect. Until she found Penny and closed this case, time was at a premium. Meg had a list of things to do. Number one? Talk to her parents.

They must have heard her drive up because her mother met her at the door. "Meg, darling…"

Meg pushed past her into the house. "Don't *darling* me, Mom. Where is Dad? We have to talk."

"Oh, dear."

"You can say that again."

Soft music rose from the veranda. Barbara caught up with Meg. "We're under the portico. You should hear the coyotes tonight."

Meg turned on her mother. "I never expected you of all people to stop supporting me. Why?"

Barbara stepped closer. "Is taking a chance on your life worth one case?"

"You know what it's like to establish yourself in a male world. You're a metallurgist, for goodness' sake. Not too many women in that field."

"My career never put my life in danger."

"I'm trained, damn it! I know how to take care of myself."

"It's just one case, Meg."

"Don't you understand? Dad has just trashed my career. Even with Penny missing, Eric wouldn't have been so quick to take me off if Dad hadn't insisted. Taking me out as team leader discredits my abilities to my team. Even if they know the truth, I can't be relied on to be present for my men if Dad yanks me off a case every time he gets nervous. I just lost my job."

Barbara's light blue eyes grew harsh. "You are

more important to us than any job. I support your father in his decision."

"I hope you both don't regret your choice."

Meg barreled onto the veranda, her mother following in her wake. If Don Francisco recognized the anger in Meg's face, he didn't react to it. He remained seated, cigar in hand. The only concession he gave to Meg's agitation was to place his cognac snifter on the table.

"You'll excuse me if I don't get up. You are about to fillet me, so I'd prefer to remain comfortable."

Barbara returned to her seat across from him. "Really, Francisco. Can't you be more understanding?"

He puffed on his cigar. "No." He looked at Meg. "You are my flesh and blood. This case has dragged on for months, and while one woman from this case turned up dead, two others disappeared. My car was tapped, no doubt from one of the many times I've visited Eric. Now your friend—your roommate—has been abducted. Mitchell Blake, who is the primary suspect on this case, is gunning for you. This case has gotten too close to our family, and I'm not taking any chances."

"Dad! I am trained to take chances."

"Not this time."

"This time? How about forever in Adobe Creek."

He reached for his drink. "There will be other cases. You haven't been fired."

"Oh, so you've decided how far my career should

go? If I climb too far out on a dangerous limb, you'll slap me down to keep you and Mom comfortable? Not on my watch, Dad."

"You are overreacting, Meg."

"No. You've just sealed my fate. I can't work in this town and keep any credibility as a detective. I'm going to leave Adobe Creek to pursue my career without your interference."

"Meg!" Concern creased her mother's brow. "You don't mean that."

Tears threatened, and she fought them back. "I most certainly do."

"Where would you go?" Don Francisco made light of her threat, as she expected he would. He knew how much she loved Adobe Creek, especially Rio Plata Ranch.

"I'll go to New York with Tico when this case is done."

Don Francisco's cigar stopped halfway to his mouth. He focused on his wife as if confirming an understanding between them. He puffed his cigar. "So I was right."

"And you were also wrong. I turned him away because he wants marriage and children."

Barbara frowned. "There's nothing wrong with those things."

"Well, I disagree. Why have kids if you're going to lock them up and hide them from the world? I refuse to undermine a child's independence the way the two of you have always undermined mine. Even now."

She made her way from the house, relieved to finally hear dead silence behind her.

MEG COULDN'T SLEEP. She'd changed out of her work clothes and into pajamas, only to get dressed again. There was no way she could rest while her friend was missing. The house was too quiet without her. Even Bruno sensed the dire situation behind Penny's absence and trembled in Meg's arms as she carried him from one empty room to another.

Penny's perfume still lingered in her dressing room. The clothes she'd worn on her date were draped over a chair, a hairbrush tossed on her bed. All for what? Pen hadn't been missing twenty-four hours, but given the circumstances, everyone knew she was in trouble. Especially since her car had been discovered abandoned.

Meg returned to the back patio to watch the sunrise. She racked her brain for answers. Replayed yesterday's events minute by minute. Bill had tracked down Pen's new love interest. He had been truly distressed at the news of her disappearance. When questioned, he'd said he'd attended business meetings after Pen left his place, so he had names and numbers to verify his whereabouts.

Pen had called her from the Quarry after ten, but Meg hadn't listened to her message until four-thirty. For that entire day, Pen had been in distress, and Meg had been oblivious. The thought made her sick to her stomach.

Okay. Next. Tico arrived at the Quarry. They set off in search of Penny. Climbed on the Harley. Rode to the top of the Quarry.

Meg stopped pacing.

What if Penny had never left the Quarry? The memory of the light from the setting sun hitting the side of the foothills made Meg's skin tingle. Of course! Chances were good Enrique and Mitchell stashed their drugs and human cargo in an old mine shaft. The foothills were inhospitable for travel and considered dangerous terrain. Since that small mountain range didn't lead anywhere, the area had been overlooked during the searches.

Meg practically tripped over herself trying to tug on her sturdiest jeans. She slipped into a camouflage shirt. Slid a gun into her boot holster, a sheathed knife into the other boot. She filled a canteen with water, swiped up her phone, grabbed a cowboy hat from the hook and headed out the back door. Whisper could use a good run.

Angry as she was, every ounce of training pushed her to alert one of her team to her whereabouts. Grudgingly she dialed Bill's number. When he didn't answer, she hung up without leaving a message. She'd call again later when he'd be more likely to be awake.

Meg would find Penny and bring her home. Her father would soon understand how capable she was to do her job in the face of danger. Tico would be furious with her for taking off without him, but damn it all, he'd walked away from her, too. Besides, calling in and waiting for the team would take too much time. Time was one luxury they no longer had. Penny needed to be rescued. Once Meg evaluated the situation, she'd call for backup. This rescue required stealth. Chances were good she'd be in and out before anyone knew what happened. She squashed her pinging conscience for not leaving Bill a message.

Only one consideration seriously bothered Meg as she headed to saddle Whisper. Penny was most probably drugged, which meant Meg would have to carry her out. Meg could do it, but it would all depend on how far in she'd have to hike. She'd assess the situation then and call for backup once she'd pinpointed the location.

The sun had only been up about thirty minutes when she reached the upper perimeter of the Quarry. The trail she had spotted yesterday was invisible again. The fallen tree offered the only marker to lead her in the right direction.

The boundary fence butted up against the mountain. At the junction between fence and land, a twisted mesquite tree offered sparse shade for the horse. Better than nothing. Meg looped the reins once around a branch, giving Whisper enough room to graze. She poured water in her cupped palm for the horse to lap and then kissed her on the muzzle. "Wait for me, girl. I'll have you home for breakfast."

She hiked the incline toward the fallen tree. Not knowing how far in she'd have to go, Meg moved as silently as she could, pacing herself to keep her breath soft and even. Her boots found purchase in the sun-bleached gravel and dirt. She'd pulled on a pair of leather work gloves that protected her hands when she grasped prickly grasses and small branches to keep her balance. The whole way she silently chanted, "I'm coming, Penny. Hang in there."

She hauled herself along the carcass of the dead tree, skirting the spindly branches, her acutely tuned senses registering the splitting, grayed bark, brittle from the merciless sun. She scrambled up to the trail, checking both directions before exposing herself.

The trail looked unused, overgrown. No sign of footprints, but that didn't mean anything. Traffickers often tied squares of carpeting to their shoes to scour their footsteps.

The lack of any cover made her nervous. If anyone approached in either direction, she'd be visible. She listened. Only the breeze. A hawk flew overhead. Otherwise, no unusual activity. She checked her watch. Fifteen minutes since she'd left Whisper. The horse looked fine below. The sun rose higher, increasing the morning heat. Meg moved forward, staying close to the side of the mountain.

The trail snaked around the back of the mountain, putting Meg in complete shade. With perspiration already drenching her shirt, she was grateful for that small blessing. She removed her gloves and tucked them in her back pocket. Moving cautiously, alert to any motion or activity, she still sensed nothing. The trail leveled out for about five hundred feet where it met another trail from the other direction.

Meg inspected the second, much wider trail. This path must have been used by the mining company for hauling ore to the other side of the mountain. It made easy access for an all-terrain vehicle or anyone willing to hike the distance from the other side of the Quarry—if they knew the trail existed. From where she stood, it looked as if the path led directly behind the spa. And, she realized, the trail was peppered with recent footprints leading ahead on her path, which no one had bothered to conceal. Either someone had been in a hurry or didn't believe anyone would come up here.

How had she and her team missed this? Tico had questioned them about the Quarry from the very first. He'd come without preconceived notions or prejudices about anyone or any one area in Adobe Creek. None of them, however, had considered the foothills behind the Quarry. A surge of embarrassment filled her. She'd been so focused on protecting her position that she hadn't thought things through.

She wished Tico were here now. Instead, she moved farther along the trail. Every instinct told her to be wary. Footsteps to follow confirmed her guess that she'd stumbled upon the answer they'd been looking for for months.

The trail came to a bend leading toward the other side of the mountain. Meg started in that direction but stopped when something caught her eye. Right in the elbow of the bend, rocks were piled high, as if they'd been dug out. The usual scraggly growth crowded around the pile, but the formation looked contrived, like a barrier—no, like pilings from a reopened mine shaft.

Her heart pounded. She secured her gun from the holster in her boot. Silently and carefully, she threaded around the pile, stopping when a rock shifted. The area looked clear, so she kept moving. Sure enough, an overhang shielded an opening in the mountain tall as a man. The shaft gaped, dark and quiet. She listened for breathing. Nothing.

"Penny?" she whispered.

No sound came from the cave. She needed to see past the blackness. She sniffed the air. The cloying smell of cannabis wafted through the gap. Holding the gun in one hand, Meg slid her phone from her jeans pocket and swiped the flashlight icon. With her back to the mountain, she aimed the light into the cave. An upturned aluminum bucket stood in the center of the deep, narrow cave. Several cigarette butts littered the floor, but no scent of freshly smoked tobacco lingered on the air.

To the right, strips of burlap remnants were scattered across the floor. Casting the light toward the wall, Meg sucked in a breath. Bales of marijuana and stacks of bricks, either cocaine or heroin, were piled there. She turned the light to the left.

Penny!

Bound hand and foot in the dirt, Penny lay in the same clothes she'd worn from the house yesterday. Sweat-stained and dirty, but alive!

Meg cast the beam of light to the back of the mine shaft. Darkness. She'd have to trust her gut that no one lingered out of sight. She covered the few steps to Penny and holstered her gun into her boot to check Pen's pulse. Strong. Good. Inspecting her arm, Meg found the point of dried blood where the syringe had been inserted. She could do nothing to make her friend comfortable, but had to get her out of here. She'd need the team to meet her. She could cover a decent distance with Penny over her shoulder, but backup would help secure the situation. She checked her phone, but there was no reception inside the cave. Laying the phone down next to her, light side up, she slid the knife from her boot to cut the ropes at Penny's wrists.

Meg froze. A tingle lifted hairs on her neck as she sensed movement behind her. She should have confirmed that the deeper part of the cave was empty. Meg reached for her gun, turned to roll onto her back and shoot. But she wasn't fast enough. Pain and sharp light seared her skull. Then nothing.

## CHAPTER EIGHTEEN

TICO'S PHONE RANG. Though he seemed calm, sitting in the porch rocker, inside his senses were jumping. It was already midmorning, and he'd hoped to hear from Meg. He checked the caller ID—Bill. Well, if it wasn't Meg, he couldn't think of anyone else he'd rather talk to.

He put his coffee mug on the table. "Good morning, Bill."

"Tico. Things are getting hot."

He sat up. "Like what?"

"Two things. First, remember that bug you snuck under that poolside table at the Ripleys'? Jose just overheard a conversation between Enrique and Katrina Ripley. How fast can you get to the station?"

"I can leave now. What's the second thing?"

"Meg called and didn't leave a message. That's not like her."

Tico sighed. "She's angry, man. Let's give her some slack."

"Okay. I left her a message. I'll try calling again in an hour."

Tico sped the whole way to the station. Bill was

waiting for him in the hallway. He looked at his watch. "Fifteen minutes from the ranch. Nice job."

"My bike moves, man. Beats a horse any day."

"Today, I'll agree to that." Bill led him to a small room where surveillance equipment was set up. Jose sat at the desk, printing out the transcripts from the recordings.

"Play the meeting for him, Jose," Bill said.

Jose handed Tico and Bill headphones, then tapped the keyboard.

Katrina's voice sounded irritated.

*"I didn't like your tone of voice over the phone, Enrique."*

*"Well, we have a problem, Katrina."*

*"I'm sure you'll have no problem fixing it."*

*"Oh, I can fix it, all right. How about some jail time for accessory to kidnapping, drug trafficking and, oh, I don't know...murder?"*

*"What are you saying, Enrique?"*

*"Don't act like you don't know."*

*"That awful whore you took from the party? The one the police were asking about?"*

*"She's dead. Your fault, Kat."*

*"Oh, no. You can't pin that one on me. I just asked you to make her disappear."*

*"And the other women over the past two years who you asked me to politely remove?"*

*"I didn't tell you what to do with them, Enrique. That was your business."*

*"There's a lucrative market out there for beautiful, young American women. Thanks to you, I had a steady stream of them. You knew exactly what I was doing."*

*"You'll never prove it."*

*"But you did. You couldn't stand having pretty women around to tempt Josh."*

*"You can't put the blame on me, Enrique. I have plenty of money and excellent attorneys."*

*"You're already a target, Katrina. You shot your stupid mouth off in front of Tico and Meg."*

*"Who?"*

*"Mick and Amelia. I told you to be friends with them, but I also told you to be careful."*

*"They were cops?"*

*"Yes."*

*"Why didn't you tell me that?"*

*"If you'd known who they were you wouldn't have been your sweet, charming self, and I was trying to keep you out of this mess as much as possible."*

*"You could have told me to keep the drugs hidden."*

*"The drugs didn't matter. They expected you to be using. What mattered was that you bragged to your friends about getting them from me."*

*"So, you'll claim I was in on everything else, just for revenge?"*

There was a momentary pause. The sound of a device being turned on filled the silence.

*"I have you recorded on my phone, my dear Kat."*

Katrina's voice sounded angry and harsh as he replayed their conversation. *"I don't care if she dies, Enrique. Get that black-haired bitch out of my house!"*

Katrina interrupted the recording. *"Turn that thing off! How dare you? I was angry and high as a kite when I said that."*

*"You say a lot of stupid things when you're high, Kat. Now it's time to shut your mouth. If you betray me, you'll go down, too. Your best bet is to get your sweet, expensive ass out of town as fast as you can and don't come back until this blows over. I'll be gone for good when you return."*

THE THREE MEN watched each other while they listened. When the tape ended, Tico said, "We can use this as evidence, correct?"

Bill nodded. "Yes, indeed. It doesn't get better than that."

Tico removed his headphones, disgusted. "I can't believe those two destroyed other people's lives for such stupid reasons."

"Do we go for Enrique?" Bill asked.

"Absolutely." He picked up the desk phone and called Eric to fill him in on the latest. He hung up the phone.

"You two bring in Enrique. Maybe we can get him to tell us where they're holding Penny." He headed for the door. "I'm headed to the Ripleys' before Katrina has a chance to pack her suitcase."

Bill stopped him. "Wait. Take a squad car. You can't arrest her on a motorcycle."

MEG'S HEAD ACHED. She opened her eyes only to close them again. Even the small circle of light in the dark was too much. She felt dizzy. Nauseous. She took a deep breath, remembering. She'd been hit. The coppery smell of earth invaded her nostrils. She was still in the cave. She lay on her side, her hair and face in the dirt. Her head throbbed just below her hairline. She tried to touch the spot, but found that she couldn't move. Alarm zinged through her. The corded pattern of rope confined her wrists. Her ankles were bound the same way. Her boots? Her gun? Gone. Her eyes shot open. She forced herself to focus.

A lantern stood on the upside-down pail in the middle of the cave. A small dome of light glowed from it, casting a circle on the cave floor. Meg's boots stood by the cave opening in a patch of sun, which told her that the morning was progressing. Where was her gun? Who had struck her? Something was different.

She checked for Penny. Still unconscious, lying behind Meg, close to her feet. Meg sent up a small prayer that she hadn't been drugged, too. Yet. What was different? Her senses kicked in, and she focused on the other wall. The bales of marijuana were gone. Only the smaller bricks of heroin and cocaine remained.

A movement by the entrance caught her eye. Recognizing the voice of the speaker, she squeezed her eyes shut. *Damn it all!* Mitchell Blake walked directly over to her and kicked her foot. "Open your eyes, Meg. You can't still be unconscious."

She opened her eyes. Mitchell crouched down. "There, that's better. Have a nice nap?"

"You slimeball."

Mitchell wiped dust from her cheek. "You're in no position to call me names now, are you?"

He pulled her gun from his waistband. "Terrible for a cop to lose possession of her gun. Not going to look so good for you, Detective. Losing your gun. Losing your team. Your career just might be over."

Behind Mitchell, another man, sweaty and dressed in dirty clothes, picked up an armload of bricks. He looked over at her. His dark eyes seemed malevolent. He must have been the one who attacked her. Her best guess was that he had been guarding the drugs and Penny, heard Meg coming in and hid deeper in the cave until he could subdue her. She should have paid closer attention when she saw the drugs. No one would have left them unguarded.

Mitchell thumbed to the man behind him. "You're lucky this clown is a drone. If he'd known there was a bounty on your head, you'd be dead already, minus a few fingers as proof of reward."

Meg sniffed in disgust. "I'm surprised you're not collecting the reward for yourself."

He sucked in a breath. "I'm enjoying ruining your life too much to see you dead, Meg. Besides, I don't need the money. My reward is knowing I'm the one bringing you down."

"The day isn't over yet, Mitchell."

Mitchell grinned and looked more evil than Meg had ever seen him. "Sweetheart, your *life* is over. Your timing couldn't be better. We just got our latest load of cargo. You and your pretty little friend here are going on a long trip. You have new careers ahead of you. Just wish I could be there when your first john arrives. If you're lucky, you won't speak the same language, so you won't have much to talk about."

Meg's first reaction was to lash out, but she caught herself. Mitchell loved to goad her into anger. She wouldn't let it happen now, especially if this was her last chance to get him between the eyes.

"I'm not worried, Mitchell."

He looked disappointed. "Oh, no?"

"When Eric called Tico and me into his office, it wasn't about taking me off the case, you moron. Eric told Tico and me how you'd been fingered by the feds. They've been tailing you for days now."

He laughed. "Nice try, Detective. I'm a pro, remember? If I was being tailed, I'd know."

She considered telling him about the locker key to prove her point, but realized she didn't need to make one. All she needed to do was wait for Tico to figure out where she'd gone, because she knew he would. Until then, she had to keep her wits about her and do everything in her power to escape.

Mitchell sat, making himself comfortable. "Let me tell you how this story is going to end."

"Must you?"

He flicked a piece of dirt from the knee of his pants. "Oh, yes. I find it incredibly interesting."

Penny stirred. Mitchell pointed to her friend. "Looks like her sedatives are wearing off. No worries. We'll be giving her another injection soon. You, too, Meg."

If he'd wanted to see shock in her face he was disappointed. She watched him, keeping her face blank. But damn it all, if he drugged her, she was screwed. She couldn't let that happen. "Then what, Mitchell? You assault me because that's the only way you can get a date?"

Anger flared in his eyes, but he calmed. He watched her a long moment. "You know what I like best about this situation, Flores? Your father is going to spend the rest of his life wondering what the hell happened to you. He's going to know you were sold into the black market. He's just never going to know if you're dead or alive. I can't think of a better revenge on the good mayor."

"Revenge for what?"

"Come on, sweet cakes. Tell me you don't know."

Meg moved the ropes with her hands. Damned they were snug. She didn't have to fake anything this time because she was speaking the truth. "Honestly, Mitchell. I have no idea."

He laughed. "And all those times you razzed me about drinking I thought you were rubbing it in."

"Rubbing what in?"

"That your father found me unconscious at my desk late one night. He carried me from the department over his shoulder and I woke up with him staring at me lying on my living room couch. That's when he told me I was done."

"If that's true, my dad would never have let you back on the force."

Mitchell grinned. "You'd think so, but your old man is too dedicated to his cartel task force to take away his best investigator. I went to rehab and he took me back as a consultant. It was the perfect setup because by then my priorities had changed."

The sarcasm in his voice filled the small space. Meg laid her head back on the ground. Her head was still pounding, but she ignored the pain. "Believe me when I tell you, Mitchell, I had no idea. I kept digging back at you because I couldn't understand why you were always putting me down."

He watched her a moment longer. "Really?"

She closed her eyes. "God's honest truth."

He clucked his tongue. "Well, that's a shame. Best I can do now is send you off without killing you. You should know that I did think about killing you for the bounty reward. But guess what? The smugglers will pay me more for you." He stood. "I'm leaving for Costa Rica right after I send you off."

"You'll be able to live with your conscience while sipping those margaritas, Mitchell?"

"Funny you should ask that, Meg. You see? I started out just like you. Full of good intent. Out to get the bad guys. But you know what? The more I tried to do good, the worse it got. I watched the bad guys get away with murder, literally, over and over again. And after your father threw me off the job, it didn't take long to see what a sweet life I could lead by taking a few bucks here, a few bucks there. In a year, I was a rich man." He exhaled a long breath. "No, my dear, I worked hard for my success. I'll enjoy every minute of my Costa Rican hideaway."

Meg chuckled. "Well, I'll send you off with a warning."

"And what would that be?"

The other man returned for the last of the narcotics without looking their way.

"Check your shoes every morning, Mitchell. No one ever expects the scorpion sting."

He laughed. "I'll be sure to wear sandals." He headed for the mouth of the cave. "I have a few things to do. I'll be back with your injection. Meanwhile, you can ponder your new life."

She heard the men move farther down the trail. With no time to waste, she pulled herself around to face Penny. She wanted to make sure her friend was okay, but even more, Mitchell hadn't mentioned the knife she'd had tucked into her boot. Either the other man had taken it and Mitchell didn't know, or...

There! The blade lay beneath the folds of Pen's skirt. Without the lantern, Meg never would have seen it. Her body had probably shielded the small weapon from Mitchell's view while they were talking. She sent another prayer skyward and inched over until her fingers reached the knife. Turning the blade upside down between her fingers, she turned the sharp edge onto the rope binding her wrists. The knife fell. She tried again. This time, she slipped the blade between her hands to work from inside the rope outward. She moved slowly using as much pressure as she could. The first threads began to fray. Sweat broke out on her brow. She concentrated, careful not to lose her hold on the knife. Time dragged by. She heard the other man grunting as he moved the load of drugs to the other side of the rock barrier, but Mitchell had left the area.

Penny stirred again. Her eyes fluttered open. "Meg?" Pen's voice was hoarse.

"Yeah, sweetheart. I'm here."

Pen worked her mouth. "I'm thirsty."

Meg whispered, "Shh, honey. We'll get you something to drink soon."

Penny tried to focus. "Where are we?"

Meg felt the rope around her wrist giving way. "We're in trouble. Please, stay quiet, but I need you to try to wake up."

Penny sighed. "You came to save me." She drifted back to sleep.

Meg sawed harder on her ropes. She'd come to save Pen. She wouldn't let her down now. Her heart pounded in her chest, but she stayed calm, letting the adrenaline surge work for her. Pressing the knife more firmly, she pulled her wrists apart to keep tension on the rope. One. Two. Three more slices and the rope gave. She untied her wrists and sat up. She would have loved to work the circulation back into her arms but had no time. She immediately went to work on the rope around her ankles.

The small blade performed beautifully. Her ankles were freed in no time at all. Now to prepare for attack. She wrapped the line around her feet once, and draped the rest to look as though she was tied. She did the same with the rope around her wrists, holding the open ends with her hands, the hilt of the knife pressed into her palm. She positioned herself where Mitchell had left her, tucking the blade between her knees to shield it from view. And waited.

Tico took the desert road to the Quarry, speeding the whole way there, lights flashing. As he neared the uphill climb to the Quarry, Tico spotted a cherry-red Jaguar XKE barreling down the road toward the private airstrip used by the Quarry residents. Josh had spent as much time showing Tico Katrina's classic car as he had his Harley Fat Boy the night of the party. He careened the car onto the access road. He switched on the siren to go with the lights.

The Jag could easily outrun the police cruiser, but that didn't matter. There was no way Katrina would be able to get the jet in the air before he arrived. But it seemed she wasn't even going to try. Tico pulled up next to Katrina as she parked her car. She was gathering a large purse and an overnight case from the passenger seat.

"What's the fuss all about?" She looked at him from over the top of her sunglasses, cool and composed.

"Leaving in a hurry, are you?" Tico asked, getting out of the cruiser.

"Well, Mick. Surprise, surprise. Or should I call you Tico?"

He didn't answer but showed her his badge. "Where are you going?"

"Home to Los Angeles. My mother is sick. Is anything wrong?"

"We're still investigating the Melissa Collins

case and would like to ask you a few more questions."

She pointed to the jet on the tarmac. "Terrible timing. I have to go."

"Your mother isn't ill, Katrina," Tico said. "I know about your discussion with Enrique this morning. I also know he told you to get your expensive little ass out of town. Things might go easier on you if you come to the station willingly."

"I didn't have anything to do with that missing woman," she said. "I want my attorney."

Tico led her to the backseat of the cruiser. "I think that's a great idea, Mrs. Ripley. I'm sure Enrique Comodin will say the same."

Taking the road back toward the Quarry, Tico slowed the cruiser. A saddled horse was walking along the outside perimeter of the Quarry wall with no rider. He rolled down his window for a better look. "Whisper?"

Tico pulled over and called Meg's cell phone. It didn't even ring. The call immediately went to voice mail. This morning he'd been so upset over their argument last night that he'd thought she was avoiding him. Now he thought differently. Meg never turned off her phone. Damn it all. If Whisper was here, he had to believe that Meg was in the foothills investigating that trail they'd seen from the bike.

He dialed one more number. Don Francisco answered on the first ring. "Tico, good morning."

"Don Francisco. I don't want to alarm you, but is Meg with you or at her house?"

"No. She's not. Barbara rode over there this morning to have a chat with her, but she was gone. Looks like she's out on a ride."

"We may have a situation here, sir. I see Whisper now with no rider. I'm outside the Quarry."

"If anything—"

Tico cut him off. "Sir, I'm heading into the foothills behind the Quarry."

Katrina raised her voice from the backseat. "If you think I'm climbing into those mountains with you…"

"Excuse me, sir," Tico said into his phone. He turned to Katrina. "I'm not talking to you, Mrs. Ripley. You need to keep quiet for a moment before I charge you with obstructing justice."

Katrina snapped her mouth shut.

Tico returned to the phone call. "Do you know anything about the layout of those foothills?"

"Of course I do. I used to own that mine. The Quarry was my development."

Tico's brow rose. That was news. "Is it possible to get a helicopter in there?"

"Probably not. Anyone coming out has to use the back pass unless they come through the Quarry side of the mountain. If they hole up in the foothills, they could hide indefinitely, but when they come out? There's nowhere to hide. The desert is flat for miles behind those mountains."

"I'm going in."

Katrina yelled. "Hey!"

Tico silenced her with a look.

Don Francisco spoke again. "I talked with Eric before you called. He said the feds have a lead on Mitchell Blake."

"Did they say where?"

"Hell, no. You know the feds."

"If we're lucky, they're headed in the same direction."

"Tico, I'm on my way. Don't let anything happen to my daughter."

"Your daughter can handle herself, sir. Bring help. I don't have time to call Eric."

Whisper had reached the Quarry road when Tico drove up. Like a faithful animal, she was heading home. Tico radioed the police station dispatch. "I'm on the road into the Quarry. I'm leaving the squad car here and heading into the foothills to look for Detective Flores. Send a unit immediately to retrieve Katrina Ripley. I'm detaining her in the vehicle. Bring extra car keys."

The dispatcher began to argue, but Tico turned off the radio. He opened all the windows, pulled handcuffs from the glove box and pocketed the car keys. Climbing into the backseat, he hooked one handcuff to the wire grill separating the backseat from the front and beckoned Katrina to give him her hand.

"You're not shackling me to this car."

"Look, sweetheart, I don't have time for this. You're in deep trouble. You can have my hand slapped for leaving you uncomfortable, but the more you cooperate with me, the better it will be for you. Trust me when I say that when it comes to drugs and human trafficking, your attorney won't be able to help you. The feds don't take kindly to those two particular offenses."

"I didn't kill anyone."

"Then you can be an excellent witness and save yourself some serious jail time."

She let him cuff her hand. "I'm so disappointed. I thought you were a tough gang leader who liked to live dangerously."

He grinned at her. "I am living dangerously, if you haven't noticed. A squad car should be here in ten minutes, tops. Thanks for doing the right thing."

Tico whistled for Whisper and ran to meet her. The horse seemed hot but rested. Meg hadn't been riding her for a while. A frisson of fear zapped through him. Meg knew how to handle herself in the desert. If she'd left the horse this long, something was seriously wrong. He hoped he wasn't too late. He jumped into the saddle and headed for the foothills.

# *CHAPTER NINETEEN*

ALL HER SENSES on alert, Meg felt the tremor in the ground beneath her, and knew from the weight of the approaching footfalls that Mitchell, not the other jerk, was returning.

This was the moment of truth. She could take these two men, one at a time. But together? It was doable, but she'd need the element of surprise. Right now that was all she had. Surprise, her knife and a deep-seated drive to haul this bastard in. When she was done with him, Mitchell Blake would be going to jail for life.

His eyes would have to adjust to the shadows from the bright outdoors again, giving her precious seconds. Now she needed to distract him.

"Miss me that much, you jerk?"

He chuckled. "Should I kiss you goodbye now, or after you're unconscious?"

She spit into the dirt. "Definitely after. Couldn't imagine any conscious being would want you to touch them."

He crouched down next to her and opened a black leather case. A collection of syringes and hypodermic needles, two of them already prepared.

Meg counted the seconds. Mitchell had become too cocky. He wasn't protecting himself. He lifted the syringe to see in the dim light.

Meg struck.

She buried the knife blade deep into the muscle of his upper left thigh. He cried out and fell backward onto his ass. "You bitch!"

Not wasting a second, Meg jumped to her feet. With both hands still together, she punched him on the side of the head, hitting him squarely in the temple. He fell sideways, the syringe flying. Meg scrambled for it; right now that was her worst enemy. With a grunt, Mitchell pulled the knife from his leg and lumbered to his knees to use it on Meg.

"No way, you son of a bitch!" Meg whispered. Needle in hand, she kicked him in the face. Mitchell swung the knife, slicing her calf muscle, but the motion set him off balance just enough. She lunged, jammed the needle into his neck and squeezed the plunger.

He fell like the lump of lard he was. She pulled her gun from the back of his waistband. Her leg burned something fierce. She felt the wetness of blood running down her ankle, but she couldn't look now. Someone was coming into the cave.

She took a shooting stance. Her heart pounding, the taste of survival in her mouth. Nothing would please her more than to put a bullet between the eyes of the little weasel who'd subdued her and hurt her friend.

The intruder stopped at the mouth of the cave. The shadow of a man fell across the ground in the opening, the outline of an extended gun clearly visible. She would have to shoot or be shot. The rumble of all-terrain vehicles rose on the air.

"Meg, are you in there?"

*Tico!* A rush of breath escaped her lungs. "I am. We're secured in here." She lowered her gun, moved to make the lantern brighter.

Tico stepped through the opening. "We're in the cave. I'm in contact with Meg," he said into his phone. He looked at it in his hand. "I lost the connection."

"Phones don't work in here," Meg said.

He took one look at Mitchell unconscious on the ground, and Penny unconscious against the wall.

"Is Penny all right?"

Meg swiped hair from her cheek. "Sedated but fine."

He let his focus roam over Meg from the top of her head to the blood pooling around her right ankle. He holstered his gun. "Well, I'll be damned, Detective Flores. Nice job."

She blew out another breath, steadying her pulsing heart.

"Your father and the feds are right behind me. I apprehended the other man. Our job is done." He moved toward her, grinning, and opened his arms. She fell gratefully into his embrace.

He held her close, squeezing tight. Meg squeezed back. No one had ever felt so good to her. Felt so right. His familiar, fresh clean scent mingled with the raw heat and wind from riding in the desert. Pure Tico. Everything she loved about the man.

The thought stopped her. *Loved* about the man? Yes. The truth had hammered itself into her heart while she lay there waiting to get free. She wanted to laugh out loud, but instead she gripped Tico harder. "You know, while I waited for this bastard to come back, all I could think about was you. And how desperately I wanted to tell you that I love you."

Tico held her face with both hands. "I love you, too, Meg. More than life itself. We can work out the rest." He chuckled. "Ah, there's nothing more romantic than a good drug bust. Makes a woman appreciate her man so much more."

Penny sighed from against the wall. In a thick voice, she said, "Happy to hear you two lovebirds getting along. Can somebody get me some water? And these ropes…"

Outside Meg could hear her father's voice rising. "Where are they?"

Tico smiled. "Looks like the cavalry has arrived."

Meg laughed, and for the first time ever, she felt as if her life had finally fallen into place. "Thank you for coming for me, Tico," she whispered. "But what took you so long?"

He answered quietly into her ear, "I was giving you a chance to beat the shit out of Mitchell."

TWO WEEKS LATER, the team gathered at Rio Plata Ranch to celebrate the closing of the case. News of the bust had already aired on local and national news stations. Enrique's good looks had his upcoming legal hearings plastered on tabloid front pages while Mitchell was getting just as much press for being a dirty cop. Both men had been charged with Melissa Collins's death and were being interrogated about the whereabouts of the other missing women, now believed to have been taken across the border.

Katrina Ripley's publicist and attorney were keeping her role in abetting the crimes as low-profile as possible, though not surprisingly, the story was a reporter's dream. Josh Ripley had filed for divorce. The detective team in Adobe Creek was simply relieved to finally close the file on this case.

While war against drug and human trafficking was still being waged along the border, the residents of Adobe Creek rested assured that, for now, their town was safe. Don Francisco wanted to recognize the Adobe Creek Police Department for a job well done.

Meg sported crutches to keep her weight off the

knife wound on her calf. While Penny did her fair share of caring for Meg, Tico took it upon himself to spend a good portion of the nights in Meg's bed, just to be sure he could meet her every need.

They sat together on one of the orange cushioned love seats under the portico; Meg in a white linen blouse and yellow shorts, her foot raised on a stool. Tico held Meg's hand, not caring any longer what anyone thought while he chatted with Eric Longwood to his left.

A brush with death was enough for Meg and Tico to live openly, wearing their emotions on their sleeves. They were professionals who knew how to take care of themselves. If they lived in fear of retribution from their enemies, they might as well live in a cave. After Meg's brief experience in one, she preferred living in the open.

Much to Meg's surprise, her parents didn't object. Barbara had told her she admired a man who wanted to have a family, and while Tico was a bit rough around the edges, she believed he was a fine man.

Meg had yet to hear from her father on the subject, but as she'd made abundantly clear before the bust, she needed to live her own life.

Meg and Tico had spent many of the past few nights sorting out their future. They'd arrived at no real conclusions, though everyone wanted to know what Tico had planned. Meg had been tight-lipped, simply saying Tico was being as stubborn as a mule in making a decision.

Jose and Julia sat nearby. Julia handed Jose, Jr. to Dove, who sat next to her. "You may want to hold the baby as practice," Julia said, smiling.

Dove hugged Jose, Jr., smelling his head. "Don't you love how babies smell?"

Bill laughed. "Sure, when their diapers are clean."

Barbara Flores came out of the house and whispered something into Don Francisco's ear. "Well, then, now is the perfect time," he answered.

He turned to the group. "If I may have your attention, everyone. There are a few things I'd like to say."

Don Francisco captured his wife's hand in his. "I want to go on record that what I am about to say is very difficult for an old man set in his ways." He smiled at Meg. "And I am grateful that my daughter is on crutches so she can't escape me easily."

Everyone laughed. Meg's eyes narrowed. "Where are you going with this, Dad?"

"Except for Tico, we've all known each other for decades. We know each other's shortcomings, yet still we love and support each other. I would like to acknowledge one of my failures."

Barbara squeezed her husband's hand, encouraging him to continue.

"Because of my personal losses, I inflicted my fears on Meg and her brother. This no longer will happen. I see now that I underestimated the ex-

KATHLEEN PICKERING 373

cellence of Meg's law enforcement capabilities and will no longer let my past interfere with using the best team this town has to get the job done." Don Francisco met the gaze of each of Meg's team members. He laid a hand over his heart. "I want to personally assure each of you that you can depend on Meg's skill as a team leader, if you still want her to hold the job."

Bill said, "I respect Meg's position as team leader. She was the first one to figure out where Penny was hidden."

"And not a moment too soon," Penny added. "When Mitchell Blake and Enrique caught me listening to their plans about the drugs and more abductions, I knew I was a dead woman."

Meg spoke up. "But wait a minute. I want everyone to recognize that Tico indicated the Quarry as a prime location for the hideout *and* suspected that we had a mole on the team from the first meeting." She lifted her hand in his. "This man understands human nature like no one I've ever met. I have no problem with inviting him to be team leader. I can learn from him."

"That's because he is half Judumi," Dove said, smiling.

Tico pointed to her. "Don't be expounding on my poorer qualities, please."

She frowned. "Why do I feel insulted when you say that?"

Bill leaned forward. "What's wrong with having

natural instincts?" He winked at Meg. "Loosen up, man. When are you going to catch on that women *love* Native American men?"

Meg threw her head back and laughed. "Ha! Guilty as charged."

Eric Longwood turned to face Tico. "Well, I guess the real question is, do you want to stay on with the force?"

Tico looked at Meg with awe in his eyes. "Now, you all know why we've been going 'round and 'round. Meg takes crime busting so seriously, she would step away from her own interests to get the job done." He clapped Eric on the shoulder. "Working for you has been an honor."

"Is that a yes?"

Tico shook his head. "This is a real struggle for me." He squeezed Meg's hand in his, making the head of his snake tattoo flex. "Meg and I are still finding our way. She's reason enough to say yes." He held a hand up to stop the enthusiastic hoot from Bill. "But I came here with so much prejudice and anger. My past has haunted me the entire summer. I don't know that I belong here."

Barbara Flores smiled. "I think we can answer that question, Tico. If you'll excuse me a moment..."

Barbara headed for the kitchen as Dawn Antiman appeared in the doorway. An older woman stood beside her, dressed in a beautiful white Indian blouse and a long skirt. A squash blossom necklace of turquoise and silver hung around her neck. Heavy turquoise earrings dangled from her ears. Her silver hair was in a long braid over her shoulder. She walked slowly, with Dawn matching her steps to lead the way.

A young man walked next to the older woman as well, supporting her other arm. His hair was tied back in a ponytail, his bearing identical to Tico's. When Tico's eyes met his, Tico let Meg's hand slide from his and stood.

He was staring at the young man but seeing his own face looking back. Dawn was beaming as she led the other two toward him. Tico felt rooted into the ground.

Family.

Dawn said, "Momma, this is Tico. Your grandson. He is Adam's boy."

The woman smiled, her dark brown eyes drinking in the sight of Tico's face. She reached out a wrinkled hand. Tico bent over so the woman could press her palm to his cheek. She started to speak in Judumi.

Dawn interrupted. "Momma, he doesn't know our language."

The older woman looked at Tico again, frowning. Then in English, she said, "Welcome home, my grandson. I have missed you for many long years." She gave his cheek a loving tap. "You are Judumi. Learn our language!"

Around him, Tico's friends chuckled. From the corner of his eye, he saw Meg cover her mouth with her hand. She was crying. He loved her more at this moment than ever before.

Dawn motioned to the young man. "Tico, this is my son. Your cousin. Marcus Antiman."

Marcus held out a hand. "Tico. Finally. It is great to meet you."

Tico grasped his cousin's hand, shaking his head in amazement. "You look just like me. It is unbelievable."

Marcus smiled. "So, you still think you don't have family here?"

Meg lifted herself to her feet. Tico opened his arm to pull her close. She wrapped her arms around his waist.

"Tell me, love. What do you have in New York that you can't find here?"

He soaked in the affection in her eyes. From their nights of conversations, he knew they were both starting to heal from their painful pasts. He never ever wanted to be far away from Meg's side. He glanced around the room at his new friends. They watched him with anticipation and caring in their eyes. This group of people wasn't afraid to hold what was important close to their hearts: family.

Don Francisco nodded at him. "A man belongs on his own lands, Tico. Think long and hard about that."

Tico smiled at Dawn. "Thank you for introducing me to your family."

He reached for his grandmother's hand. "Whil

you are busy chastising me, you have not told me your name."

His grandmother smiled. "I was named Meredith. But you call me Grandma."

"All right then, Grandma, will you give me a hug and tell me what I've missed all these years?"

She wagged a finger. "It may take many, many days and nights of talking."

Tico smiled, his heart acknowledging the woman's weathered face, alive with love. "I can stay at least long enough to listen."

Meredith frowned once more. "Well, my boy, it is a lifetime of stories."

Tico laughed. "Then we should get started very soon."

The patio erupted with clapping and laughing. Barbara headed for the kitchen. "Oh, this calls for champagne. I have a funny feeling that someday, I might even become a grandmother."

Meg smiled up at Tico. She whispered, "I have never loved anyone the way I love you. Is that how babies are made?"

He reached down, brushing her lips with a soft kiss. "We can spend the rest of our lives figuring that one out, darlin'. In the meantime, there's a Pacific Coast Highway calling our names. Care to ride with me?"

She grinned. "By Harley or horse?"

"I say we take the long runs on the Harley."

"And the short rides?"

His smile was devilish. "I'd love to hold you while riding bareback on a pony."

"Ah. A true Judumi."

"No, my sweet. I'm just a man who wants your arms wrapped around me every chance I can get."

Meg breathed a kiss against his lips one more time. "Well, then, cowboy, hold on tight. You're in for one helluva ride."

\* \* \* \* \*